THE 'BATH AT WAR' TRILOGY

'When Bombs Fell On Bath'

'Bath Ablaze'

'After the Bath Blitz'

PART ONE

CHAPTER 1

Bath, 1940

Philippe Swann awoke with a jolt as the train let out a piercing whistle, signalling its approach to Bath. He stretched and shook his head to wake himself up, realising he'd probably been snoring, smiling awkwardly at his fellow passengers who pretended to ignore him. He looked out the window at the green hills framing the bowl-shaped city and the yellow-grey rows of buildings nestling within. As the train slowed, details became clearer: the bends of the river, streets busy with buses and cars, people strolling in the sunshine on this bright April afternoon. He took his suitcase and the cardboard box containing a gas mask from the luggage rack, put on his coat and cap, left the compartment and entered the corridor of the carriage. He accidentally jostled against a woman and said, 'pardon, Madame'. She looked at him strangely while he searched for the right word, and he said, 'sorry.'

The train shuddered to a halt, steam hissing, and there was a burst of activity as Philippe and the other passengers disembarked, then the train gathered speed and with a blow of its whistle departed for Bristol. Philippe waited for a taxicab and gave the driver the address in his best English.

'Where're you from then?' asked the driver, suspicious of this foreigner.

'Paris. I came on the boat train. I'm going to stay with my English Aunt. Bath is my new home,' he said, looking out at the city's landmarks and admiring the architecture as they drove eastwards towards an area called Larkhall with its rows of attractive stone-built terraces, narrow streets and local shops. They drew up in front of a small house with a front garden turned over to a vegetable patch, full of cabbages.

'Number fifty, that's you!' said the driver.

Philippe got out the taxi, handed the driver five shillings and told him to keep the change.

'Thanks, m'dear,' said the driver, pleased with his tip, and drove away.

Philippe knocked on the door which was opened by a middle-aged woman with tightly-permed greying hair. She looked at the young man, aged twenty, of medium height, with a friendly, open face, kind brown eyes and a neat brown beard, wearing smart, if rumpled, twill trousers and a winter coat.

'Philippe Swann,' he said, taking off his cap, smiling and extending his hand. 'I am pleased to meet you, Aunt Mary.'

Her misgivings diminished at the sight of him – that tousled dark hair and ready smile made her catch her breath: his resemblance to her beloved elder brother was clear. Her heart softened towards her visitor and she shook his hand.

'So, you're Jack's boy. You'd better come in.'

He put down his luggage in the hall and followed her to the back parlour room where she gestured to him to sit down in an armchair in front of the unlit fire.

'I expect you're tired after your journey. I'll go and put the kettle on.'

'Thank you. A cup of tea would be nice.' His mother had told him about the English obsession with drinking tea.

Philippe wandered around the room, simply furnished with two armchairs, a gateleg table covered with a lace tablecloth, a wireless set and a clock ticking on the mantlepiece. A russet woollen rug covered the floorboards. In the corner a canary in a cage was on its perch, lending a flash of colour, and he ran his finger along the bars, speaking gently to the bird which began to sing. Among some framed photographs on display he recognised one of his father, Jack Swann, in his Army uniform, taken in Northern France in 1917. Although he was smiling at the camera the exhaustion on his face was clear to see.

'Jack's photo,' said Mary, as she returned carrying a tray with a teapot, two cups and saucers, a milk jug and sugar basin, and placed it on the table.

'My mother has this one, by her bed.'

Mary picked up another photograph.

'This is us with our parents and Ernest, our brother. That's me, the baby of the family.'

Philippe nodded. His mother had told him about Ernest who had been killed on the Somme.

'Thank you for having me. I am very grateful, and so is my mother. It must have been a shock to receive her letter.'

'It certainly was! I never expected to meet you.'

'And I never expected to come to England!'

They sat down and Mary poured the tea.

'How was your journey?'

'Awful. Calais was full of desperate people trying to get on the ship, to escape to England before the Nazis invade. I wanted to stay in Paris but my mother insisted I leave – she said I was half-English and must take my chance.'

'Yes…she made that clear in her letter. Well, you're here now, so let's make the best of it. At least you speak good English.'

'Maman encouraged me to learn at school – she said my father would like to know I could speak his language.'

'And you're an artist, I gather.'

'I have studied at college in Paris the last two years. And now I will go to Bath School of Art.'

Mary put down her teacup and looked at her nephew.

'I've got to be honest with you. We'd already lost Ernest, and when Jack went back to France after the war to marry your mother it was like losing him, too. My parents never forgave him. When he wrote to tell us you'd been born he sounded so happy, but we knew he'd never come home again.'

'I'm sorry.'

'Don't be silly – you couldn't help it!'

'I wish I could remember more about my father, but I was only three when he died.'

'Yes – it was terrible...'

Mary looked sadly into the distance for a moment, then continued, 'I lost touch with your mother after Jack had gone, but I did think about you both from time to time, wondering how you were.'

Then she smiled at him and said, 'let me show you your room.'

Mary took Philippe upstairs to the spare bedroom with a single bed, wardrobe, bedside table and a washstand.

'You can unpack your things and make yourself comfortable while I get the tea ready. Derek comes home at half past five and we eat at six o'clock.'

'I hope your husband won't mind me staying here.'

'To be honest he's not keen – you being foreign an'all. It's a difficult time for everyone. But don't worry, he'll come round. And he's hardly at home anyway these days.'

Mary went down to the kitchen and took a moment to draw breath. It was strange to meet her nephew for the first time and in such extraordinary circumstances. The letter from Amélie, Jack's widow, had come like a bolt from the blue. Mary had hesitated before replying – she couldn't forget her parents' hurt – but for all of it she had never stopped loving her brother. For his sake she had written back to Amélie agreeing to help their son, hoping it might make up for the years of loss.

Mary was brought back to the present by the sound of her husband's key in the lock.

'In here!' she called out.

Derek Stevens was a foreman at Stothert and Pitt, a local engineering company. He kissed her on the cheek, she asked after his day, then said, 'our visitor's arrived!'

'*Your* visitor, more like!'

'Oh, be nice to him, Derek! He seems a nice lad – and he reminds me so much of Jack…'

'Well, if you're prepared to look after him that's up to you. At least he'll be company for you in the evenings and it will give you someone to talk to besides that bird…'

Just before six o'clock Philippe came downstairs and Mary introduced him to her husband. The two men shook hands and sat down together at the kitchen table while Mary served their meal.

Philippe said, '*bon appétit!*'

Mary and Derek looked at him curiously, then Philippe took a forkful of potatoes and meat and declared, 'but it is my favourite! *Hachis parmentier!*'

'Well, I'm pleased you like it,' said Mary, 'we call it shepherd's pie.'

'My mother told me English food was bad, but she was wrong!'

They ate the rest of their meal in silence, then Derek got up.

'I'll be off then – we've got a meeting tonight.'

'Derek's part of the local Air Raid Precautions team,' explained Mary, 'he's out to all hours some nights, then working again all day. You overdo it, dear.'

'Well somebody's got to. You never know when those Jerries are going to strike.'

'You have air raids here?' asked Philippe, surprised.

'We've had the odd explosion, but no raids. But we've got to be prepared.'

Philippe needed an early night, so leaving Mary listening to the wireless he went upstairs to his room, undressed and got into bed, trying to get comfortable on the lumpy mattress. He took a cigarette from the packet of Gauloises he'd brought with him, lit up and was immediately reminded of home. He pictured his mother sitting in their apartment, her father dozing in his armchair, and knew she would be pleased that he'd arrived safely in England – tomorrow he would write and tell her.

Philippe was grateful that Mary had welcomed him into her home, knowing it must be difficult for her – he may be her nephew but he was *l'étranger* in both senses of the word – a stranger and a foreigner. Needing to sleep, he stubbed out his cigarette in the ashtray on the bedside table and put out the light, wondering what the next day would have in store.

CHAPTER 2

Bath, 1940

Bath School of Art had recently moved to Green Park Buildings in the centre of the city, having been ousted from its previous home by the Admiralty. Philippe made his way there, passing a railway station, a different one from where he had arrived yesterday. He found the entrance to the School on the left side of the street, asked the way to the office of the Head and knocked on the door.

'Philippe Swann, from Paris. I hope you are expecting me.'

'Indeed! Delighted to meet you. I'm Richard Cross - I run the School with my wife, Ann.'

Richard, a kindly man in his forties with a receding hairline, stood up to shake Philippe's hand.

'I'm pleased you made it here safely. I received the letter of introduction from your tutor - full of praise! I'm looking forward to seeing your work and hearing about your studies in Paris.'

He ushered Philippe into the corridor, saying, 'we have a life class today so you may as well get started. I'll take you along to the studio and you can fix yourself up with whatever materials you need. Don't go too mad on the paper, though, it's in short supply.'

Philippe followed him to the back of the building to a high-ceilinged studio and a large window framed by thick, heavy curtains for the blackout. Ten students, the majority female, were standing at their easels in a semi-circle, sketching a naked young woman with long red hair, lying on her side on a couch.

Richard introduced the newcomer to the other students then returned to his office. Philippe helped himself to one sheet of paper and pencils, set up an easel and proceeded to sketch the model. Life drawing was one of his strengths and as he concentrated on his subject, all thoughts of home and war vanished from his mind. After an hour they stopped for a break and Philippe followed the others into a refreshment room where they queued up for mugs of tea and cake. The student in front of Philippe turned and spoke to him.

'The tea's all right, and you may as well grab the cake while you can, we don't get it very often nowadays…I'm Daniel Johns, by the way.'

'Philippe Swann, good to meet you.'

He sat at a table with Daniel, a friendly fellow with dark, wavy hair. They drank their tea then Philippe offered him a cigarette.

'Thanks,' he said, inhaling the strong tobacco and erupting into a coughing fit. 'Gauloises,' he croaked, examining the packet, 'I've heard of them but never tried one before…' He took another drag and started hacking again, then another student joined them and sat down next to Philippe.

'Michael, you must try these!' said Daniel, taking the cigarette from his lips and passing it to his friend who inhaled and also began to cough.

'Hey, they're strong! Got any more?'

'I have a few packets - I brought them with me from home,' said Philippe, amused by the effect his cigarettes were having, 'but I think they are too much for you!'

'Not at all!'

The second student, a tall, thin, fair-haired lad, introduced himself. 'I'm Michael White. So, you're our new Frenchman. Where were you studying in Paris?'

'The Ecole des Beaux-Arts, near the Louvre.'

'Sounds impressive.'

'It's the best art school in Paris. But now I've come to live here with my Aunt - my father was English. I wanted to stay in Paris but my mother insisted I come, it's becoming dangerous over there.'

'Well you should be safe enough here,' said Daniel, 'no one wants to attack Bath! And this is a good school - I started last year. The staff are great.'

'…and the models…' added Michael. 'What did you think of her this morning?'

He grinned suggestively and nudged Philippe with his elbow.

'She was very good, she stayed very still. But I'm having trouble with the shape of her foot - I always find feet difficult!'

'…I wasn't thinking about her feet…'

The class resumed, then afterwards Daniel showed Philippe around the school which extended over all four storeys of the Georgian terraced house, with studios for ceramics, sculpture, graphics and textiles as well as painting and drawing. The basement provided a storage area for art materials and the students' work, but more importantly had been converted into an air raid shelter for the duration.

'The Head and his wife are very ambitious,' Daniel said, 'they have loads of ideas about Art and Design in the future and see it as a community effort. They like the idea of students living and working in the same place - Michael has his own room up on the top floor which doubles as a studio.'

A girl passed them on the stairs and introduced herself to Philippe. The new French student was arousing attention.

'There are a lot of women here,' commented Philippe, as she carried on down the stairs.

'Yes - mostly arty types from posh schools whose parents can afford the fees. Of course, most of the men in our age group have been called-up.'

'Yes...so what about you?'

'My family are Quakers so we're exempt on religious grounds.'

'So you are a pacifist?'

'Yes. Does that bother you?'

'No, not at all. And in my position I can't criticise. I'd like to do something to help the war effort, though. What about Michael - is he a Quaker, too?'

'No - he couldn't join up because he suffers from migraines, but you'll have to ask him about that. If you want to do something useful you could volunteer for fire watch - Richard Cross will put you on the roster.'

Back in the studio a couple of girls came and chatted to Philippe about life in Paris, then went on their way. Michael, observing, said, 'you'll have no trouble attracting the local girls - they go weak at the knees when they hear your accent!'

Philippe shrugged. 'It's just the way I speak!'

'You must come out with us one night, have a few drinks.'

'Thank you - I'd like that.'

Philippe left Green Park Buildings and walked to the Guildhall to catch his bus back to Larkhall. As the bus moved slowly through the traffic he looked out curiously at the busy streets, happy with his day's work, feeling less of a stranger. He had plenty to tell his Aunt when he got home - yes, he was beginning to get used to the idea - this was his new home now, here in Bath.

Paris, 1940

Amélie Swann was sitting by the window of the small but comfortable apartment in the east of Paris, close to Place de la Bastille, that she shared with her widowed father, Louis Duvalier. She had lived there all her life among a changing population of native Parisians, Jewish émigrés and other foreigners who had arrived during previous times of conflict and stayed to make their homes. She looked out at the familiar row of houses opposite which mirrored her own with their mansard roofs, thickets of chimneys and wrought iron balconies, a typical Parisian scene set against a clear blue sky with the top of the Eiffel tower visible in the distance.

In her hand she held a letter - the precious letter she had been hoping to receive ever since she had waved her son goodbye at the Gare du Nord. She whispered a silent prayer of thanks for his safe arrival in Bath, grateful that Mary had accepted him into her home without rancour. She was also pleased Philippe liked the Art School and that the money she had telegraphed to cover the first term's fees had been received.

She read Philippe's letter once more and sighed. She missed him but knew she had done the right thing in sending him away. News was that the Nazis were advancing by the day and held the Netherlands and Belgium in their sights. Pessimists warned they would be in Paris by the Summer; the thought filled her with dread.

Leaving the letter on her chair, Amélie walked over to a bookshelf, picked up her framed wedding photograph and looked at the young couple, so in love, so happy. They had met on the Western Front when Jack had suffered a shrapnel wound to his leg and she had nursed him back to health. He was sent back to England just before the end of the war, but as soon as peace was agreed he had left his parents and sister in Bath and headed to Paris. Within weeks they were married.

Amélie's father owned a garage and employed Jack as a car mechanic, putting to good use the skills he had acquired in the Army, while Amélie resumed her nursing career at the nearby hospital at St Antoine. Their neighbours looked curiously upon the Englishman, the ex-soldier who had chosen to settle in

Paris, and some had doubts about Amélie, too. Madame Duclos, the old woman who lived next door to them, was particularly hostile, muttering, 'aren't our boys good enough for you, that you want to marry a foreigner?' But Amélie ignored the barbs and after a while the residents got used to seeing Jack, always cheerful and polite, as he slowly climbed the spiral staircase to their first-floor apartment.

When Amélie gave birth to their son, Philippe, the couple's joy was unconfined. Life had been wonderful, until that dreadful day when two gendarmes knocked on the door to tell her Jack had been killed in a road accident. All these years later she still felt the injustice, that her husband had survived the war only to meet his death on the streets of Paris, run over by a speeding car.

Amélie put the wedding photograph back on the bookshelf. So much had changed; she looked at the young couple as if they were friends from long ago, people once known and loved, but who belonged in the past. She came back to the present as her father cried out, 'can you get me a drink, *chérie?*'

She went to the kitchen and took a glass of water to her invalid father who was resting in bed.

'I have good news, Papa – I've had a letter from Philippe – he's arrived safely in England and is settling in well.'

'That's good, you did the right thing. And what he doesn't know can't harm him.'

CHAPTER 3

Bath, 1940

Philippe received a letter from his mother, expressing her relief that he had got to Bath, and just in time - his had been one of the last passenger ferries to leave Calais. He went to Mass at St John's, the Catholic church, feeling the connection with his mother and grandfather, praying to God to watch over them.

At the Art School, Richard Cross directed his students to record Bath in the wartime conditions, depicting the Royal Crescent, Circus and the Abbey with sandbags piled high, signs to the nearest air raid shelters and people in military uniform. Philippe loved working outdoors, *en plein air*, and took the opportunity to get to know his adopted city and its famous buildings of Bath stone. He favoured an Impressionist style, working quickly in oils to portray busy street scenes, bringing light and movement into his pictures. Standing at his easel he grew used to passers-by taking an interest in what he was doing, and in the typical English Spring weather he sought shelter under shops' awnings, painting people as they hurried along under their umbrellas and the colourful reflections on wet paving stones as the rain poured down. His favourite subject was Pulteney bridge with the River Avon flowing over the weir alongside the Parade Gardens, a tranquil spot amongst the hustle and bustle of the city.

Daniel and Michael befriended Philippe and one Friday night, keen to introduce him to Bath's nightlife, they took him on a pub crawl. With the novelty of his accent and strong cigarettes the Frenchman proved quite a draw, and his friends used him like bait to attract the girls. In one of the pubs Michael spotted a familiar face.

'See that redhead sitting in the corner with her friends - do you recognise her? She was our model the other day.'

'Looks different with her clothes on!' said Daniel, as they went over to chat to her.

'The art students!' she said, recognising them. She was used to such attention and batted off the lewd comments, saying 'it's just a job.' She accepted one of Philippe's cigarettes. 'I remember you coming into the studio, on your first day. How are you getting on?'

'Very well, thank you - Bath is a friendly place, although I still miss Paris.'

Then the girl turned her attention to Michael and asked, 'why aren't you in the Services, anyway?'

'I get migraines. They come out of nowhere and I have to lie down in the dark until they pass. I tried for the Army but failed the medical - they said I wasn't any use to them like that.'

'How horrible! And you don't know what causes them?'

'No. They started when I was twelve and haven't gone away. They're very painful – I've just had to learn to live with them.'

'It sounds awful,' she said, sympathetically, turning and sitting closer to him. She liked his blonde hair and piercing blue eyes, and spent the rest of the evening flirting with him.

The model's friends chatted to Philippe and Daniel but in truth Philippe didn't find English girls that attractive; they were either brash or giggly, whereas he preferred someone he could have a proper conversation with. He thought of his old girlfriends at the Ecole des Beaux-Arts and smiled at the memory – they'd had a lot of fun, and suddenly he missed them. Also the room was beginning to spin - this local cider was stronger than he'd realised - and he wasn't sorry when they called it a night.

They left the pub and wandered down the street to Fishy Evans to buy chips, then Daniel began his walk home to Lower Weston, a couple of miles away, leaving Philippe with Michael and the model who were in a clinch. Philippe wished them goodnight and caught the last bus back to Larkhall. He entered the back parlour room just as Mary was putting a cover over the birdcage and was going to tell her about his evening when she turned to him and asked, 'have you heard the news?'

'No...'

'It's been on the wireless. The Germans have invaded France.'

Paris 1940

Amélie returned from the market, her head buzzing with the latest rumours. She found her father and said, 'Papa, everyone is saying the Germans are coming! Our forces have given up the fight.'

'Yes, *chérie*, I know. The German Army by-passed the Maginot line and are attacking through the Ardennes. It won't be long till they reach Paris.'

At the hospital everyone was discussing the events. One of the doctors, Gérard Moreau, said resistance was futile, and it wouldn't be long before Great Britain was conquered as well.

'Never!' Amélie protested.

'But the Nazi war machine is powerful, and our Army is weak,' Dr Moreau replied. 'We can't rely on the British to save us – their forces in Belgium are on the run. You must be realistic, Nurse Swann.'

'But we can't just roll over, we have to fight back!' countered another doctor, Jean-Pierre Fournier.

There was no answer, and the discussion ended. Amélie and Dr Fournier exchanged a glance and as they walked down the corridor he said, quietly, 'we must be very careful, Amélie. Trust no one.'

'Can we still meet?'

'Yes…but be cautious. Come to my office tonight, after my secretary's gone home. I don't think she suspects anything, but…'

Amélie understood.

As they entered the orthopaedic ward he said, at normal volume, 'thank you, Nurse Swann, that will be all,' and left her to resume her duties.

Within days Paris became flooded with Dutch, Belgian and French refugees arriving from the battle zone searching for somewhere to stay, their cars laden with all their worldly goods. They told terrible stories of villages in flames, packed roads and being attacked by low-flying aircraft that fired straight at them as they ran for cover in ditches and under vehicles. As each day passed, news from the front worsened; there was nothing to stop the German advance. Amélie went to Mass the next Sunday to pray for peace, but the congregation knew it was too late. She told her father about staff at the hospital who had gone to stay with relatives in the south.

'Do you want to leave Paris, *chérie*?' he asked.

'Of course not, Papa! You're not up to travelling and we have nowhere to go. We'll stay and make the best of it. There is one thing, though. I want to telegraph some money to Philippe while we still can, but our savings aren't enough. I'll have to sell another piece of Maman's jewellery.'

Over the years Amélie and her father had got by on her nurse's pay and his pension but expensive items, like medical treatment and Philippe's education, had required extra funds.

'That's all right – your mother would be pleased to know the money's being put to good use. Go and pay Monsieur Rosenberg a visit.'

Amélie went to her bedroom and took a jewellery box from a drawer, the one her mother, Raisa, had brought from East Prussia when she had fled with her parents sixty years ago. Amélie had heard the story many times: how the family were forced to escape from the Russian invasion of their homeland with what they could carry and made a new home in Paris. At the age of twenty Raisa had fallen in love and married Louis Duvalier, a native Parisian. They moved into the apartment and were overjoyed when Amélie was born, but when Raisa was thirty she succumbed to scarlet fever, leaving Louis to bring up their daughter alone.

Amélie opened the jewellery box and examined what remained – a sapphire and diamond brooch and a pearl necklace. The necklace was pretty but the brooch would fetch more money. Her decision made, she wrapped the brooch in a handkerchief, put it in her handbag then walked briskly to the Marais, the Jewish quarter of Paris, about a mile from her home. She found Monsieur Rosenberg's shop down a quiet side road, glanced around and opened the door. A bell rang as she entered the room which was in semi-darkness save for a circle of lamplight on the counter where an old man with a white goatee beard was sitting on a stool, peering through a magnifier, repairing a pocket watch. When he saw Amélie his face broke into a smile and he stood up to greet her.

'Madame Swann! How nice to see you! How may I help you?'

She greeted him in turn, took a seat by the counter and showed him the brooch.

'Aah, another fine piece. This also belonged to your mother?'

'Yes. There is very little left now…'

He put his jeweller's loupe to his eye and examined the brooch carefully.

'These are fine sapphires, from the East. Beautifully cut. And the diamonds are exquisite. It is a good brooch. I will give you a good price.'

The transaction completed, Amélie got up to leave and shook the old man's hand.

'I am very grateful to you for helping me all these years, Monsieur Rosenberg. The Germans, when they come…you must take care. One hears such dreadful stories…'

He shrugged. 'We must put our trust in God.' Then, gripping her hand tightly, he added, 'and you, Madame Swann, you must take care also.'

He looked meaningfully into her eyes; he knew her secret.

Amélie said nothing but acknowledged him with a slight nod of her head. She left the shop and hurried away from the Marais to the Bank where she deposited the money and arranged to a transfer to England. Back home she wrote to Philippe telling him about the payment, saying how much she loved and missed him, praying her letter would reach him. She had done all she could.

CHAPTER 4

Bath, 1940

At home in Larkhall, Philippe told Derek he had volunteered for fire watch at Green Park.

'That's good, they'll give you some training, show you what to do. And you could help out with my ARP team if you like…'

They were interrupted by a knock at the door. Mary went to answer and returned followed by a pretty young woman carrying a cake tin.

'Derek, it's Clare, Eric Pargetter's daughter. She's got a message for you.'

'Dad's not well and he can't do his fire watch tonight – it's his bronchitis. He's really sorry. Mum's made some buns and thought you might like them - it won't make up for Dad though…'

'Sorry to hear that, thanks for letting me know.'

Clare noticed Philippe, and Mary introduced him. He stood up and shook Clare's hand, admiring her clear blue eyes, shoulder-length fair hair and curvy figure.

'You're from France! Goodness!' she said, taking in his good looks and friendly smile.

'Yes – I'm studying at Bath School of Art.'

'Thank your mother for the buns, Clare, and I hope your Dad feels better soon,' said Mary, showing her out.

'Thank you, Mrs Stevens. Goodbye, Philippe, nice to meet you.'

Derek said, 'well, Philippe, looks like this is your chance to learn about fire watching! You can take Mr Pargetter's place with me tonight. Oh, and don't get any ideas about his daughter – she's married. Her husband's in the Army.'

Philippe overslept after being on watch and the next morning he caught a later bus than usual. He spotted Clare among the passengers and when she saw him she gestured to him to come and sit next to her.

'Philippe! I haven't seen you on the bus before.'

'No - I normally catch an earlier one, but after the fire watch...'

'Of course! You've probably been awake half the night. It was quiet, though?'

'Yes. It gave Derek the chance to show me how to work the - how do you call it - stirrup pump? And he told me all about different ways to put out fires.'

'At least it wasn't raining. I reckon that's how my Dad got his bronchitis, standing up on the roof, wet and cold!'

She glanced over the shoulder of the passenger in front to read the headlines in the newspaper.

'The Army's in retreat. Reg, my husband, is out there with the British Expeditionary Force – he's a Sapper in the Royal Engineers. I do worry about him.'

'It must be very difficult for you.'

'We got married last year on my eighteenth birthday. Reg said we may as well get on with it, and he joined up soon after so we were only together for a few weeks. I still live with Mum and Dad so it doesn't seem any different, really. Strange what war does, isn't it?'

'Yes – it's only because of the war that I've come to Bath.'

Clare listened with interest as Philippe told her his family story, then the bus arrived at Green Park where they both dismounted.

'And where do you work?' asked Philippe.

'Here, at the railway station.'

'So we're neighbours! I hope to see you again, Clare.'

'And you, Philippe!' she said, turning to wave as she walked away.

Over the next week the news worsened. British forces were in full retreat and massing at Dunkirk on the French coast, trapped by the German army. At the end of May a rescue operation began and over the next nine days Royal Navy ships, merchant vessels and an armada of small boats sailed across the English Channel to save thousands of stranded soldiers, under intense attack from German forces.

In Larkhall, Clare returned home one evening to find her husband, Reg Watkins, sitting in the back parlour room, drinking tea with her parents. Thin and utterly exhausted, she was shocked by his appearance but flung her arms around him and gave him a kiss.

'I've been so worried about you, Reg! Thank goodness you're safe!'

He kissed her. 'It's good to be home.'

She sat next to him on the settee, looking at him, noticing how he had changed. His sandy hair was cropped short and his face weathered.

'Tell me what happened.'

He wiped his face with his hands.

'To be honest I don't remember much. We walked for miles and miles, all through Belgium, then into France. We walked in our sleep. There wasn't anything to eat. It was horrible, babe.'

She'd forgotten he called her that. She held his hand, tightly.

'When we reached Dunkirk we were sent to the beach - it was massive, there were thousands of us, all along the coast. There were planes flying overhead, firing at us…the noise! Then we had to queue up, on the sand, and I fell into this little boat and they transferred us to a ship moored offshore. Then I passed out. Woke up when we got to England!'

'It sounds horrific. You're so brave! Thank heavens you made it home!'

'Yes… plenty didn't…'

He'd never be able to tell her the terrible things he'd seen and done. He knew he wasn't the same man who'd set off from Bath what seemed like an age ago, a keen recruit to the Army…she didn't need to know.

'How long are you back for?'

'We're awaiting orders. But I think I'll be staying in England for a while - we have to do some training, up North.'

'At least you'll be a bit closer. Oh, I'm so pleased to see you...'

'You, too, babe.' He squeezed her hand, then fell quiet.

Clare wasn't sure what else to say to him and knew she would have to be patient. She had a horrible feeling that the young, carefree lad she'd married had vanished on that beach as surely as if he'd been shot down by a Nazi plane, and this man beside her was a stranger.

Paris, 1940

One warm night in June, Amélie awoke, sure she could hear gunfire in the distance, and caught her breath with fear. The next day out on the streets the atmosphere was unnerving, expectant, the calm before the storm.

'The Germans are coming!' shouted a child, running down the road.

Amélie left her father and joined the throng of people who were making their way towards the Place de la Bastille, and there she saw them – a line of tanks rumbling along, followed by rows of German soldiers marching in step, their rifles on their shoulders, the crunch, crunch of their boots on the road. The citizens of Paris stood in silence, not knowing what to make of this invading force. Even in the First war the enemy had never come this far and there was a sense of disbelief that their leaders had allowed this to happen.

'So what now?' asked a woman, of no one in particular.

Another shrugged her shoulders. 'Go and buy bread, while we still have some.'

Amélie returned home and told her father what she had seen.

'There is nothing we can do,' he said, resignedly, 'just sit it out and see what develops.'

Paris was cut off from the world. The last ship to England had sailed, petrol was rationed and the roads were empty apart from enormous convoys of German vehicles, many carrying the booty of war back to Germany. Amélie caught the Métro to the Place de la Concorde to find that it had been turned into a huge car park for German military vehicles. She walked down the Champs-Elysées watching German soldiers on a spending spree, buying fashions, clothes and food to take home. In one of the stores an assistant told her they had gone through the place like a plague of locusts and not one pair of stockings was left.

Amélie glanced up at the Eiffel tower standing defiantly over Paris, strong as ever, and was cheered by the rumour that the Führer had been unable to ascend the tower because a tool essential to the safe operation of the lift had mysteriously gone missing.

A curfew was put into effect from nine in the evening until five in the morning; the City of Light was in darkness.

*

At the cinema Philippe watched newsreels of the Nazis occupying Paris in despair, anxious for his family, prisoners in their own city, and felt ashamed when he heard English people say the Frogs were cowards who had given up the fight. He read about General de Gaulle, the leader of the Free French in exile in London, who was urging the French people to resist German occupation and work with the Allies to defeat the enemy. But what could he do? Just as he'd started to feel at home in Bath he suddenly felt alone, cut off in the cruellest way from the people and places he loved the most and unable to do anything to help.

CHAPTER 5

Paris, 1940

Amélie and her father continued their daily lives as normally as possible, hating the sight of Nazi soldiers on the streets but learning to live with it. They grew accustomed to seeing the flag of Nazi Germany with its black swastika flying over every government building, street signs written in German and even the clocks were set to German time. Paris became the favourite place for Nazi soldiers' rest and recreation and certain hotels, cinemas and theatres were set aside for their use only.

Amélie felt sick at the takeover of her country, shuddering as she walked past the pavement cafés where soldiers were sitting at tables, drinking beer and scrutinising the local talent, feeling their eyes upon her. She'd heard of women who were prepared to sell themselves to the enemy in exchange for money or extra rations, and was ashamed of them.

Paris was governed by the German military and French officials approved by the Germans, and those who resisted were denounced for anti-Nazi activities. Every day Amélie and her father read about rebels who had been executed in public, a terrible lesson to others. Daily living became difficult with food, tobacco, coal and clothing being rationed while supplies grew scarcer and prices higher. The French press and radio contained only German propaganda, although in October word filtered through that the Royal Air Force had bravely defended the skies and won the Battle of Britain, leaving the defeated Nazi forces to turn their attention elsewhere.

At the hospital, people divided into two camps: those who were willing to work with the Nazis, and those who were determined to resist at all costs. In this atmosphere of distrust the one bright star in Amélie's life was her relationship with Dr Fournier. As she left for work one morning she said to her father, 'don't forget, I'm working late tonight. I've prepared your meal, you just need to heat it up.'

'All right, don't worry, I'll manage!'

After a busy day attending to her patients, Amélie finished her shift then walked to the end of a corridor to Dr Fournier's office. She knocked on the door and he let her in, looked out surreptitiously to make sure no one was around, closed the door and locked it. They embraced, passionately, his hands travelling down her back and over her hips. She undid his shirt and pushed it off his shoulders, caressing his back, his chest. They moved towards his desk and she lay against it, then he lifted her up, running his hands under her uniform and up her black-stockinged legs. With a gasp of pleasure she held him close, panting with desire as their lovemaking grew to its climax.

Afterwards, they adjusted their clothes and he fetched a bottle of cognac and two glasses from a cupboard. He poured generous measures and made a toast.

'To you, my beautiful Amélie.'

'Good health, Jean-Pierre.'

They faced each other, savouring the smooth, amber liquor. Warmed by the alcohol they put down their drinks and she sat on his lap, putting her arm around his broad shoulders. He was in his early forties, a couple of years older than herself, and in good shape. She ran her fingers through his thick, dark hair, greying at the temples, lending him a distinguished look which she found very attractive. They kissed, lingeringly.

'We can't stay late tonight,' he said, 'you must get back before curfew.'

'I'll be fine – we have to show that it's still our city, not theirs.'

'Yes - but we must be careful. And don't go anywhere near the Arc de Triomphe on Armistice Day. There's going to be a big demonstration against the occupation and it might get nasty.'

'But how do you know…?'

'Amélie, it is important, and secret. You are to say nothing, understand? I know people in the Resistance movement who are ready to fight back, to reclaim our country. They are in contact with England. It is very dangerous - the Germans have already shot some of our men. Will you join us?'

'Yes! But what can I do?'

'There may come a time when I need you to deliver a message, or to cover for me. Will you do that?'

'Of course!'

He looked at his watch and sighed.

'We'd better go.'

They kissed again, reluctant to part. She left the room first, and Jean-Pierre followed a few minutes later.

On the Métro on her way home Amélie imagined Jean-Pierre going back to his apartment near the Eiffel tower to be welcomed by his loving wife and three children. Their affair had begun two years ago, the same time as Philippe had started at the Ecole des Beaux-Arts. After years of being a daughter, a mother and a widow she had felt an overwhelming need to be herself - Amélie. She had known Jean-Pierre Fournier for years and one evening their mutual attraction had boiled over. The timing was right; the arrangement suited them both, and Amélie soon overcame any guilt she felt about borrowing another woman's husband. It was his choice, and a common enough practice in Paris at that time.

Over the months, she and Jean-Pierre had become friends as well as lovers, but now, with what he had told her, their relationship was taking another turn - they were fellow-conspirators, fighting the enemy.

Bath 1940

Through the Autumn term the students painted scenes of Bath in the parks and woods in the countryside around the city, capturing the seasonal colours, but the horrors of war were never far away.

Victory in the Battle of Britain had boosted morale, but a number of properties in Bath were damaged when bombs intended for other targets went astray. Bathonians grew used to the drone of enemy aircraft flying overhead to bomb factories and ports in South Wales, and in November, Bristol underwent a devastating attack, wiping out the mediaeval centre of the city and leaving many hundreds dead.

But life went on, and come December the students started talking about Christmas and planning some modest celebrations, given the restrictions of rationing and the blackout. At home, Philippe asked Mary how she and Derek marked the festive season.

'It's different, now, with the war, but we used to have such fun!' she said, her eyes misting over with nostalgia. 'When I was a girl, before the First war, when Jack was still living at home, we'd play games, and charades, and mother would play the piano. Your father had a fine singing voice, you know. And one year Ernest got us a goose from a farm up the road, it fed us for weeks! Then when Derek and I married we always went to his works 'do' – Stotherts' always put on a good party for its workers. It's been quieter in recent years, though. We normally see Derek's sister who lives in Box, a village just outside Bath. She and her husband will come over on Christmas Day, so you'll meet them.'

Mary sighed. 'They say Christmas is a time for children, but when you don't have your own you make your entertainment in other ways...'

Philippe looked at her, with interest. It was the first time she'd mentioned the lack of children in her and Derek's marriage. He didn't say anything, but she knew he was curious and added, 'it was one of those things - it just never happened for us. I was sad at first, but you get used to it, and fill your life with other things…'

She glanced around the room and her gaze fell on the canary. Aware of her underlying loneliness he wanted to cheer her up, and said, 'well this year we'll make Christmas special!'

Borrowing some materials from the School, Philippe made some colourful Christmas garlands and put them up in the back parlour room, and Derek acquired a real fir tree, filling the house with its fresh, piney scent, which they decorated with lights, tinsel and baubles from previous years. On Christmas Eve, Mary invited some neighbours around, including the Pargetters, and Philippe was delighted to see Clare again. With Derek he helped play host, handing round glasses of sherry and plates of mince pies, a strange English delicacy he had never heard of before.

'I thought they were made of meat, but they are sweet!' he said to Clare.

She laughed. 'Yes, I don't know why it's called mincemeat because it's dried fruit. Do you like it?'

'Yes, I do!'

The subject of food gave a good opening for Philippe and Clare to chat and the time passed quickly. When the guests came to depart Philippe helped see them out, shaking their hands, and looking into Clare's eyes he said, 'merry Christmas. I hope to see you again soon.'

Under his gaze she blushed, and said, 'thank you. Merry Christmas to you too.'

That evening Philippe went to midnight Mass at St John's and said a prayer for his mother and grandfather, wondering what sort of a Christmas they would be having under Nazi rule. Normally he would have spent the day with his family preparing a feast of oysters, roast meats, foie gras and cheeses but now, such fine foods and the company of those he loved were an impossible dream.

On Christmas Day Philippe exchanged gifts with Mary and Derek, presenting them with one of his paintings of Pulteney bridge which they loved, and Derek hung it on the wall above the fireplace. Philippe was equally appreciative of the pairs of woolly socks Mary had knitted him. Derek's sister and her husband arrived and together they tucked into roast chicken and vegetables from the garden, washed down with cider, a memorable treat for them all. Derek stood to make a toast to 'absent friends', then they clinked glasses and Philippe declared, '*Joyeux Noël !*'

CHAPTER 6

Bath, 1941

In the new year Richard and Ann Cross announced that the School would hold an exhibition of their students' work in the Summer with the theme 'Bath at War'. Spurred on to produce some new paintings Philippe decided to portray the industrial side of Bath and was discussing ideas with Richard when they were interrupted by the sudden, shrill blast of a train whistle.

'Now that would be a good subject for you - the railway station! There's plenty of activity there!'

On a cold January day Philippe went along to Green Park station, happy to immerse himself in a new project to take his mind off events in Paris. He found a suitable spot at the far end of the platform and spent a couple of hours sketching the archways of the vast wrought iron and glass roof which sheltered the platforms while trains steamed past. He was grateful for his new socks but nevertheless by midday had had enough of the freezing temperatures and went to the refreshment room in search of warmth and a sandwich. He spotted Clare sitting at one of the round, marble-topped tables, wearing her working uniform of dark navy serge trousers and a jacket, with her hair tied back into a knot underneath a cap. She saw him and beckoned him over.

'Come and join me. What are you doing here?'

'How nice to see you! I'm making some sketches of the station for our new exhibition.'

He sat down and offered her a cigarette which she took. The Gauloises had long gone and he'd grown used to Woodbines which were less satisfying but better than nothing. They lit up and she said, 'I enjoyed the party at your house – Mr and Mrs Stevens are such a nice couple.'

'They are, they've been very kind to me. Did you have a good Christmas?'

'Yes - Reg, my husband, had a pass for a week's leave. He's been posted to a training camp in Lincolnshire so he's going to be in England for a while. He…he hasn't got over Dunkirk yet…'

She looked sad for a moment, then Philippe asked, 'so what do you do here?'

Brightening up, she said, 'I'm one of the platform staff - I keep everything clean and look after the Ladies Waiting Rooms. I love it! I've been here over a year now - they don't employ many women but with the war they were short-handed. I could ask one of the station staff to show you around if you like, might give you some ideas for your drawings.'

'That would be very useful - thank you!'

They paused while they ate, then Clare said, 'right, I'd better get back to work. It's been good to see you again.'

He watched as she walked away, admiring her shapely *derrière* which even the unflattering uniform couldn't disguise, then she turned back, smiling, and he reddened slightly, as if caught looking at something he shouldn't.

The next day Philippe was approached by the Assistant Station Master.

'You must be the artist! Mrs Watkins said you were interested in looking round the station, so if you'd like to follow me…'

They walked along the platform towards the goods yards, sidings and train sheds where carriages were cleaned and maintained, and the repair shop where engines were dismantled, serviced and fixed by an army of workers, their faces and hands blackened with coal dust.

'This station services the Somerset and Dorset railway,' the guide explained. 'We run trains up to the Midlands and down to the south coast. If you think it's busy now, just wait till you see it in the Summer! The 'Pines Express' has them queuing out the door!'

There was a stable block with horses and carts used to transport goods around the station, and the Fish House, a large, airy stone building which hadn't been used for years but still retained a distinct smell. Further down the line were the engineering works of Stothert and Pitt, where Derek worked. Finally his guide said, 'now I'll show you the vaults.'

He unlocked a door next to his office and Philippe followed him down a steep staircase at the bottom of which a vast vaulted area extended under the platform into the distance.

'About half the cellars are Bonded Stores, used by our friends in HM Customs and Excise to store wine and spirits.'

He opened the door to one of the cellars to reveal a long, narrow space with a small, barred window at the end, stacked high with barrels. The walls of the vault were coated with a dark film due to the alcoholic vapours.

'You can't stay here too long, the fumes go to your head! In the other cellars we store lamp oil and coal – there's a trapdoor from the main road for deliveries – you've probably walked past it without noticing.'

He was interrupted by a loud crashing noise above their heads.

'It's all right, just the 12:42 heading out. Time to get back up top.'

Back in the office Philippe said, 'thank you for the tour, it's been fascinating!'

'You're welcome. Always happy to do a favour for young Mrs Watkins.'

Over the next weeks Philippe divided his time between the station and the studio, building up a fine series of paintings of life on the railway. He found inspiration in the men he observed working among the noise, smoke and grime who clearly had a sense of pride in keeping the trains running in wartime conditions. He sketched busy scenes on the platform with passengers arriving and departing among clouds of steam, the porters, guards and platform staff. He asked Clare if he could paint her as she went about her work and she happily agreed, posing with her broom as she swept the platform, pinning up notices and helping the public with a cheerful word and a smile. They had lunch together at the refreshment room most days and the more he saw her the more he liked her. Lunchtimes with Clare became the highlight of his day.

Searching for inspiration for the 'Bath at War' exhibition, Michael returned to his old stamping-ground of Oldfield Park, the residential area to the west of Bath where he'd grown up among the terraced streets and alleyways. His parents had died when he was small and he'd been brought up by his sister. Showing an early interest in art, he owed everything to a teacher who had spotted and nurtured his talent, encouraging him to apply for a scholarship to Bath School of Art where Ann Cross took him under her wing, offering him a room when his sister married and moved away to Plymouth. Michael walked down to the Scala cinema and when he saw the large public air raid shelter which had been built opposite, knew he had found the subject of his next painting.

As for Daniel, he headed home to Lower Weston with 'Dig for Victory' as his theme. He painted people working in their allotments, sowing seeds in every spare inch of their gardens, and the vast areas of Victoria Park which had been turned over to growing vegetables and fruit. As a pacifist he felt an instinctive aversion to themes of war, but providing food for the population seemed to him a worthy subject.

Paris, 1941

The atmosphere in Paris was tense. Shortages were becoming worse, the black market was flourishing and stories abounded of collaborators, businessmen offering their services to the enemy to increase their profits and women using sex to obtain extra rations. In the apartment block people watched each other suspiciously and Amélie overheard her neighbour, Madame Duclos, say of her, 'well, she married one foreigner. Who knows, she might want to marry another?' But Amélie didn't confront her and put the cruel remarks down to the bitterness of an old woman.

The landlord was forced to put up the rent and as money became short Amélie and her father decided to sell the last piece of Raisa's jewellery - the pearl necklace. Amélie walked the mile to the Marais and was horrified to find buildings painted with yellow stars with the word *'Jude'* scrawled above the doors, homes wrecked, their owners nowhere in sight. Monsieur Rosenberg's shop had been ransacked, the windows broken, the counter and glass display cases smashed to pieces. As she stood there in disbelief a neighbour emerged from his door.

'Where is Monsieur Rosenberg?' she cried.

'He was taken away with the others in the raid last month. I'm still here because I'm Catholic, but there's no Jews left in this street.'

Appalled and disgusted, she turned on her heel and fled. In her haste she rounded a corner and ran headfirst into a German soldier coming the other way.

He took her arm, forcefully. 'Why are you in such a hurry, Madame? Show me your papers!'

Beginning to panic she fumbled in her handbag and in doing so the necklace, wrapped in a handkerchief, fell out onto the pavement. The soldier bent down and picked it up.

'Mmm...a fine piece. I wonder why you are carrying a pearl necklace around in your bag?'

'I...I took it for repair...it's broken...'

He looked her up and down and examined her papers.

'So you went to the Marais. Interesting, when there are other jewellers closer to where you live.'

She looked away from him, fighting her anxiety, then he said, 'Madame Swann. That's an unusual name.'

'Not really,' she shrugged, knowing she had already said too much.

The soldier looked at her, suspiciously.

'Thank you, Madame Swann. I will keep this,' he said, putting the necklace in his pocket. 'It's broken. You don't need it any more.'

'But...'

Anger overtook her fear and she moved towards him to remonstrate, but the soldier pushed her away and fixed her with a steely stare.

'Go home, Madame Swann. I will not forget you.'

Trying to maintain some dignity she drew herself up to her full height, turned on her heel and walked away from him, defiantly, but her eyes were brimming with tears.

CHAPTER 7

Bath, 1941

By Easter, Philippe's work at the railway station was almost complete. It seemed as good a reason as any to show his gratitude to Clare, so he said, 'I want to thank you for your help - you and your colleagues have made me very welcome here. Would you like to have tea with me at the Pump Room?'

Philippe had asked Mary's advice for a suitable venue, and her suggestion was right on the mark.

'Thank you, I'd love to! I've lived in Bath all my life and never been there.'

'Shall we say Saturday? If you're sure that would that be all right…'

'You mean, taking a respectable married woman out to tea? I'm sure Reg couldn't object to that. I think it would be lovely.'

The following Saturday they caught the bus into town together. Clare had chosen a tea dress with a rose pattern, nipped-in at the waist to accentuate her figure, and was wearing her hair loose. When Philippe saw her his heart skipped a beat and he said, 'you look beautiful!'

She laughed and twirled around, while he admired her shapely legs.

'Makes a change from the serge suit!' she said. 'And you look nice too.'

He had trimmed his beard and was wearing smart twill trousers and a jacket.

They walked together through the city, enjoying the Spring sunshine, and made their way to the Pump Room next to the Abbey. A waiter guided them to a table laid with a white linen tablecloth and bone china, close to the stage where a string quartet was playing. They looked around the room with its high ceiling and ornate plasterwork and voiced the same thought – 'it's better than the refreshment room at the station!'

The waiter brought a pot of tea, served with a flourish.

'*Bon appétit!*' said Philippe.

Clare gave a little giggle at the foreign expression. '*Bon appétit!*' she responded, smiling.

They ate, hungrily, and spam sandwiches and fruit cake had never tasted so good. Philippe watched Clare as she told him about the Pump Room and the Roman Baths, but wasn't really listening to what she said.

'So that's why Bath is called Aquae Sulis,' she concluded, 'it means 'waters of the sun' - because of the hot spring water.'

'Fascinating!' he replied, noticing how her blue eyes sparkled when she smiled, her regular features he had found such a pleasure to paint, that way she had of brushing her fair hair back from her lovely face…

When they had finished their tea Philippe paid the bill and they wandered outside, walking through the Orange Grove towards the Parade Gardens.

'This is my favourite part of Bath,' said Clare, leaning on the stone balustrade overlooking the gardens and beyond to Pulteney Bridge and the River Avon.

'Mine too – it's beautiful. I painted the view from here, last year, when I first arrived. It seems a long time ago.'

They stood, side by side, watching the water rushing over the weir. Further down the river a pair of swans glided by serenely, children were playing on the riverbank and people were strolling around, relaxing in the warm weather. Clare took a deep breath and held her face up to the sun, her eyes closed; it felt good to be away from the smoke and dirt of the railway station, out in the fresh air and with a handsome man for company.

They stayed for a while then Clare said, 'I'd better be getting home. Thank you for the tea, it's been wonderful - and a good excuse to wear a dress!'

They caught the bus back to Larkhall and he walked her to her door.

'Thanks again. You're a good friend, Philippe.'

She gave him a kiss on the cheek and lingered for a second, loving the feel of his smooth beard against her skin, aware of the scent of him. Then she smiled and reluctantly went indoors.

He walked away, touching his face where she had kissed him, thinking how lucky he was to have Clare as his friend, and wishing she could be more.

Paris, 1941

One night in July, Amélie was woken by screams and flashing lights and rushed to the window to see groups of German soldiers with rifles storming into the apartment block opposite, seeking out Jews and forcing them from their homes at gunpoint. The commotion awoke Louis who joined his daughter and they watched, aghast, as men, women and children were lined up, pushed into the backs of lorries and driven away. Amélie went out onto the landing where the neighbours were discussing the events, saying, 'thank God we don't have any Jewish families here.'

Amélie learnt that over a thousand Jews had been arrested that night and taken to an internment camp in Drancy, a north-eastern suburb of Paris. At the hospital the next day most of her colleagues expressed their disgust, although some reserved comment or said, plainly, that Jews had always been a problem and it was high time action was taken to get rid of them.

Amélie was appalled, saying, 'but they're just people! Why do you hate them so much?'

'They are money-grabbers, always have been,' said Dr Moreau. 'Look at the de Camondo family! They came here, made all their money by milking the rest of us then bought great houses in the best streets in Paris! It's time they had their come-uppance.'

'It's dreadful,' interjected a nurse, 'but many of them are foreigners. There's nothing we can do.'

Amélie looked at her colleagues in despair.

'Come, Nurse Swann, back to the ward,' said Dr Fournier, ushering her away, then he whispered, 'don't take any notice of them. They are ignorant. Come and see me this evening, I've something for you.'

After her shift Amélie went to Jean-Pierre's office. He locked the door, they kissed, then he said, 'I have a letter which must be delivered tonight to an address near the Place de Bastille. It's close to your apartment - would you mind?'

'No, of course not! I'll do it on the way home.'

Amélie had run several errands for Jean-Pierre under cover of delivering medicines to patients, riding her bicycle as the soldiers were less likely to stop her. He suddenly let her go from his embrace, put his finger to her lips and crept over to the door. He listened, then, satisfied there was no one outside he returned to Amélie, but they were both on edge.

'I'm sorry, it's difficult here and I don't want to put you in any danger. I have an idea of somewhere we can meet away from the hospital. My friend has a room in Montmartre he is willing to let us use. We would be able to spend more time together. What do you think?'

'It sounds wonderful, if you are sure it is safe.'

'Good, I'll talk to him. But now you must go.'

They kissed again, then Amélie left the hospital and delivered the message. At home she went to see her father who had gone to bed.

'Are you all right, *chérie*? They work you too hard at that hospital.'

'I'm sorry, Papa,' she said, feeling her usual rush of guilt at leaving him. 'I had to work late, unexpectedly. Sleep well.'

She kissed him on the forehead and went to her room. She hated lying but couldn't stop thinking about what Jean-Pierre had said, and in her mind she was already inventing reasons to leave the house so that she could spend precious time with her lover.

In August more than four thousand Jews were arrested in a series of raids led by the Gendarmerie, acting on Nazi orders. One afternoon Amélie witnessed Monsieur Veber, a Jewish man who owned the local shoe shop, being forced at gunpoint into a lorry with a dozen or so others. Shocked to the core, she cried out, 'Monsieur Veber, what's happening?'

In her anger she confronted one of the gendarmes, a young man about the same age as her son.

'What on earth do you think you are doing? Monsieur Veber has been selling shoes here since before you were born! What right have you got to treat him like this, herding him into a truck, like an animal! What is the matter with you?'

He looked at her, his eyes full of confusion, but as soon as he hesitated his sergeant came up and said, 'he's following orders. Now get out and let us get on with our job.'

'But…'

'Please, Madame…'

He took her by the arm and steered her away and she watched, powerless, as the lorry drove off.

Outraged by what she had seen, Amélie quickly made her way home, unable to contain her distress. She ran up the stairs to the apartment, seeking her father, leaving the front door ajar in her haste.

'I'm so angry, Papa, but I'm scared, too - what if they find out? Will they come after us? It's a nightmare coming true - all my fears for Philippe - I was right to send him away, wasn't I?'

'Yes, you were. He'll be safe in England. But don't worry, nobody knows around here, it's all so long ago. Tonight, we will say a prayer for our brothers and sisters. There is nothing more we can do. They are in God's hands.'

In her anguish Amélie hadn't noticed Madame Duclos following her into the building. Now, the old woman stood in the shadows, by her front door, listening attentively. She'd always had her suspicions about Madame Swann and her parents - something was nagging at her memory from long ago. She remembered when the Duvalier's had moved in - Louis and his foreign wife Raisa, a lady who kept herself to herself and shunned contact with her neighbours, almost as if she had something to hide. Once, on the stairs, she'd caught her by surprise and Raisa had tried to conceal the necklace she wore... Yes, she remembered now.

With a surge of satisfaction, Madame Duclos quietly let herself into her apartment. She sat down, her hands folded in her lap, and smiled to herself. She decided to keep this useful information to herself - for the moment. Because she remembered now, what she had seen around the woman's neck: a Star of David.

CHAPTER 8

Bath, 1941

With great excitement, Richard and Ann welcomed their guests to the private viewing of the 'Bath at War' Summer Exhibition, prior to the formal opening. Their students had done them proud, producing over a hundred paintings and sketches of Bath and its people.

Philippe invited Mary and Derek to the *vernissage*. 'It means the day when artists put the finishing touch to their works by varnishing them,' he explained.

'But I'm not really interested in art,' said Derek.

'Oh, go on!' said Mary, 'it will be interesting to see what Philippe's been up to. We'd love to come!'

The guests, who included the Mayor of Bath, sponsors, art critics and a journalist from the *Bath & Wilts Chronicle*, were welcomed with glasses of sherry and there was a happy buzz about the place as the visitors wandered around with copies of the catalogue, scrutinising the pictures. Their reaction was enthusiastic, and the exhibition seemed sure to be a favourite with critics and public alike.

Mary was impressed with Philippe's work.

'I wonder what Jack would have made of it — you, from Paris, painting scenes in Bath! I love the ones of the railway station, although those cellars give me the creeps,' she said, looking at a gloomy picture of the vaults in semi-darkness. 'I had no idea they were there!'

Mary also admired the painting of a young woman in her working clothes, sweeping the platform.

'It's Clare Watkins, isn't it — you've captured her so well, very authentic.'

Mary didn't say, but noticed something special about the expression on Clare's face as she looked at the artist, a softness in her eyes, and could sense the rapport between them.

Daniel's parents came to the exhibition accompanied by a pretty young woman with auburn hair who turned out to be Daniel's girlfriend.

'You kept her quiet!' said Michael.

'Emma? Our families have known each other forever — we go to the same Meeting House. But...'

He looked coy.

'...I suppose, lately, we have been seeing more of each other...'

Michael said, 'God, I wish my life were that simple!'

He'd recently been ditched by the model who had become bored with penniless artists and turned her attention elsewhere. He found some consolation in the response to his work, though — he won the overall prize for his painting of the Home Guard practising drill by the air raid shelter, opposite the Scala in Oldfield Park.

Richard gave a short speech praising his students' work and the Mayor responded, saying the paintings represented a fine record of Bath during this difficult period of its history. Philippe had invited Clare to the exhibition and was anxiously looking out for her, but when she finally arrived she wasn't alone – a soldier was at her side. Philippe went over to greet her and rather nervously she said, 'this is Reg, my husband – he came home last night, unexpectedly.'

Philippe extended his hand and said, 'pleased to meet you.'

Reg Watkins shook Philippe's hand without enthusiasm.

'I didn't want to miss the opening, so I persuaded Reg to come with me. I hope that's all right?'

'Of course! It's good to see you. Help yourselves to a glass of sherry and take a look around.'

In his Army uniform Reg looked out of place among the students, their families and the local worthies. He clearly didn't want to be there. Clare spotted Mary, pleased to see a friendly face, and Mary said, 'have you seen Philippe's painting of you? I love it - so natural.'

Clare found the painting and pointed it out to her husband.

'Look, Reg, it's me!'

He looked at the portrait of his wife in her working clothes, leaning on a broom on the platform. Something about her expression rattled him and he said, 'surprised you had time to stand there while he drew you – I thought you were always so busy!'

He looked at Philippe's other pictures of the station, observing that Clare appeared in several of them.

'Looks like you've been seeing quite a lot of this Frenchman while I've been away…'

'Well, it was interesting, having an artist working there.'

He was unimpressed. In the crowd, Reg accidentally jostled a man's elbow and he spilt his drink.

'You idiot, you've made me spill sherry down my shirt!' exclaimed the man who was short, fat and wore glasses.

Reg snapped. All the resentment and jealousy that had been building up inside him exploded.

'You pompous bastard!'

'How dare you!'

Reg made to take a swing at him but Daniel stepped in and restrained him before the blow could land.

Clare was appalled.

'Reg! Stop it!'

'No, I won't! Look at you all! Standing here with your sherries, looking at the pretty pictures…Bath at War…you've got no idea what war means!' he sneered. 'You haven't seen men with their innards spilling out, their heads blown off in front of you…but I have! I'll show you what I think of your exhibition…'

He took a knife from his pocket and made to slash one of the canvases but Richard grabbed him from behind and the knife fell to the floor.

'Somebody call the police!' cried a woman.

'No, it's all right,' said Richard, calmly, 'we'll just get our soldier friend out of here, nice and quietly…'

Clare, upset and embarrassed, apologised to everyone and said, 'come on, Reg, we're going home!'

Philippe looked on, feeling that somehow this was all his fault, but unsure what to do. After the couple had left, among the general murmuring of condemnation Richard said, 'it is difficult. And he has a point – what do we know, living quietly here in our lovely city? We haven't been subjected to the awful things our soldiers have seen. Who are we to judge?'

'Our servicemen are under a lot of strain,' commented his wife, Ann.

But many people disagreed, and Derek said, 'bloody rude I call it!'

After Reg returned to Lincolnshire, Clare came round to see Mary, Derek and Philippe to apologise. She was mortified by her husband's behaviour but Mary made some tea, told her not to worry, and talked of other things. When Clare got up to leave, Philippe walked her to the door.

'I'm sorry, Philippe - I really enjoyed having lunch with you while you were at the station, and going out for tea. But…well, Reg did get funny about me being friends with you. I feel awful, but I think I'd better not see you again.'

'But Clare…'

He touched her gently on the shoulder and she looked up at him, sadness clouding her eyes. She kissed him on the cheek, hating to leave him, and walked away.

At the start of the Autumn term Richard set his students to produce self-portraits, working at their easels in the studio. Philippe sensed a wistfulness in his painting which he put down to missing Clare. Teased by his friends who told him to get over her, he sought new amusements, chatting up other girls in the pubs on his nights out, but it wasn't the same. He threw himself into his work, and when the artists progressed to painting portraits of each other Philippe and Michael showed a real talent for the genre. One day Richard called Philippe into his office.

'I think you're ready for your first commission. I've had a request from a Government official called Legge who wants a portrait of his daughter to mark her twelfth birthday. It would be a good one for you - are you interested?'

Pleased of the diversion and the challenge of something new, the next Saturday morning Philippe caught the bus to Claverton Down on the south side of Bath where Mr Legge lived with his family in a grand Victorian mansion. The housekeeper showed him into the study where Mr Legge, a thin, balding man wearing horn-rimmed spectacles, was seated in an armchair, reading the newspaper. He stood up to greet his visitor.

'How interesting to meet a Frenchman! Tell me, how do you come to be in Bath?'

Philippe explained briefly, then Mr Legge asked, 'and what do you know of the situation in Paris?'

'Only what I read in the newspapers. I haven't received a letter from my mother since the Nazis invaded. I am very concerned about her and my grandfather - he is quite frail. My mother is a nurse at the hospital St Antoine. I think about them every day.'

'It can't be easy for them - or for you.'

Mr Legge hesitated for a moment; the young man seemed a reasonable sort and had come highly recommended by Richard Cross whom he knew and respected. He sympathised with his plight and said, 'Monsieur Swann, in my line of work I occasionally hear reports from abroad. If I learn anything of interest I'll let you know.'

'Thank you! To know something - anything at all - would help.'

'Indeed. Now, I'll take you to meet my daughter, Angela. You can speak to her in French if you like - she could do with the practice.'

Philippe followed Mr Legge through to a pleasant, sunlit drawing room where a brown-eyed girl with rosy cheeks and freckles was standing, looking out the window. Her dark hair was in plaits and she was wearing a lemon yellow party frock.

'Angela, this is Monsieur Swann, the artist. Say *bonjour*.'

Angela did so and her father left the room. Philippe asked Angela to sit down so he could arrange her pose, tilting her head back slightly and asking her to relax her shoulders to improve her posture. He encouraged her to speak a few words of French and she told him, in a dreadful accent, that this was the dress she was going to wear at her birthday party. Then, sighing, she said, 'I really can't see the point of learning languages. Mummy says the best thing to do with

56

foreigners is speak loudly and keep repeating yourself until they understand!'

Philippe gave up and reverted to English. He began sketching, then asked, 'what does your father do?'

'No one knows *exactly* what he does - not even Mummy. He works in an office in Whitehall and sometimes he gets phone calls at the weekend. I think he's quite important.'

Angela began fidgeting around and Philippe tried a few topics - family, school - but failed to engage with her. Then he said, 'your father tells me you have a pony.'

Her eyes lit up.

'Yes! He's called Marmalade because he's got a browny orangey coat and he's an absolute darling!'

He'd cracked it; from then on, Angela was the perfect subject.

CHAPTER 9

Paris, 1941

In Montmartre, Jean-Pierre Fournier was looking down at Amélie sleeping beside him. She was beautiful; her well-defined dark eyelashes and eyebrows stood out against her pale skin; a few fine lines around the corners of her eyes and mouth indicated her maturity; her dark hair fell around her shoulders and onto her small breasts. She was thin - everybody was, now - and he could see the outline of her ribs, leading down to her pelvis and the curve of her hip.

For him, it had started much in the traditional manner of the *cinq à sept*, the hours when French men met their mistresses for a brief liaison between finishing work and going home to their families. But Amélie was special, and as the months had gone on, occasional sex in his office at the end of the day was no longer enough. He was fortunate that his friend - one of his Resistance contacts - had offered him the room in Montmartre so that he and Amélie could spend more time together. Jean-Pierre still loved his family but had grown apart from his wife and used the opportunities war afforded him to be away from home without explanation. All he wanted now was Amélie. There were still things about her he didn't understand, but it didn't matter. He would do anything for her.

She stirred, opened her eyes and he kissed her. They made love, again, enjoying the luxury of privacy, a proper bed and time to do all the things they had yearned to do to each other for so long. Time was not limitless, however. Jean-Pierre looked at his watch and said, 'I'm sorry, *chérie...*'

'I know.'

She got out of bed, pulled a robe around her and went over to the window, peeking out through the shutters. The late Autumn afternoon was drawing to a close and the sun was low in the sky, glinting on the golden cupola of Les Invalides in the distance. From the attic room high up in Montmartre, Paris lay at their feet. The narrow alleyways and cobbled streets provided the perfect place for a liaison; nobody knew or cared about the lovers who met there. The couple left the building and walked, hand in hand, through the artists' quarter towards the shining white domes of the Sacré Coeur, then down the steep hill to the Métro where they went their separate ways.

Amélie lived for these moments with Jean-Pierre and found it hard to disguise her joy – their affair had blossomed into something much stronger and serious. Her father noticed and finally asked, 'I don't know where you go when you disappear on Saturdays, but tell me - are you seeing someone special?'

Her excuses had run thin and she confessed. 'Yes, Papa - I can't deny it. I am in love!'

'At last, she tells me the truth! If he makes you happy, that is fine with me. I won't ask any more. It is your business. Take your happiness while you can.'

Madame Duclos also observed her neighbour's comings and goings at the weekend, the blush on her cheek when she came home, her eyes sparkling, a smile she couldn't hide. The old woman was delighted to add to her dossier another reason to be suspicious of her neighbour, the half-Jewess…

Bath, 1941

Towards the end of the year, Richard hit a snag: there were so many canvases in the basement the School was running out of storage space. Philippe had an idea and went to Green Park where the Station Master was happy to help.

'There's an empty cellar at the end of the vaults you can use. It's dry in there and they'll be perfectly safe. I'll get someone to give you a hand.'

Philippe packed the canvases into boxes ready for storage and pushed them on a trolley to the station where he was met by none other than Clare. At one look he knew how much he had missed her.

Reddening slightly, she greeted him.

'The Station Master asked me to help someone with storage - I didn't realise it was you! I've got the key to the vaults - let me help you.'

They spent the next hour carrying the boxes down the stairs and stacking them in one of the gloomy rooms below ground, Clare carrying a gas lamp to light the way. After they finished the first batch Philippe said, 'I think we deserve a break - let me buy you a cup of tea.'

They went to the refreshment room together, each reminded of the pleasant times they had spent there in the past, and at last they could talk properly.

'I'm sorry I had to break off our friendship. I was worried about what Reg might say - he gets so jealous, although he hasn't been home for ages. I've missed seeing you, Philippe.'

She looked at him, remembering his kind brown eyes, his lovely smile, and how much she enjoyed his company.

'I've missed you too,' he said, touching her hand. 'My friends told me to forget you but I can't.'

It was true: none of the other girls he'd been out with interested him like Clare, and seeing her again he wanted her more than ever.

'Well, now we have a good excuse to meet! How many more of those boxes do you have to bring over?'

'Dozens!'

Over the next days the pair carried more boxes from the School, taking their time, stacking them carefully down in the vaults. They chatted as they worked, growing closer, and being together in the gloom it was hard not to develop an intimacy. Having crammed the final boxes into place they both stood back and, in the light of the hissing gas lamp, looked at what they had achieved. Philippe put his arm companionably around her shoulders and her arm went instinctively around his waist.

'Thanks so much, this is great.'

'You're welcome. Always happy to help the School of Art!'

They stood for a moment, conscious of each other's closeness, then they turned towards each other and he kissed her on the mouth.

At first she held back, but then she found herself returning his kisses, feeling herself melting inside. She put her arms around him, pulling his firm body close to hers as they grew more passionate. They whispered each other's names as he kissed her neck, then he undid the buttons of her jacket, caressing her breasts, and ran his hands over her hips, his desire growing.

Suddenly a torch beam shot their way and a voice shouted out, 'are you two all right down there?'

Philippe took a deep breath. 'We're almost finished…' he shouted back, thinking, we've only just started. They kissed once more then reluctantly let each other go. Clare smoothed down her clothes and followed Philippe out of the vaults, then back on the surface she walked with him to the station entrance.

'I must see you again, Clare.'

'Tomorrow,' she said.

When the two met in the refreshment room in the cold light of day, Philippe knew things weren't going to turn out well. She looked at him, blushed, and said quietly, 'I think we got carried away yesterday.'

'I suppose we did,' he said, with a sigh. Then he drew closer and whispered, 'but you know how much I want you!'

'But we can't, can we? Reg will be coming home for Christmas and I can't have him suspecting anything.'

Philippe shook his head in frustration. Daniel had advised him against married women and he was beginning to think he was right.

'We can still be friends, though?' she asked.

He leant forward, took her hands in his and kissed them, speaking quietly but decisively. 'Clare, I want more than that. I love you. There, I've said it. I love you, I want you.'

'Philippe!'

She glanced around, hoping nobody was watching them.

'It's true! And I think you want me too.'

She caught her breath, facing her feelings and knowing he was right. She did want him but she couldn't speak the words, it was impossible - she was a married woman. She should never have let herself get so close to Philippe, no matter how much she liked him. For all his faults, Reg was her husband and she felt a loyalty towards him.

'I'm sorry, I can't...'

With a groan of exasperation he let her go. Were all Englishwomen like this, to be faithful to a husband they didn't love?

She couldn't bear it. She pushed back her chair and ran from the room, struggling to hold back her tears.

At Christmas time Philippe felt subdued, having found love then losing it, knowing Clare was nearby but out of his reach, with her husband at home.

He went to Midnight Mass, praying for his mother and grandfather, feeling ever more distant from Paris and anxious to know how his family were faring.

Reg had returned for Christmas leave bearing gifts of chocolate, cigarettes and nylon stockings he'd acquired from an American air base close to where he was stationed. He announced that in February he was being posted to the North African desert with the Eighth Army.

'I'm ready to face action again,' he said, confidently.

He took Clare out to the pictures one night but spent the other evenings in the pub with his friends, coming home the worse for drink. One night he had a terrible nightmare, shouting out and waking up drowned in sweat. He was shaking and Clare held him as he choked on his words.

'There were these bits of bodies, floating in the water, bits of arms and legs, and blood…'

When he settled down he said, 'I'm sorry, babe. I get these nightmares - I can't get those pictures out of my mind…Sometimes it stops for a bit, but then it comes back. I'm not much of a husband to you, am I?'

He looked at her and gently touched her face. For the first time since he'd been back she could see a trace of his old self.

'It's all right, you can't help it. Don't worry, we'll get through this…'

'I need you, Clare. I love you.'

She held him, stroking his hair, comforting him as she would a child, and whispered, 'I love you, too.'

CHAPTER 10

Paris, 1942

Amélie was working on the ward, dispensing medicines, when Dr Fournier approached her and said, in a stern voice, 'Nurse Swann, I need to see you in my office, straight away.'

Concerned by his tone she followed him, walking quickly to keep up. He showed her in, his face softened and he stood close to Amélie, touching her arm. In a voice barely above a whisper he said, 'you must not repeat what I am going to tell you. I have a message for you, from England. Your son, the artist, is safe and well.'

Amélie gasped. Her knees buckled beneath her and she held on to Jean-Pierre's arm to steady herself. She opened her mouth to speak but he put his finger to her lips. When she had caught her breath she looked into his eyes and said, softly, 'thank you! I cannot believe you have made contact! Can you tell him - can you tell him that I and his grandfather are also safe and well?'

He smiled and said 'yes, I will pass that on.'

Suddenly there was a knock at the door and the doctor's secretary entered the room. Amélie and Jean-Pierre swiftly let go of each other.

'Sorry to disturb you,' she said, raising her eyebrows, 'I have the letters you wanted to sign.'

'Thank you, put them on my desk.'

Then looking at Amélie he said, brusquely, 'that will be all, Nurse Swann. And remember what I told you.'

'Yes, doctor,' she replied, passing the secretary without looking at her.

Amélie went straight to the ladies toilet, locked herself in the cubicle and wept, silently, with relief. She would say nothing, not even to her father, but after two years of worry she had received the news she was so desperate to hear.

Her son, the artist, was safe and well.

Bath, 1942

At the beginning of March it was Michael's turn to be offered a commission. Richard told him, 'it's an urgent job for a Mrs Mason who wants her husband's portrait painted while he's home on leave – he's a Captain in the Royal Navy.'

The next day Michael climbed Lansdown Hill, an affluent area on the north side of Bath, to a large, detached house called The Oaks. Mrs Mason, a tall, slim woman of around forty with neat blonde hair and pale blue eyes, greeted him and led him to a sunny conservatory where she had placed a chair in front of a bamboo screen for the subject, and another chair and table for the artist.

'This is perfect, thank you,' said Michael, smiling at her. Mrs Mason noticed his remarkably white teeth.

'I'll go and fetch my husband.'

Captain Mortimer Mason, medium height, stocky, with an impressive bushy brown beard, was wearing his uniform for the occasion. He wasn't keen on his wife's suggestion to have his portrait painted ('I can't be sitting still for hours while some whippersnapper weighs me up!') but she'd persuaded him it would give him an interest while his ship was in dock, and a perfect way to mark his fiftieth birthday. Michael quickly got to work making preliminary sketches while the Captain relaxed and related tales of his life at sea. Two hours later the artist announced that he had sufficient for the first sitting and the Captain went outside to get some fresh air.

Mrs Mason offered Michael some tea and he followed her into the kitchen. He watched her as she moved around, admiring her shapely calves and the way her tight tweed skirt clung to her buttocks, while she fussed over the kettle and reached up into a cupboard to fetch a packet of biscuits.

'There's no cake, I'm afraid. Since I lost my housekeeper I have to do everything myself and I'm not very good at baking!'

She poured the tea and the two sat at the kitchen table.

'The Captain was telling me about the war, up in the North Atlantic. It sounds very exciting, but dangerous. You must worry about him.'

'I do, but one gets used to it. It's what he's always done - the Navy is what he loves the most. I grew up with it, you see - my father was an Admiral…'

Michael listened attentively as she told him about her happy childhood at The Oaks. Her elder sister had married an Army officer and lived abroad, so when their parents died she had stayed in the house and made it her home.

'Bit big for you, isn't it?'

'It's fine when my husband is here. But yes, it is rather large when I'm alone.'

'No children then?'

'No…'

A shadow crossed her face, and Michael sensed the sorrow that lay beneath her answer.

She took a breath and continued, '…but my charity work keeps me busy, especially now, with the war on. I can't take paid employment, you see, it wouldn't be appropriate for a Captain's wife.'

'Of course not.'

They finished their tea and she showed him to the door. As they shook hands she noticed his long, artistic fingers which held hers in a firm yet gentle grip.

'Good day, Mrs Mason.'

Under the gaze of his piercing blue eyes she found herself saying, 'Rosamund. You can call me Rosamund.'

She watched his tall, slim figure as he walked back down the driveway, then closed the door and went to find her husband.

'How did it go, dear? Not too painful?'

Mortimer harrumphed and said, 'it was all right, I suppose. Now, what's for lunch?'

That evening, alone in the kitchen, Rosamund thought about Michael - a perceptive young man whom she knew had recognised the loneliness that lay within her. Her charity work helped fill her empty life but nothing compensated for her basic, primeval, want of a child. Her friends tried to be sympathetic but when they chatted about the ups and downs of their own families she couldn't help but feel envious and excluded. Years ago, she had gone to see an obstetrician at the local hospital, a charming man around her own age called Dr Roberts, who could find no sign of infertility on her part but suspected that the problem lay with her husband.

'I could arrange for him to come for some tests, if you wish,' he had told her.

Rosamund was shocked. 'Mortimer would never let himself be subjected to that!'

'I'm afraid in that case, Mrs Mason, there is nothing more I can do.'

She had noticed a framed photograph on the doctor's desk of his lovely wife and two young sons and felt a wave of jealousy. She looked crestfallen, and, fearing he may have sounded harsh, Dr Roberts added, 'but do keep trying - nature is a strange mistress. Don't give up hope.'

Rosamund came back to the present and sighed. Yes, one must never give up hope.

She turned her attention to what to cook for herself, as Mortimer was eating out with his friends from the Admiralty and wouldn't be home until later. She picked up the well-worn copy of Mrs Beeton's *'Cookery and Household Management'* she had inherited from the housekeeper. Skimming through the recipes in search of inspiration for her evening meal she noticed a recipe which began, 'Take six fresh eggs…'

Rosamund laughed. 'In my dreams!' she said, out loud.

*

Pushing thoughts of Clare to the back of his mind, Philippe completed Angela's portrait and delivered it to the Legge's house in time for her birthday. He unveiled it with a flourish, declaring, *'et voilà!'*, and the family applauded. Angela was thrilled that he'd made her look so pretty and her father said, 'it really is very good. You've captured that mischievous look in her eyes!'

Angela giggled.

'What a marvellous birthday present!' said her mother, 'this deserves a drink!' She signalled to the housekeeper to pour whiskies for the adults and a lemonade for Angela. While the family inspected the portrait more closely, Mr Legge took Philippe to one side and said, 'actually, I'd like a word with you if you'll come into my study.'

He followed him across the hallway and Mr Legge gestured to him to sit down.

'First of all, here's your payment', he said, passing the artist some bank notes, 'but more importantly, I have a message for you - from Paris.'

Philippe caught his breath.

'Now, you must tell nobody about this - *nobody*. Understand?'

'Yes…'

'Your mother and your grandfather are safe and well. And they know that you are, too.'

Philippe was staggered. 'But how…?'

'That's all I can tell you. But I must warn you - things are difficult over there, and life is hard. Monsieur Swann, if ever, in future, you feel able to do something for your country - and they need all the help they can get - then ring this number.'

He gave him a card with a London telephone number written on it.

'Thank you for this information, Mr Legge. I am very grateful.'

They got up and shook hands.

'It's been good to meet you, Monsieur Swann. Good luck.'

Philippe walked away, his mind reeling with questions. Somehow, Mr Legge must be in touch with the French Resistance movement, and moreover his mother must know someone in Paris with access to Resistance communications. The situation over there sounded dire. He touched his pocket containing the card, doubting whether he would ever be brave enough to call the number. What role could he possibly play in helping his country? All he knew was how to paint pictures!

CHAPTER 11

Bath, 1942

Rosamund Mason was with her friend Prudence in a poor area of Bath near the quayside, giving out clothes to the needy. They made their way swiftly along the rows of houses, trying not to breathe in too deeply - the stench was appalling and Prudence swore that she'd just seen a flea jumping out of a boy's hair. At the next house a woman with a cigarette dangling from the corner of her mouth and a babe in arms willingly took the offerings. Rosamund looked at the baby - a remarkably healthy boy with fair hair and blue eyes - and couldn't help but say, 'what a darling boy.'

The woman looked down at her son with a sigh of resignation and said, 'number seven! As if I didn't have enough on my plate!'

Rosamund felt an extraordinary impulse to grab the child and take it away, imagining the brighter future she would be able to give him, but the woman closed the door and the fantasy faded away.

'Come on,' said Prudence, 'only four more houses to go. Then we can go home and have a nice hot bath.'

Her good deed completed, Rosamund returned to The Oaks and did just that, luxuriating in her bathtub, washing the grime from her skin and the stench of cigarette smoke and coal dust from her hair. She thought about the baby boy, wondering what sort of a life he would have, and how unfair it seemed for a woman like that to have seven children when she, Rosamund, couldn't even produce one.

The sittings progressed and Rosamund got into the habit of serving Michael tea in the kitchen while Mortimer took a turn around the garden to stretch his legs. She enjoyed Michael's visits, getting to know him better and finding his youthful company stimulating.

'I expect you've had enough of Mortimer and his stories!' she said. 'You must be a good listener.'

'It helps. Most people present a certain face to the world, but I'm interested in what lies beneath. You see, when you're painting a portrait it's the subject's character you want to capture as well as how they look.'

'Yes…how fascinating!'

Resting her chin on her hand, she watched the young man who was probably half her age, but so sensitive, and, with those blue eyes and blonde hair, really quite attractive.

'Tell me about yourself. You're a local boy?'

She listened as he spoke about his background, explaining how he'd been unable to join up because of his migraines.

'They sound horrid,' she said, sympathetically, touching his hand.

'It's something I've had to learn to deal with.'

'And you have no relatives?'

'No – there was just my sister but she moved away to Plymouth and was killed in a raid, last year.'

'How sad! You poor thing, you're all alone in the world.'

He smiled and held her gaze. She was rather lovely for an older woman, he thought, empathetic, nice looking and with a great figure.

'Right, I'd best be going,' he said, getting up. 'I'll be back on Monday.'

She watched as he walked away, carrying his easel and paints, and at the end of the driveway he turned and waved. She smiled and waved back, feeling an odd sensation within her, then closed the door.

That night, Mortimer wound the grandfather clock in the drawing room and went upstairs to join his wife. It was that time of the week again. Mortimer mounted her and began moving, pushing himself against her. She felt the familiarity of his bushy beard rough and scratchy on her face, smelt the tobacco on his breath and the salt embedded in his skin, but in the darkness her thoughts strayed to Michael and her imagination took flight. What if it were him, doing this to her? She pictured his long fingers caressing her, his gentle voice whispering endearments, his young, lithe body moving in harmony with hers.

She suddenly gave a sigh of pleasure, surprising herself, as well as Mortimer, who exclaimed, 'goodness!

That hasn't happened for a long time, old girl!', then rolled off her and went straight to sleep.

Rosamund turned away, her mind in a whirl.

After the final session Michael packed up his kit and said to Rosamund, 'it will take me about a month to finish off the painting in my studio. I'll bring it up to you when it's ready.'

'Thank you, I'll look forward to seeing it - and you. I've enjoyed our chats!'

'So have I.'

Mortimer wasn't the most communicative or affectionate of men but Rosamund had grown used to him being at home and was saddened when, one morning at the end of March, she answered the telephone to hear the clipped tones of a naval officer asking to speak to the Captain. She called Mortimer and after a brief conversation he replaced the receiver, turned to her and said, 'the ship is repaired and ready for sea. I must leave this evening.'

Rosamund spent the afternoon packing Mortimer's kit and before they knew it they were standing in the hall, saying goodbye.

'I'll miss you!' she said.

'And I you, my dear.'

'You'll be able to see your portrait next time you come home!'

'Indeed! I suppose it wasn't too much of an imposition. I'm sure he'll do a good job. Goodbye, Rosamund, take care of yourself.'

He kissed her on the cheek, then he was gone.

Paris, 1942

It was April in Paris, normally the most romantic time of year in this most romantic city, but now devastated by Nazi soldiers patrolling the streets, random episodes of violence and a shortage of food and other essentials. For Amélie and Jean-Pierre their moments together in Montmartre were all that mattered. Lying entwined around each other in bed they would dream of a time when the war was over, when Jean-Pierre would leave his family and they could begin a new life together in the south of France where the weather was warm and the skies always blue.

Amélie lay on her side, looking at her lover as his chest rose and fell with his breath. With her forefinger she gently traced the pattern of dark hair on his torso, admiring his muscular frame, then, aroused, he reached out to her and pulled her towards him. They made love again, quietly, beautifully, until it was time for them to part. They washed and dressed then left the building, walking away with their arms around each other, lost in their own world.

They didn't notice the steely-eyed soldier standing opposite, watching them, curious about the couple he'd often seen meeting here at the weekend, so wrapped up in one another. He recognised the woman and finally remembered where he'd seen her before – down in the Marais. She'd dropped a pearl necklace, a very nice one, too, which he'd sold for a good sum. She had told him it was broken, but it wasn't. He lit a cigarette as he contemplated what was going on: adultery, obviously, but he had the feeling there was more to it than that. He wondered who owned the building where they met - he must check it out. The woman had an unusual name - Swann, wasn't it - he'd made a note of it at the time. He took a deep drag of his cigarette, then exhaled, saying to himself, 'so, this is an interesting situation. What are you up to, Madame Swann? And who is this handsome man that you are so in love with?'

Bath, 1942

Since receiving the message from Mr Legge, Philippe's thoughts turned more and more to Paris and his family. He was relieved to know they were well but frustrated that he could do nothing to help them, and the newsreels showing Nazi cruelty, shooting members of the Resistance, filled him with horror. He read the newspapers with growing concern, thinking of his friends from the Ecole des Beaux-Arts, wondering what they were doing, knowing that his previous life had gone for ever. He couldn't turn to Clare for comfort – he hadn't seen her since that day in the refreshment room before Christmas when he'd proclaimed his love for her and she'd run off in tears. He had left her alone to make up her mind who she really wanted, and although she hadn't been in contact he still clung to hope.

The one thing that cheered Philippe during those lonely months was his discovery of *Radio-Londres*, the voice of the Free French Forces, which broadcast daily. He tuned it in on Mary's wireless set and the first time he heard the words of his native tongue crackling over the airwaves he caught his breath; it was like oxygen to him. From then on he listened whenever he could, revelling in the comfort of his own language, enjoying the music and singing along to French *chansons*. Some evenings when Derek was out Mary would listen with him and occasionally the two would dance together. As he twirled her around Mary laughed like a young girl, saying to Philippe, 'this is just the sort of thing your father would have done!'

One such evening Philippe was waltzing Mary up and down the parlour room when there was a knock at the door. Mary went to answer and showed in their visitor.

'Philippe – there's someone to see you,' she said, discreetly going into the kitchen so the two could be alone.

'Clare! This is a surprise!' exclaimed Philippe, switching off the wireless. They stood for a moment, looking at each other.

'Sorry to disturb you.'

'Not at all! Have a seat.'

'Thanks, but I won't stop. There's something I want to talk to you about. I wondered if you'd like to come for a walk with me, next Saturday? I could bring a picnic.'

'Yes, of course,' he said, intrigued.

'Good. We can meet at mine at one o'clock.'

'I'll be there. Thank you, it will be nice to catch up with your news.'

'Yes…and yours too.'

He showed her out and Mary came back into the room.

'She wants to see me, next Saturday.'

Mary had observed their friendship from a distance and could see that Philippe wanted more than Clare could give him. She'd grown to love her nephew and didn't want him to be hurt, so she said nothing, but squeezed his arm and smiled at him, kindly.

Then he said, 'shall we dance again?'

CHAPTER 12

Bath, 1942

The next Saturday, Michael was on his way out of the School carrying a large package tied with brown paper and string when he passed Philippe in the hallway.

'Just delivering this to Mrs Mason!'

'Ah, you finished the portrait of the Captain. Well done! I hope she likes it. Have a good day.'

'I intend to!' he said, with a wink.

Michael strode through the city and up Lansdown Hill with an air of expectancy. When he'd rung Rosamund to tell her the portrait was ready she sounded excited, and keen to see him. Had he noticed something between them, or was it his imagination, playing tricks?

Rosamund opened the door wearing a cream silk blouse tucked into her skirt, her hair neatly brushed and lipstick freshly applied. She greeted him and he followed her into the drawing room where he carefully unwrapped the package and held up the painting to show her. Rosamund gasped at the stern, dark-eyed, sober face staring at her, proud in the uniform he wore like a second skin, born to the Senior Service.

'My goodness, you've captured him perfectly! That intensity he has, that seriousness – he'll love it, and so do I. You've done a marvellous job. I'd thought I'd hang it here, above the fireplace. Would you be a dear and put it up for me?'

'Of course.'

'Thank you. I'll go and fetch your payment - thirty pounds, wasn't it - I took some cash out the bank yesterday, especially.'

She returned and counted out six white fiver bank notes.

'Thank you, it's been a pleasure,' he replied, folding the notes and putting them in his trouser pocket. He had never possessed such a large amount of cash.

'…and here's a receipt for you. I do like to keep proper accounts,' she said, handing him a note and placing the carbon copy under the frame at the back of the picture.

Michael positioned the picture hook and knocked it in with the hammer. Rosamund watched as he lifted up the painting with its heavy gilt frame and placed it carefully over the hook, admiring the shape of his muscular arms underneath his white shirt.

'That's marvellous. Now, I thought we should celebrate with a glass of sherry.'

He followed her into the kitchen where a bottle and two glasses were on the table, and sat down in his usual place. Rosamund poured their drinks and they clinked glasses.

'To the artist!'

They sipped the sherry.

'The Captain's back at sea, then?'

'He left a month ago. He sent me a letter from Scapa Flow but the ship's on convoy duty now so I don't expect to hear from him for a while. Do you have any more commissions for portraits?'

'Yes - a lady in Batheaston wants a portrait of her brother, a Brigadier. I'm due to start it next week.'

'You're so talented. You'll be famous one day!'

'I don't know about that!'

'I've missed our chats – it's good to see you again.' She touched his hand, admiring those lovely, artistic fingers. 'I enjoy your company - you make me feel ten years younger!'

'And you're a very attractive woman. I'd love to get to know you better…'

They looked into each other's eyes, then, feeling slightly awkward, Rosamund picked up her glass and Michael followed suit but as he raised it to his lips he suddenly cried out in pain, his hand jerked and he dropped the glass which smashed on the floor.

'Whatever's the matter?' she cried out in alarm.

Michael grimaced, his hand to his head. The colour had drained from his face and he looked as though he was going to be sick.

'It's one of my migraines - they come on suddenly, I'm all right one minute and the next…'

He squeezed his eyes shut, in pain, and held his throbbing head.

'It'll pass, but I need to lie down in the dark.'

'Come with me.'

She led him upstairs and along to the end of the hallway.

'This was my housekeeper's room. It's not used any more so I leave the blackout curtains up all the time. Why don't you lie down on the bed and rest until you feel better.'

'Thank you,' he said, weakly.

She helped him get comfortable, took off his boots and covered him with a blanket.

'Close your eyes and I'll bring you some water.'

When she returned, Michael was asleep and she left the glass on the bedside table. Knowing there was nothing more she could do she went downstairs and swept up the broken sherry glass. She looked at her watch - four o'clock. She would leave him for a couple of hours then go and see how he was.

*

Philippe was spending that same Saturday afternoon with Clare. It was a lovely, clear day and at her suggestion they were taking a walk from Larkhall up to Little Solsbury Hill. As they climbed the path Philippe told her about his successful commission for Mr Legge but said nothing about the message from Paris. When they reached the top they sat down on the grass to admire the view of Bath, nestling peacefully among the hills. A skylark hovered above them and they watched, entranced, as it filled the heavens with the trills and chirrups of its song, then flew away.

Clare unpacked their picnic and they ate the sandwiches she had made. Philippe was grateful, even though he thought English cheese tasted awful, and he told her about the joys of camembert and brie, feeling a rush of homesickness as he spoke. With her fair hair lit by the sun she looked lovely and he longed to kiss her, but something was clearly on her mind and finally he asked, 'what did you want to talk about?'

He waited with a growing sense of foreboding.

'Philippe – I'm pregnant.'

His stomach lurched.

'Pregnant?'

'I thought you should know. I haven't told anyone else yet – not even Mum and Dad. I've written to Reg – it was when he came home at the end of January, just before he went to North Africa. I'm sorry, I don't want to hurt you. But he is my husband. He wanted me and I had to let him…'

She looked up at Philippe but he couldn't meet her gaze. Although he was the one in the wrong, he felt betrayed.

'And are you pleased, to be carrying his child?'

'I don't know…I think I am, I like children – but oh, Philippe, in a different world…'

He put his arm around her waist.

'Clare – I still love you. I want you for my own!'

'But I can't! I'm married, and now I'm expecting his baby. Please try and understand.'

'I will never understand! Do you really want to spend the rest of your life with *that man*?'

He spit out the words, scornfully.

'He doesn't love you like I do!'

'I have to! He's my husband.'

Angry and frustrated, Philippe stood up, swearing under his breath in French, and lit a cigarette.

'It's time you thought about your own happiness, Clare.'

'It's too late for that…'

She started to cry. She knew in her heart she'd been attracted to Philippe from the day they'd first met, making a connection she would never feel with Reg, but there was nothing she could do to change things. She took a hanky from her pocket and wiped her eyes.

'I'm sorry, but I can't see you again. I really mean it this time.'

'But Clare…!'

'No! I'm sorry Philippe. It's no use. It's over between us. I want to go home.'

To distract herself she started packing up the picnic basket. He looked again at the view of Bath, unable to believe the day had changed from heaven to hell in a matter of minutes. He struggled to contain his hurt and anger, but there was no point in arguing with her. They walked back down the hill in silence until they reached Clare's house.

'Goodbye, Philippe. Thank you for everything. You're a lovely man, you'll find someone else…'

'I don't want anyone else!'

'I'm sorry, I have to go…'

She kissed him on the cheek, went inside the house and straight upstairs where she threw herself onto her bed and wept. She loved Philippe and knew he loved her, but they both had to accept that there was no future for them together.

*

Towards six o'clock Rosamund made a cup of tea and took it up to Michael, who was awake. She switched on the bedside lamp.

'I hope that's not too bright. How are you?'

'Much better thank you.'

She sat down on the bed next to him and put her hand to his forehead.

'You've cooled down.'

She moved closer to him. The lamplight flattered her, accentuating her fine bone structure. He gently touched her face and she caught her breath as he traced the outline of her cheekbone and her jawline, her chin and finally her lips. Then he put his hand to the back of her neck and gently pulled her towards him, and they kissed.

She felt as if a madness had invaded her and driven all rational thought away. She put her arms around him and they held each other close, kissing all the while. They undressed and she got into bed with him, caressing his smooth chest, filled with the urge to feel her body next to his. Their mutual desire unleashed at last, they made love, overwhelmed by their passion, she moaning with pleasure under his touch. He couldn't believe the desire he had aroused in her, loving her warmth, her femininity, enchanted by the scent and the taste of her. Time went away until, exhausted, they fell into a deep sleep in each other's arms.

A few hours later, Rosamund awoke to a droning sound in the distance.

'What's that?'

Michael stirred.

'Bombers, I expect - heading towards Bristol. Just ignore them.'

He held her tightly and started kissing her again.

CHAPTER 13

Bath, 1942

Confused and angry, hating Reg Watkins with a passion, Philippe stomped along the main road into Bath and went to the School to paint, the prime outlet for his emotions. In the early evening the fire watch team started to arrive and as it grew dark it became apparent that Michael wasn't going to turn up for his shift. Richard asked Philippe if he would take his place and he agreed, with some resentment as he'd been on shift the night before, but he had nothing better to do. The team took up their usual positions on the roof in the narrow passage behind the balustrade on top of the building. It was a clear night and the city was bathed in the light of the full moon – 'a proper bomber's moon!' commented one of the men.

All was quiet until around eleven o'clock when they heard the drone of bombers approaching in the distance. At first they didn't take much notice – it had become a common sight, seeing bombers flying over Bath on their way to Bristol and South Wales to bomb ports and factories. But as the planes came closer it became clear that this was the prelude to something else entirely.

Michael and Rosamund's kisses were interrupted by the wailing of the air raid siren.

'My God, they're not going to attack us, are they?' she cried.

'Could be…' said Michael, as the drone of the planes grew louder. Suddenly there was an explosion and the house shook. Rosamund screamed and they clung to each other, under the covers, then Michael said, 'Christ, I've just remembered! I'm supposed to be on fire watch tonight!'

'They'll have to manage without you! You can't leave now…'

He held her even tighter.

'I'm going nowhere. One of the others will stand in for me.'

'They're going to have a busy night!' Rosamund said, clutching her lover as another bomb exploded nearby. 'We ought to go down to the cellar…'

'It would be safer…but I'd rather stay here, like this…'

As the bombs rained down around them Rosamund fleetingly thought of Mortimer and the horrors he must face at sea when under fire, feeling a surge of guilt at her infidelity, but the sound of gunfire from an enemy plane roaring overhead concentrated her mind on the present. The only thing that mattered now was survival.

The School of Art was directly in the path of enemy attack. Up on the roof of Green Park Buildings, the fire watch team had a bird's eye view as reconnaissance planes flew directly over their heads in groups of two and three, dropping incendiary bombs. One landed next to them and they rushed to action, promptly putting out the flames with water from the stirrup pump as they had been trained to do.

'I can't believe it's come to this! Why do they want to attack Bath of all places?' cried Philippe, shocked by his first contact with the enemy.

'Who knows what goes on in their evil Nazi minds...get down!' a warden cried as a plane flew straight at them, firing its guns, and they dived for cover.

Fires were breaking out all over the city, turning the sky orange and lighting up targets beautifully. The bombers swept over the city from west to east, dropping their deadly cargo on the railway, roads and bridges, then there was an enormous explosion as the gasworks became a fireball. Another fire broke out on the roof and as the team struggled to put it out some debris fell, injuring one of the students who was taken down to the cellar for first aid.

The city was totally unprepared for an attack of this scale and there was little resistance. The planes criss-crossed the city until their supply of bombs was exhausted, then they flew low, aiming their guns at civil defence workers and firemen on the streets who were struggling to control the raging fires. After two hours of unremitting violence the bombers droned away into the distance. The all-clear sounded and the exhausted fire watch team were left to assess the damage, amazed that Green Park seemed to have escaped the worst.

Michael extracted himself from Rosamund's grasp, went over to the window and lifted the blackout curtain slightly so he could see out. He gasped - the sky was ablaze and from down in the city he could hear shouts, cries, and the wail of sirens.

'We'd better check that the house is all right,' said Rosamund, getting out of bed and trying to find her clothes. Downstairs everything seemed in order apart from some smashed crockery which she proceeded to sweep up. The cold water tap spluttered but she managed to fill the kettle, only to find that the gas supply wasn't working. Michael went outside where broken glass was glinting in the moonlight and he could make out some damage to a garden wall. He heard the neighbours checking their properties and it seemed that although there had been explosions nearby, their area had suffered only minor damage.

He went back indoors. 'It doesn't look too bad round here. I'll have a proper look in daylight. There are fires everywhere, though, all over the city, and it looks as if the gasometer exploded. We've been very lucky.'

Rosamund went to him and he held her tight in his comforting arms.

'Oh Michael, I've never felt so scared! I can't believe they want to come here and kill us – it's inhuman!'

'I know – it's horrible, but it's over now. There's nothing more we can do until the morning. Let's go back to bed.'

The fire team at Green Park had a brief respite but towards four o'clock they heard the chilling sound of the siren and rushed up to the roof to resume their positions. The look-out watched through his binoculars as a second wave of aircraft approached, the noise of their engines becoming louder. This time, guided by the raging fires, the enemy's job was even easier. They began by bombing the railway line and factories along the riverbank, then proceeded to attack the Oldfield Park area where rows and rows of terraced housing fell under the bombs, collapsing like packs of cards.

Once more the planes flew low, machine gunners aiming directly at people fleeing in the streets, falling like ninepins to the ground. The planes zipped back and forth, unleashing all the destructive power they had on the citizens of Bath. Philippe watched, stunned at the cruelty inflicted on innocent people, staring at the fires raging all over the city in disbelief, praying that those he loved were safe.

Rosamund and Michael clung together in terror as the planes tore overhead, dropping their lethal cargo, hoping against hope not to be the next target. The house shook as bombs exploded nearby, fires took hold and fierce orange flames filled the sky. At five-thirty the all-clear sounded and the last of the planes droned away.

Dawn rose on this Sunday morning like no other and a deathly yellow pall of smoke and dust hung over the city. The lovers got dressed and went downstairs to inspect the house which, by some miracle, was still intact. Some windows at the back had smashed, scattering shards of glass, and one of the mature oak trees had been severed, but compared to the destruction wrought on the rest of the city they were fortunate. Rosamund checked the drawing room where Mortimer's portrait was still hanging on the wall, undisturbed. She looked up at him, guiltily, and shut the door.

They spent the morning clearing up and shared a tin of corned beef, then Michael said, reluctantly, 'I really ought to go and see how things are down at Green Park. There's so much smoke, it's impossible to identify which buildings have been hit, although I'd say it looks like Oldfield Park's taken a pounding.'

'Yes, you really must go – they'll need your help down at the School. And you'd better take your turn on fire watch tonight!'

'God, yes…let's hope it will be quieter than last night…'

'I'm sure it will be. The Germans have done enough damage to our city. They won't come back.'

They embraced and kissed, longingly, holding each other, then at last Rosamund pushed him away saying, 'now, go! You really must.'

'All right. But I'll come back and see you tomorrow, if that's all right.'

'Of course it is! You don't need to ask. All I want is to see you again.'

They kissed one final time and Michael left the house, Rosamund standing at the door watching him as he walked down the drive. She noticed Mrs Marston and her daughter Eileen, who lived in the house opposite, sweeping up broken glass and it crossed her mind that the neighbours might be wondering what the young man was doing at her house, with her husband away. Mrs Marston stared at Michael and even at a distance Rosamund could sense her disapproval. I'll have to be careful, she thought, then Michael turned towards her, smiled and waved. Rosamund's heart leapt and she said to herself, to hell with it, I don't care what anyone thinks, he's the best thing that's ever happened to me. I love him.

CHAPTER 14

Bath, 1942

Michael walked down Lansdown Hill feeling like a different person from the boy who'd walked up there only yesterday, carrying the portrait wrapped in brown paper and string. He couldn't believe what a change twenty-four hours could bring. The bombing had been horrendous, the most terrifying experience of his life, and he was afraid at what might have happened to the people and places he knew. But next to those feelings of dread he held a diametrically opposed elation, a happiness which he had not thought possible. Rosamund's passion for him had surpassed his wildest fantasies. Together they had survived the raids, and with the confidence she gave him he felt he could achieve anything.

As he neared the bottom of the hill the damage inflicted on the city revealed itself. Thick yellow dust hung in the air and fires were still burning. The Civil Defence teams were out in force, searching in ruined buildings for survivors, for bodies, and the stench of death in the air made him feel sick. At the bottom of Lansdown Hill he saw that the Paragon, a curved

Georgian terrace, had a huge section blown out of it, and a pub they frequented was just a gaping hole. With a rising sense of panic he wondered if the School and his friends had survived. It was unreal - how could this be happening in Bath, his home city, of all places?

He picked up the news as he walked along, hearing as he suspected that Oldfield Park had borne the brunt of the second attack, and that many people had been killed there. He passed the large air raid shelter in Queen Square which looked as if it had served its purpose, but the Francis Hotel along the south side of the square had taken a direct hit. His heart in his mouth he turned down towards Green Park to meet a scene of ruin. Familiar landmarks were gone, the road was covered with masonry from fallen buildings and he couldn't find a way through. He spoke to one of the wardens.

'I'm a student at Green Park. Are they all right? How can I get down there?'

'The Art School's still there but the station roof's gone and the railway track is damaged. Several people have been injured and some reported missing – you're probably one of them! You'd better get along - look, you can follow the path we've made through here…'

Michael thanked the warden and made his way carefully between teetering buildings on one side and heaps of rubble, planks of wood, roof tiles, broken furniture and crushed cars on the other. At last he reached Green Park Buildings and found Philippe and some of the other students sweeping up debris.

Philippe spotted him and turned on him, angrily.

'Where the hell have you been? You were meant to be on fire watch and I had to do it instead! We reported you missing last night, after the first raid.'

'I'm sorry, I was up at Lansdown…'

'Mrs Mason! I thought as much! Too busy, were you?' Philippe said, sarcastically, 'happy for others to do your job while you were having fun?'

'I couldn't leave her after the raid started, could I? By the time I remembered I was supposed to be on watch it was too late…I'm really sorry I didn't make it. Thank you for standing in for me.'

'Well, you can take my place tonight. I've been working for twenty-four hours. It was hell, I tell you - there were fires everywhere, it was horrific. I need to get to Larkhall to see if my Aunt and her husband are still alive. And *you* can take *this*.'

Philippe thrust a broom into Michael's hands and turned away to start the long walk home. Michael stood, looking after him and shouted out once more, 'I'm sorry!', but Philippe ignored him and carried on walking.

Michael sighed and started sweeping up. Richard appeared, the second person to give him a hard time for disappearing, and said, 'look, it was pretty hairy last night. If you're not going to be around at least let us know. But the good news is that everyone's safe, the building's not too badly damaged and we should be able to resume classes tomorrow. You can take your turn on watch tonight. Let's hope the Jerries have had enough of Bath and don't come back!'

It took two hours for Philippe to reach Larkhall, picking his way through the ruined streets full of displaced people whose homes had been blown apart, steering clear of craters in the roads, smashed glass and chequered flags marking the sites of unexploded bombs. He was worried about Mary and Derek, and Clare - he refused to believe she'd finished with him and was desperate to know she was safe. At last Philippe approached his Aunt's road and saw with relief that the house was still standing. He let himself in and Mary rushed to meet him.

'I've been so worried about you! When you didn't come home last night I wanted to try and find you but Derek said I should stay here in case you came back - and here you are!'

Philippe hugged her tightly.

'I'm pleased to see you, too. And is Derek all right?'

'Yes - he had a busy night, as you can imagine. We had some bombs here, but not as bad as the city centre. Tell me, what's it like?'

They sat down and Philippe told her as much as he knew, then Derek returned and Philippe asked, 'how are the Pargetters?'

'They're all right - he was on duty with me last night. I've just left them - you could go and see them if you want - Clare was asking after you.

'I would like to see them - if you don't mind…'

Mary smiled at him. 'Off you go, love.'

Philippe went round straightaway, finding Clare in the kitchen. She ran to him and in the emotion of the moment they embraced, thankful to be alive.

'I was at Green Park, on fire watch. It was very frightening, but it's over now.'

'I've never been so scared in my life! Our neighbours down the road were killed – I was friends with the daughter. It's awful, their house took a direct hit. How's the Art School?'

'Some minor damage but it's still standing.'

'Well thank goodness you are all right.'

He looked at her, with hope in his eyes, but then she said, as gently as she could, 'I'm sorry - it doesn't change anything between us. I still can't be yours…'

Philippe's elation at finding her dissipated as he finally grasped that she meant what she said. He saw no prospect of changing her mind, and with the heaviest of hearts he held her one last time, then returned home. Derek had gone to bed to catch up on his sleep, but Mary was there and made her nephew some tea. He looked despondent, and not just because of the raids, she suspected. Gently, she asked, 'did you see Clare?'

'Yes – all the family are fine, and there's no damage to their house. But…'

Mary waited.

'…but she doesn't want to see me again. She's worried about Reg getting jealous…'

'I see. That's a shame, when you're such good friends. But he is her husband…although, for what it's worth, I never did like Reg Watkins.'

She put a reassuring hand on his shoulder.

'I'm sorry, love. Life is cruel and we can't always get what we want. And then Hitler drops bombs on you!'

He tried to smile.

'Don't worry, you'll find someone else.'

'That's what she said!' he said, miserably.

Exhausted, Philippe had an early night and fell into a deep sleep, but around midnight he became aware of the distant drone of aircraft. He thought he was dreaming, but the siren wailed and he awoke with a start. The bombers were back. Derek, Mary and Philippe quickly got dressed and met downstairs.

'We'll have to get into the Morrison shelter!' cried Derek, as the first of the bombs came flying down.

The large steel cage was in the kitchen, covered with a cloth to double as a table. They swiftly got inside, squashed like sardines in a can, and Derek fastened it. The three of them lay together in the darkness, terrified, while bombs exploded over their heads. Among the crashes and bangs Philippe's mind went to Clare, and also to Michael. Your turn tonight, he thought.

Michael was indeed in position on the roof of Green Park Buildings, watching as the planes approached, guided by the moonlight shining on the river. It was an awesome sight, he thought, like a theatrical display, until the bombs started to drop. An incendiary landed close by and Michael grabbed the hosepipe and quickly put out the flames, but that was just the beginning. Daniel, who was also on watch, shouted out as another fire took hold and the team swiftly brought it under control. The bombs flowed down, the planes targeting the railway and industrial sites, and the city was ablaze once more. Two planes flew low, directly at them, and the team ran for cover, all except Daniel who stood rooted to the spot. Michael grabbed him and yanked him to safety behind a large chimney stack, a split second before the pilot fired. Daniel was shaking from head to foot and the head of the team shouted, 'get him inside – he's no good to us like this.'

Michael said, 'lean on me,' and got Daniel to his feet. Together they reached the top of the staircase and Michael helped him down to the cellar where the others were sheltering. He took him to Ann Cross and said, 'he's in shock, look after him, will you?' Then Michael took a deep breath and went back up to the rooftop. He found the courage from somewhere, and his thoughts went straight to Rosamund, hoping she was safe.

Rosamund had returned to the bed in the housekeeper's room where she and Michael had spent their night of passion. He had been in her mind all day and she pictured him now, on firewatch, wishing with all her heart that he was here, with her. The scent of their lovemaking lingered on the sheets and she breathed it in, replaying in her mind every moment with him, every word and sigh. As bombs exploded nearby and planes flew low over the house she cowered under the covers, imagining his arms around her and saying his name. Suddenly there was an almighty explosion close by, the house shook to its foundations and there was a deafening crash. Part of the ceiling caved in on top of her and she passed out.

As yet another wave of bombers approached Green Park, Michael and his colleagues stood with hosepipes at the ready, hoping the planes would change direction, knowing that the water supply was running low. But a particular group of three planes continued, unremittingly, straight towards them.

'Take cover!' ordered the team leader, but it was too late.

The planes released their deadly cargo directly above their heads. Michael and the rest of the team threw themselves onto the ground and into oblivion.

CHAPTER 15

Bath, 1942

The all-clear sounded at 2am.

Philippe, Mary and Derek crawled out of the Morrison shelter. Peering through the dust they were aware of a cold draft and realised they could see outside - there was a gaping hole where a wall used to be. They heard a voice and a warden appeared, shining his torch around.

'You've had a narrow escape! Better get yourselves outside before the house collapses.'

The three spent the rest of the night in the local church which was being used as a shelter. They looked around anxiously at their neighbours, relieved to see them, but learning with horror that two households nearby had been completely wiped out. At daybreak Derek went to survey the situation and when he returned said, 'there's a lot of damage in Larkhall but it could have been worse. The Pargetters are all safe, but there are reports that Green Park took a bad hit. I think you ought to get over there, Philippe, and see what's going on.'

Philippe resisted the temptation to see Clare and began the long walk into the city which was in an even worse state than the day before. Water pipes were leaking all over the road, many more buildings were in ruins and thick, choking dust hung in the air. He finally made it to Green Park to a scene of utter devastation. He couldn't believe what he saw: the row of buildings to the left was torn in two and the Art School had been obliterated. His heart thumping, he clambered over the debris towards what remained, finding Richard with a shovel, desperately digging, searching for survivors.

Philippe recalled his angry words with Michael and felt terrible.

'Richard! What's happening? Where's Michael and Daniel?'

'The School took a direct hit - the people on the roof didn't stand a chance. Michael's gone - they all have. I was sheltering in the cellar - most of us down there survived. My wife's over there –' He gestured to Ann who was comforting the remaining students. 'Daniel was in the cellar with us. He was in shock and Michael brought him down from the roof - he saved his life. I've sent Daniel home, he's in a bad way.'

Richard handed Philippe a shovel.

'We've got to keep searching, you never know…'

Rosamund regained consciousness, covered in white dust, among a heap of plaster that had fallen onto the bed and all over the floor. She sat up, shaken and with cuts and bruises, and stayed in the housekeeper's room until dawn broke when she ventured downstairs.

Hearing a commotion outside she opened the door to see that the house opposite wasn't there. A warden, who knew Rosamund, approached her.

'What on earth happened?' she asked, stunned.

'Your neighbours' house was destroyed. I'm afraid we found the couple there, both dead.'

'My God! What about their daughter, Eileen?'

'A daughter? No, we didn't find her.'

'Then she must still be there! We must look for her!'

Rosamund was horrified: the house had been there for years, like The Oaks, but now there was just a gaping hole in the ground surrounded by heaps of broken glass and masonry. The rescue party dug, removing timber and stones, until they heard a faint cry.

'She's here!'

They carefully shifted the debris that was trapping the young girl and extracted her from the ruins. She was bleeding heavily from a head wound and the warden despatched her immediately to hospital.

'The poor girl!' exclaimed Rosamund, 'she has no parents and no home. Let me know how she goes on, won't you?'

'Yes, Mrs Mason.'

'Is there much damage down in the city?'

'Too early to say yet but it's pretty dreadful. The railway and the area around Kingsmead was badly hit. Green Park, too.'

'Green Park?!'

She felt the blood drain away from her face.

'I must go there!'

Rosamund took the long walk down Lansdown Hill, following in Michael's footsteps the day before, meeting a sea of destruction. Kingsmead was ravaged and she had to follow a path that had been carved through the rubble to reach what remained of Green Park Buildings. When she saw that a huge chunk had been blown out of the left side of the terrace her heart went to her mouth. She pushed past rescue workers, panic rising, and accosted a warden.

'I'm looking for one of the art students, Michael White. He was on fire watch last night.'

'If he was in the fire watch party he didn't stand a chance, poor sod - blown to bits.'

Rosamund gasped. Her knees buckled under her and she fell to the ground. Someone helped her up and said, 'you were asking for Michael White?'

'Yes…do you know him? Where is he? He must be somewhere…'

She looked around, desperately, unable to take in the scene of devastation.

'My name is Philippe Swann. I'm a student, and a friend of Michael.'

There was something about this woman which made him ask, 'are you Mrs Mason?'

'Yes!'

'I'm so, so sorry…Michael's dead…' His own voice was hoarse with emotion.

He held her while she sobbed, and he cried with her.

*

Philippe walked back to Larkhall in despair at the loss of his friends and the School to find Mary and Derek in the church surrounded by the belongings they'd managed to salvage from their house, the canary in its cage on the pew beside them.

'The house has been declared unsafe so we're not allowed to go back again,' said Derek. 'Mary and I are going to stay with my sister in Box for a while - she can squeeze in the two of us…'

'I'm sorry, Philippe,' said Mary, 'I did ask but they've only got a small house…the vicar says you can stay here for the moment. We brought your things…'

She stared wistfully at a suitcase and some shopping bags.

'It's all right, I understand.'

He was displaced, homeless, and felt a sudden empathy with his countrymen who'd been forced out of their homes by the Nazi invasion.

'I never thought it would come to this…' said Derek, his face in his hands.

'Now, come on!' said Mary, 'one day we'll find another house and get back to normal.'

The men were doubtful; 'normal' seemed a long way away.

The night passed peacefully, everyone hoping the Nazis had done their worst and wouldn't come back. The next morning Philippe decided to go and see Daniel at home in Lower Weston on the other side of Bath. As he walked through the city the scale of the destruction was apparent, people's homes lost, the gasworks still smouldering, bomb craters in the roads.

As he neared Locksbrook cemetery the road was cordoned off and he had to go the long way round, crossing over the river and back again, to get to Daniel's house. Philippe walked past a row of Victorian villas, the lottery of bomb damage clear to see. He noticed one called Eagle House with stone eagles on pillars by the front gate which was relatively unharmed, whereas the houses opposite were in ruins. People were searching among the debris, owners or looters, it was hard to tell, looking for anything worth taking. He noticed a woman carrying a babe in arms and wondered whether she had a home to go to.

Philippe finally reached Daniel's home which he had visited before when invited for tea, and when Mrs Johns answered the door she remembered him.

'Come in, Philippe! Daniel's in the front room.'

'You haven't suffered too much damage?'

'No, we've been lucky - just some broken windows.'

She showed him to her son who was sitting in a chair, silently staring into space.

'He's all right physically, but he's still in shock. The doctor said he'll come round, in time. Daniel's girlfriend Emma has been to see him, but he didn't seem to recognise her.'

Philippe could see the worry etched on her face. He sat beside his friend, gently took his hand and spoke to him, but he didn't respond. Mrs Johns brought some tea and she listened in horror as Philippe told her about the School, and Michael who had saved Daniel's life but later perished.

'The war has come to Bath with a vengeance. We must pray to the Lord to spare us any further damage.'

When Philippe got up to leave he shook Mrs Johns' hand and said, 'thank you for letting me see him. I will pray with you for his recovery.'

As he returned to Larkhall, Philippe reflected on the maelstrom of the last few days. The level of destruction on the city was hard to comprehend and his own life was shattered. Everything in Bath that he had grown to know and love had been destroyed. The School of Art had gone, wiped out by the bombs, and his work with it. His friend Michael had been blown to pieces and Daniel had been left in a state of trauma. Clare, the love of his life, had rejected him. He was homeless.

He had seen the enemy, up close, with his own eyes, and witnessed their cruelty. He felt an overwhelming anger that the Nazis had dared to bomb a civilised city like Bath, attacking ancient buildings, gunning down innocent people in the street, taking a sadistic pleasure in destroying a place of beauty – was there no limit to their wickedness? They had even bombed St John's church, where he had been to Mass. He wondered, if that's what it's like here, what is it like in France, living with the enemy? Mr Legge had told him the situation in Paris was dire and he imagined the horror of occupation with foreign soldiers in control, basic freedoms gone and the constant threat of violence.

That night Philippe lay on a pew in the church, trying to get comfortable. He had put on his jacket for warmth and fumbling in his pocket found the card Mr Legge had given him with a telephone number. He turned the card over and over in his fingers. As the night wore on he kept thinking, 'what do I have to lose?'

By morning he reached his decision. He found a telephone box, dialled the number, then after a *click* a man's voice said, 'hello, who is this?'

Philippe spoke into the mouthpiece.

'My name is Philippe Swann, I am French. Mr Legge in Bath gave me this number. I want to fight the enemy in whatever way I can. I want to help my country. Tell me what I have to do.'

PART TWO

CHAPTER 16

Bath, 1942

Mary was intrigued to receive a letter with a London postmark, delivered to her new address. She opened it and read:

> *'Dear Aunt Mary and Derek,*
>
> *I thought you should know that I have decided to move to London, temporarily. I will always be grateful to you for taking me in as my mother requested and thank you for the love and care you have shown me for the last two years. But I need to move on now. I cannot tell you what I will be doing but hope one day when the war is over to come to Bath and see you again.*
>
> *Yours affectionately,*
> *Philippe Swann'*

She showed the letter to Derek.

'I suppose he felt there was nothing for him here, with the Art School gone, and Clare...'

'Clare?'

She waved it away. 'It doesn't matter now... I'm going to miss him. I do hope he'll come back one day.'

'You did all you could for him, Mary. We have to get on with our own lives now.'

Most Bathonians were battling to do just that - get on with lives which had been changed forever by the Bath Blitz. The attack had killed over four hundred people and injured many more. Swathes of terraced housing had been destroyed, famous Georgian landmarks had suffered extensive damage which would take years to repair, churches were in ruins and the cityscape would never look the same again. The Blitz had brought the horror of war to Bath, exposing civilians to scenes of death and destruction they had never imagined. Everyone hoped and prayed that the enemy had done their worst and would never come back.

For all of it, a sense of what had become known in London as 'Blitz spirit' prevailed. Businesses and cinemas re-opened, and at Green Park station, after an extensive clean-up and repairs to the damaged rails, the trains began to run again.

Hertfordshire, 1942

After making the telephone call that would change his life, Philippe went to London to report to an address in Baker Street where he was interviewed by an executive and asked to sign a copy of the Official Secrets Act. He was told to stay in the capital, on expenses, while awaiting orders, so he booked into a modest hotel and spent the next few days walking the streets, discovering London, comparing it with his home city and deciding that while each had its merits, Paris was far superior. The destruction wrought by the Blitz was everywhere and he was impressed by the resilience of the people who carried on with their lives amongst the bomb damage, going to work dressed in their smart clothes, picking their way through the rubble.

One morning the hotel receptionist handed him a message. As instructed he caught a train to a small town in Hertfordshire where he was met by an Army driver and taken to a country estate. A sentry waved the car through the gates and they entered the grounds, passing a group of people in shorts and T-shirts running in step behind a military instructor, then the driver stopped in front of the mansion where an Army corporal was waiting to show him inside. They walked through the wood-panelled hallway, past the foot of a grand oak staircase to an office where a man in civilian clothes was sitting behind a desk.

'Thank you, corporal,' he said, getting up to greet the new arrival. 'Welcome, Monsieur Swann, delighted to have you among us. I'm Hugh Goodwin, the course director. I'm sure you'll soon settle in - there are several other Frenchmen and women here, people like yourself who want to help their country. I cannot stress enough the need for absolute secrecy about what you see and do while you are with us: the future of the war is at stake. Right, I'll take you to join your group.'

They went to a room where about a dozen people were seated, reminding Philippe of his first day at Bath School of Art, but this time there were desks instead of easels and the nude model was replaced by an Army sergeant demonstrating how to strip down a Lee-Enfield rifle.

Philippe spoke to one of the men, Yann, from Brittany, about how they came to be there.

'My parents run a restaurant in Quiberon,' said Yann. 'I hate the thought of Nazi soldiers being there. I was teaching in London when France was invaded, but now I must do something to help our country.'

Philippe found that most of the other students had been working happily in England until war broke out and everything changed. After dinner that evening they were addressed by an Army Colonel.

'You have all been chosen as candidates to join the Special Operations Executive - the SOE. Our mission is to conduct clandestine operations in occupied Europe to help defeat the enemy. We will train and equip you for your task, and if you prove yourselves capable you will be flown to France where you will work with the Resistance. Your mission may include sabotage and combat, doing whatever is necessary to defeat the enemy. It will be dangerous and some of you may not return.'

The group were undaunted. Philippe knew, more than ever, that this was what he must do.

Bath, 1942

Richard and Ann were devastated at the loss of the School and so many of their students. They were thrown a lifeline by the family of Walter Sickert, a well-known artist who had died earlier that year, offering their home in Bathampton as a temporary refuge for the School. The Cross' accepted gratefully and moved there with the surviving students.

Richard went to visit Daniel, walking through the bomb-damaged streets, past fallen trees and workers busily clearing rubble, repairing roads and fixing telephone wires. He thought of Reg Watkins, the soldier who had tried to wreck the Summer exhibition, and felt he could look him in the eye now that the brutality of war had come to his very own doorstep.

Mrs Johns welcomed Richard and showed him into the lounge where Daniel was in an armchair, completely still and silent, staring at nothing.

'The doctors say he will return to us, when he's ready. We are praying for him.'

Richard was shocked by the shell of a man he saw. He hoped Daniel might find solace in art, so pulled up a chair next to him, took out a pad and pencils from his bag and proceeded to sketch a vase of flowers on a table by the window.

'Look, Daniel,' he said, gently, 'start by outlining the shape of the vase, then the surface it's sitting on. Think about the direction the light is coming from and add shading to give it depth. Look at the flowers – carnations, aren't they – the petals, the stems, the forms they make.'

He drew a few more lines, then left the pad and pencils on a table in front of Daniel and said, 'now you have a go. It will soon come back to you.'

Daniel made no movement, but Richard turned to Mrs Johns and said, 'your son is a very talented artist. I'll leave these here to give him another way to communicate. Daniel may not want to talk, but when he's ready he'll be able to express his feelings by doing what artists do – draw!'

*

In the aftermath of the attack on Green Park, Rosamund was bereft. In twenty-four hours she had gone from ecstasy to agony, from the thrill of finding love to losing the very person who had made her so happy. That terrible Monday morning she had left the kind Frenchman who had comforted her in the smouldering ruins of the School and somehow got herself home. She shut herself away in her grief, struggling to come to terms with her loss, staring at Mortimer's portrait in disbelief that the young man who had painted it was gone.

As she looked at the picture she became aware of her dilemma: for all his eccentricities, she still loved her husband and wanted to stay married to him. And yet, she had totally fallen for Michael. If he had lived…well, things would have been different. But he was dead, and she had everything to lose and nothing to gain by ever revealing that they had been lovers. She felt disloyal to Michael, but came to the conclusion that, for the sake of her marriage and reputation, she had to keep her all-too-brief love affair a secret.

A neighbour called on her, offering to repair damage to the house and garden. She gratefully accepted and he fixed the damage to the ceiling in the housekeeper's room and gave it a lick of paint. Rosamund went in there, stripped the bed - the one where she and Michael had made love that night - and burnt the bedding. The portrait was the only piece of him that remained.

Towards the end of May, a month after the raids, Rosamund answered the door to find the warden who had rescued Eileen from the wreckage of her parents' house, opposite The Oaks.

'I thought you'd like to know that young Eileen has responded well to her hospital treatment. She'll never be completely right, but should be able to lead a reasonably normal life.'

'I'm pleased to hear it. What will happen to her?'

'Well, it's difficult - we can't trace any relatives nearby. The only person we've been able to find is an elderly uncle in Kent, and he isn't well enough to look after a fifteen-year-old girl. It will be up to the Council to find foster parents for her. They're keeping her at the hospital for now, but she's not the only child in that position, unfortunately…the Nazis made orphans of so many.'

'How awful.'

Then, almost without thinking, Rosamund said, 'I suppose she could always come here. She would be company for me while Mortimer's away and I could do with a hand with the housekeeping! At least she'd have a roof over her head, and it would be familiar – I've known her all her life.'

The warden was taken aback.

'That would be most generous, Mrs Mason! It's a wonderful idea, and sounds like it could suit you both.'

'Why don't you see what she thinks?'

Eileen arrived at The Oaks with nothing but the clothes she stood up in. A shy child, she came in, cautiously, and Rosamund took her into the kitchen for tea.

'There's no cake, I'm afraid – I'm not very good at baking!' Rosamund said, suddenly remembering Michael's first visit.

'That's all right, Mrs Mason. I love baking! Mother says my pastry is very good…'

She stopped in mid-sentence.

'I mean, she used to say…'

Her eyes filled with tears and Rosamund took her hand and gave it a squeeze.

'That sounds wonderful, Eileen! Once you're settled in I'll let you loose in the kitchen!'

Rosamund gave Eileen the housekeeper's room, revamped with new bedding, curtains and a rug. She kept some clothes which had been donated for charity and presented them to the girl, along with some books and games to keep her amused, and Eileen was thrilled. It was a new start for them both.

CHAPTER 17

Bath, 1942

On a sunny June day Mary caught the bus from Box into Bath to do some shopping and get her hair done. Her sister-in-law was very kind, but Mary missed her old home and neighbours. It was her first visit to Bath since she and Derek had moved away and she was struck by the changes - unsafe buildings were being demolished leaving gaping holes in familiar terraces, and she heard that in Oldfield Park whole streets were being cleared to make way for new.

Mary walked over to Green Park and caught her breath when she saw that the entire left side of Green Park Buildings had gone, leaving the right side completely exposed to view. She spoke to some workmen there who explained that what remained after the bombing was just too dangerous and had to be pulled down.

'My nephew was at the School of Art,' she told them. 'He wasn't here that awful night, but he lost several of his friends.'

'Tragic,' replied one of the workmen, sympathetically.

'Bloody Germans,' said the other.

Mary walked on, past the railway station, shaken by what she had seen. She crossed over the road and went towards Kingsmead Square which was still in ruins. It would take years to sort this out, she thought, and who was going to pay for it all? As she pondered these difficult questions she turned towards the main shopping area and was brought back to earth when she noticed a pregnant Clare walking towards her.

'Clare! I didn't know you were expecting! Congratulations!'

'Thank you, Mrs Stevens. I'm due at the end of October. I've written to tell Reg - he's in North Africa - but I haven't heard anything from him…'

Mary listened, sympathetically. 'It must be difficult for them, out there in the desert - communications can't be easy. Well, I'm pleased for you both. I'm feeling out of touch myself! – we're living with Derek's sister out in Box for the moment.'

'Yes, I'm sorry you had to leave Larkhall. Do you have any news of Philippe?'

'I had a letter from him a couple of months ago. He's moved to London.'

'London?'

'Yes. I don't have an address for him. I think after the raids he needed to get away, what with the School being lost, and so many of his friends…'

Clare felt her face flush, but continued, 'I can understand that. The damage to Green Park was dreadful. At the railway station it took us ages to get everything up and running again. I helped out for a few weeks but then I had to resign…they said I might put the customers off, looking like this…'

'What nonsense! Still, I suppose you shouldn't be working really. You may as well put your feet up while you can!'

With a few more words they went on their way, both women thinking of Philippe. It suddenly crossed Mary's mind – could Philippe be the father of Clare's baby? The timing was about right. But she swiftly dismissed the thought, not wanting to think badly of either of them. It was more likely to be the fact that Clare was expecting Reg's child that had driven Philippe away.

As for Clare, she wondered what Philippe was doing in London and hoped he was safe, because her feelings for him still ran deep.

At The Oaks, Rosamund hadn't been feeling well. One morning she had to rush to the bathroom where she was sick and blamed what they'd had to eat the night before. But when it happened again she began to wonder… could it be that her most heart-felt wish might be coming true?

She made an appointment to see her obstetrician, Dr Roberts. It was some years since they had met and they began by discussing the war and the Bath Blitz.

'I lost my wife, Wendy, in the third raid,' he said, sadly, looking at the photograph on his desk.

Rosamund was shocked. 'I had no idea!'

'I was in London. She'd delivered a baby girl during the first raid, but when she went back to check on the mother she was caught in the third raid, and was killed.'

'I'm so, so sorry. You clearly loved her very much. How are you managing?'

'It's not easy…I have my sons - Henry's with the RAF and Anthony's taking his exams at school. And we have our Jewish refugees living with us - they arrived just before war broke out. Quite honestly, at the moment I feel as if I'm more dependent on them than they are on me… And how did you fare?'

'I didn't lose anyone close,' Rosamund lied, 'and there was only minor damage to the house, so I was lucky. My neighbours were killed, though – I've taken in their daughter to live with me for the time being.'

'That's kind of you - you'll be company for each other. Right, let me examine you and we'll see what's going on…'

Afterwards, back home, Rosamund did some thinking. She had to get her story straight. If there was to be a baby - and she still didn't dare believe it - it was most likely that Michael, not Mortimer, was the father, but Mortimer must never suspect her of infidelity; her marriage was too precious. No one must ever discover that she and Michael had had an affair.

A week later Rosamund returned to the hospital. Dr Roberts waited for his patient to sit down, then announced, 'I have some exciting news for you. I have your test results and I can confirm that you are pregnant!'

Rosamund took a sharp intake of breath. Her heart leapt with joy to hear the news she had longed for.

'I can't believe it! That's wonderful news!'

'I'd say you're about two months, so the baby should be due in January.'

In the midst of her happiness she quickly made a vital calculation.

'No, you must be wrong there! Three months, I think - Mortimer went back to sea at the end of March.'

'Really?!' He looked at her quizzically.

She knew she had to eliminate any doubt. 'Yes, definitely March, so the baby must be due in December.'

'Well, it is hard to be precise at this early stage...'

'I'll write to Mortimer and tell him. He'll be overjoyed!'

'I'm so pleased, after all you've been through. But you must take care - as you're over forty you're elderly primigravida so I'll be keeping a special check on you throughout your pregnancy.'

'Thank you, Dr Roberts. You always told me to never give up hope.'

She stood up and as they shook hands he said, 'please, call me 'David' – I've known you for such a long time, and on a day like this it seems wrong to be formal.'

'And you must call me Rosamund. Thank you so much, David!'

She left his consulting room looking the happiest he had ever seen her. Strange about her insistence on those dates, he thought. He was sure his calculations were right, but time would tell - unless there was something she was trying to hide...

Hertfordshire, 1942

Philippe was at the rifle range, lying on his stomach, practising firing at a target. The Army instructors were giving his group a good grounding in all aspects of battle and Philippe discovered to his surprise that he had a flair for shooting. He had a good eye and a steady hand, a natural, the instructor said, and as long as he kept his nerve he would become a good marksman. He was fitter than he had ever been, taking early morning runs around the estate led by an Army sergeant and lifting weights at the gymnasium in the basement of the mansion. They were taught unarmed combat, how to use their bodies as a weapon in a defensive or offensive manner to kill or subdue an opponent. They learnt throws, holds and paralyzing attacks against the enemy and spent hours hammering the sides of their hands against wooden tables in the classrooms in order to strengthen them. Their instructor explained:

'The most efficient way to tackle your opponent is to strike him, firmly, on the side of his throat, two inches below the ear. That is where the spinal cord is most vulnerable, but for this to be effective your hands need to be hard.'

The manoeuvre sounded gruesome but the students knew that one day it might save their lives, so they kept on hammering. It was startling how quickly they had changed from civilians to warriors, keen to fight the enemy in any way they could.

'Think of someone you hate!' the instructor yelled, as Philippe ran with fixed bayonet at a straw dummy, imagining the face of Reg Watkins upon it.

Philippe revived practical skills he'd learnt as a boy, when he used to spend hours at his grandfather's garage learning the basics of mechanics, taking car engines apart under his watchful supervision. He relished the opportunity to drive again, taking motorbikes, cars, trucks and jeeps for a spin around the grounds.

As he got to know his colleagues he realised how much he'd missed his native language and the fellowship of his countryfolk. The women proved themselves to be just as tough as the men and weren't inclined to get romantically involved, so he didn't try. Every evening they would eat their meal, discussing their day, knowing they were an elite group who could trust one another completely. The days were exhausting and he slept like the dead, but in that moment between sleep and awake his thoughts always turned to Clare. However hard he tried to forget, he knew in his heart he still loved her as much as he detested her undeserving husband.

CHAPTER 18

Paris, 1942

They came in the evening, just as the late July sun sank beneath the horizon. Amélie and her father heard noises outside, a general commotion of cars drawing up, people shouting, then there was a battering upon their door. Amélie opened it to find a senior gendarme holding a piece of paper.

'I have reason to believe there are Jews living in this apartment. My officers have authority to search. Stand aside!'

The party of gendarmes forced their way into the apartment, smashing items with their rifle butts, opening drawers, taking what they wanted.

'What the hell do you think you are doing?' cried Amélie, outraged.

'We are here to arrest you, Madame Swann,' said the senior gendarme, 'you are Jewish! You will come with us. You have five minutes to pack a bag.'

'But I'm not Jewish! I'm Catholic!'

The gendarme stepped towards her, took her by the wrists and put his mouth to her ear.

'Your mother was a Jewess!' he hissed, 'so that makes you half-Jewish and that is enough for us to arrest you. Pack your bag!'

He released her and she looked in horror at her father.

'I am Louis Duvalier, and this is all a terrible mistake! My wife wasn't Jewish!'

'Don't lie, old man. We have information that she was.'

He gestured to one of his staff who showed him some papers.

'I have her details here,' he read, gleefully, 'Raisa Kosinski, left East Prussia with her parents in 1880 and settled in Paris. Religion: Jewish. Monsieur, your daughter has inherited the vile Jewish faith and she will be punished.'

Louis tried to get up from his chair but the gendarme slapped him across the face and he fell back. Amélie threw herself at the gendarme, crying out in protest, and he struck her, sending her to the floor. The neighbours heard the din and were standing outside on the landing watching in horror when a German officer arrived, pushing past them to enter the apartment. Amélie was struggling to her feet when the officer said, 'Madame Swann, we meet again.'

He looked at her with his steely eyes and she remembered him - the German soldier who had taken the pearl necklace.

'It's time I introduced myself properly. I am Leutnant Engel. I have been watching you for some time…your visits to the Marais, your liaison in Montmartre…'

She caught her breath. How did he know about that?

He stood close to her and laughed.

'Yes, we know all about you and your affair with the handsome Dr Fournier.'

'But Jean-Pierre knows nothing!'

'You mean doesn't know he's been screwing a Jewess? What a delight…I can't wait to tell him! But he can't help you now, even if he wanted to. We know about his links to the Resistance. He will be arrested with the others in his network, and we have special punishments for people like him.'

He motioned the pulling of a trigger.

Amélie was distraught.

'You should think yourself lucky, we are not going to kill you, just take you away for a while to be with your Jewish friends.'

'But I am Catholic!'

He laughed, then pulled her towards him.

'You may think that, but we know the truth!'

Glancing outside where a crowd was gathering on the staircase he added, '…and so do your neighbours!'

Amélie spotted Madame Duclos who was standing there, her arms folded, with a self-satisfied look on her face. She had traded her precious information for a generous increase in her sausage ration which in her view was a good deal.

Amélie looked at her in horror.

'Come!' said the soldier, 'we have dallied long enough.'

'But what about my father? He can't stay here, alone! He can't look after himself!'

'Then we will take him too. Come, old man.'

'But he needs his things - his medication!'

The officer sighed heavily. 'You have two minutes, but my patience is wearing thin…'

Amélie hastily packed bags for herself and her father, then Leutnant Engel said, 'one more thing… we know about your husband, the British soldier, who was killed in Paris… so sad! And you have a son, Philippe. Where is he? Where is your son?'

'He is not here.'

'We will find him.'

'Never!'

He laughed in her face.

'He has Jewish blood…he will not escape.'

The gendarmes pushed them out of the apartment at gunpoint. Amélie spat at Madame Duclos while the other neighbours looked on with a mixture of curiosity and horror. They were marched down the stairs, forced into the back of a lorry with other detainees and driven towards the River Seine, the dark shadow of the Eiffel tower looming over them.

'We're at the Vélodrome d'Hiver, the sports stadium,' said one of the men.

'That's good!' said another, ironically, 'perhaps they're giving us tickets to see a match!'

The gendarmes herded them into the stadium. In the blackout Amélie couldn't see the crowds of people before her but she could sense their presence, hear their voices, smell their bodies sweating with stress. They shuffled on, the group from her neighbourhood, just a few among many hundreds of others who had been brought there that night. They made their way towards a row of seats and sat down, exhausted. Amélie wrapped her father's coat around him, for the Summer night was cool. He said to her, 'I need the toilet.'

She looked around in the darkness and the man sitting next to them said, 'they've closed the toilets so that people can't escape from them. People are using that corner, up there. I'll take him if you like.' The man took Louis' arm, leading him carefully up the steps and returning him safely.

They tried to sleep on the uncomfortable seats and awoke to a sea of thousands of people. As the temperature rose the arena became stiflingly hot, the glass roof and windows screwed shut for security. Everyone was getting thirsty and hungry, children were crying and people asked the guards for food, but none was forthcoming. Amélie and Louis befriended a couple in their fifties called Jacques and Greta Blum, who also lived near the Place de la Bastille.

Jacques accosted a young gendarme, saying, 'you can't keep us here, herded in like animals!'

'You deserve no better, Jewish scum!' the guard scowled.

Jacques turned on him, angrily. 'I'm Jewish and French, and proud of both! I fought in the last war - I was a *poilu*! How dare you treat us like this!'

The young guard didn't know how to counter that - his own father had also been a *poilu*, a soldier in the trenches. But he had his orders, to keep these Jews in their place, so he shoved Jacques with his rifle butt and said, 'just do as you're told!' and walked away.

The next night passed, and another, the conditions worsening. On the third day, Quakers, Red Cross and medical staff were allowed into the stadium to distribute food, tend to the sick and take away the dead. Amélie was queuing for food when she recognised one of the nurses, Sylvie Lacroix, who exclaimed, 'Amélie! What on earth are you doing here?'

'It's all a terrible mistake - they think I'm Jewish! Can you help my father? He's very weak…'

Sylvie followed Amélie back to her seat. While she comforted the old man and gave him some pain killers and water, Amélie whispered, 'can you get a message to Dr Fournier?'

Sylvie's face fell.

'He was arrested yesterday.'

Amélie's heart imploded.

'I can tell Dr Moreau that you're here - he may be able to do something.'

'Thank you,' Amélie replied, knowing that Dr Moreau would be the last to help her.

Amélie was at a complete loss; she had no one to turn to. The news about Jean-Pierre was devastating, made worse by the notion that it was all her fault. They had grown careless, so wrapped up in each other that they'd failed to pay attention to the dangers of prying Nazi eyes. And it wasn't just Jean-Pierre - if he had been arrested it was likely that other members of the Resistance chain had also been taken. She was consumed by guilt but there was nothing she could do; they had no option but to sit it out in the hot, stinking stadium.

On the sixth day the prisoners were transported to Drancy, an ugly complex of high-rise apartments surrounded by barbed wire which had been commandeered by the Nazis as a holding camp for Jews. It was terribly over-crowded, built for seven hundred people but housing ten times that amount. Conditions were dire, rations were poor, it was insanitary and the French guards were brutal.

Amélie and Louis were pushed into a dormitory, given soup and bread, and told they were lucky to have a mattress to sleep on. They stayed close to their neighbours Jacques and Greta and as they talked, the two men realised they knew each other.

'You owned the garage!' exclaimed Jacques. 'When I was a boy my father used to bring his Peugeot to you for servicing and I would come with him - I loved looking at the cars and talking to the men there. That's why I became a mechanic.'

'I remember your father,' said Louis, 'he was a regular customer. And now I come to think of it, I remember you, too!'

'Such happy times... So, Louis, what on earth are you doing here? You're not Jewish!'

'No, but my wife was, and that was enough for them to arrest Amélie. I couldn't stay at home alone, so here I am.'

'This is intolerable!' said Jacques, angrily, 'we must speak to someone!'

'We've tried...'

Out in the exercise yard Amélie spotted Red Cross and medical volunteers bringing supplies to the stricken inmates. She managed to get some bread and aspirin, then spotted Sylvie, the nurse she had seen at the stadium, who was shocked to see Amélie so thin and gaunt. Slipping her an extra ration of bread she whispered, 'I told Dr Moreau I'd seen you but there was nothing he could do. I'm so sorry...'

Amélie, who had expected nothing better, asked, 'how is Dr Fournier?'

'He was shot, along with five others of the Resistance.'

Amélie gasped, almost falling.

'It was tragic, we can't believe it,' said the nurse, as a guard approached and admonished her for speaking to the prisoner.

Amélie returned to the dormitory where she lay on her bunk and wept. A short time ago she had been blissfully happy with Jean-Pierre, but now her lover was dead, the Resistance chain broken, and her life was in ruins, torn to pieces by this wretched war. Her worst fears about the Nazis - that they would hunt down anyone with Jewish blood - had been confirmed, and here she was, trapped in this hell-hole. Her one consolation was that she had made the right decision, sending Philippe to England, and in her misery she clung to the knowledge that her son, the artist, was safe and well.

CHAPTER 19

Hertfordshire, 1942

Philippe's group was learning Morse Code, practising encoding messages and using the radio transmitter until it was second nature, critical to the work they would be required to do in France. One morning the course director introduced their guest speaker.

'We are lucky to have with us Miss Beatrice Webb from Bletchley Park, the Government's secret codebreaking centre. Miss Webb is an expert in conducting communications whilst working undercover in a hostile environment.'

The tall, thin woman who stood before them wore round spectacles and had short, mousey-brown hair. Philippe reckoned she was in her mid-twenties but looked older, dressed in an unflattering brown tweed jacket with a pleated skirt and flat lace-up shoes. She spoke about the year she had spent in France working with the Resistance before returning to England to run agents, like themselves. With her tales of bravery, deception and cunning in the face of the enemy it soon became clear that what she lacked in looks was more than compensated for by her courage, sharp intelligence and quick wit.

'Secrecy is paramount. Trust no one. I survived to tell the tale; make sure that you do, too,' she concluded, leaving her audience highly motivated to go and put what they had learned into practice.

That evening at dinner Philippe sat next to their guest. In fluent French she asked Philippe about himself, then said, 'I used to love going to Paris. I can imagine how hard it must have been for you, having to leave your city and your family.'

She looked him in the eye with an air of understanding.

'Yes, it was. You are *très sympathique*, Mademoiselle,' he said, observing that she had an unsightly mole on the side of her neck.

Beatrice listened attentively as he told her about moving to Bath to live with his English Aunt, and how the Blitz had devastated the city and the School of Art, killing many of its students.

'I'm sorry to hear that - such a terrible waste. Bath was always such a civilised place.'

She went on to tell him about growing up in a rectory in Hampshire, the only child of elderly parents.

'I spent most of my time reading, then I went up to Cambridge and discovered that I was quite bright.'

Philippe looked at Beatrice as she spoke, finding her plain features strangely compelling. He imagined the challenge of painting her portrait, how to reveal the strong, empathetic woman that lay beneath the surface. She told him she adored art and they discussed their favourite pieces in the Louvre.

'They had to evacuate the bulk of the paintings and sculptures for safe keeping,' she said. 'The Germans would destroy them at the drop of a hat, but they're all in a safe place now. They have stolen art from Jewish collectors, though – in fact 'looted' is a better word for it. Terrible. I doubt whether the owners will ever get their property back.'

After their meal Beatrice spoke to some other students, then went to her room. One of the English members of staff sidled up to Philippe and said, 'you won't get anywhere with her, you know…she bats for the other side.'

Philippe looked at him blankly.

Another man said, 'what he means is, she prefers women to men.'

'Aah, you think she is *une lesbienne*… but I do not agree, my friend. I think she is just… English!'

As she lay in her bed that night, Beatrice reflected on her conversation with Philippe. There was something about the handsome young artist, half-French, half-English, so keen to fight for freedom, that sparked her imagination. Perhaps it was the way he looked at her, with a genuine interest, rather than the revulsion she usually saw reflected in the eyes of men. She knew what they said behind her back – that she preferred women – but the truth was that she had never experienced any sexual feelings towards anybody, male or female. She didn't know what it was in her background or psyche that made her like that, it was just how she had always felt.

Until now…

Paris, 1942

After two months at Drancy, Louis' health deteriorated rapidly and without medication his heart condition worsened. One morning Amélie went to wake her father, shook his shoulder and realised that he had passed away in the night. She let out a howl of anguish and Greta came to her, comforting Amélie while she sobbed, saying, 'we must get his things – here, take his wedding ring. If you don't, the guards will.' The ring came off easily, the old man's fingers having got so thin. They removed his wristwatch then Amélie took his jacket and found his wallet in the inside pocket. Greta whispered, 'hide it, quickly! We haven't got much time.'

They had just finished when a guard appeared.

'What's going on here?'

Amélie looked up at him, holding her father in her arms.

'My father is dead! You killed him, bringing him here! It is your fault!'

For that she received a slap across the face, then the guard said, 'get away from him. We will deal with the dead Jew.'

Amélie screamed at them, 'we are not Jews! We are Catholics! You must bury him in the Catholic tradition.'

He laughed in her face and took Louis away, to dump him with the others that had died during the night.

That evening when things were quiet, Amélie took out her father's wallet and examined the contents.

She found a few banknotes and two small sepia photographs, faded and worn with age. One was of Raisa holding a baby whom Amélie assumed to be herself. The other showed a little girl standing in front of a grand house, and on the back was written, '*Raisa Kosinski, Orzysz, 1879*'.

Greta came to see how she was and Amélie showed her the photographs.

'I found these in Papa's wallet – I've never seen them before. This is my mother.'

'Tell me about her.'

'She died when I was five, from scarlet fever, so I never knew her very well. But I do remember that she was beautiful and had a gentle voice. As a child she fled from East Prussia to Paris with her parents.'

'Because they were Jewish?'

'Yes - although she never spoke to me about it. I remember her wearing a Star of David necklace but I think she knew it was dangerous, even in France. I don't know what happened to it.'

'She was probably buried with it.'

'Of course - I hadn't thought of that. I was brought up as a Catholic, like my father. I never gave my mother's religion much thought until I realised what was happening in Nazi Germany. I feared then that I might be in danger - and Philippe, too - but I never dreamt it would come to this.'

Greta read the words on the back of the older photograph. 'Orzysz! I know it – it's close to where my parents came from. In their time the town was in East Prussia, but it's Poland, Amélie – your mother was Polish – like mine.'

'So I am half-Polish! I didn't know.'

Greta looked closely at the picture. 'It's a fine house. I wonder if it's still there?'

'Who knows? I think Maman's family were quite well-off. She had some beautiful pieces of jewellery, but we had to sell it all.'

'And you never saw these photos before?'

'No - Papa kept them to himself. And now they're all I have to remind me of my parents.'

'You should be proud of your mother, Amélie - Polish people are strong and resilient. Their country has been invaded many times but in their hearts they always prevail. You and I are more alike than we realised - we are French, and we share a heritage of being Polish and Jewish!'

'How extraordinary! You must tell me all about your family, Greta, it may help me understand more about my own. I am French and Catholic, but I shouldn't deny the other part of me – it's the reason I'm here, after all…'

The two women hugged, and Amélie said, 'Greta, this place would be unbearable without you.'

One dark, cold evening in October a senior gendarme came to the dormitory and made an announcement.

'Tomorrow you are going to be taken to the East where you can resettle and make a new life for yourselves. You will be given work and accommodation. You make take one piece of luggage with you. The train will leave in the morning.'

Rumours around Drancy were rife.

'That's what happened to the people who were here before us,' one man said. 'They want to ship us out so they can make room for the next lot.'

'Do you know where we're going?' asked a woman.

'No, but they took the others to a place called Auschwitz.'

*

The journey to German-occupied Poland was interminable, people herded into railway trucks like cattle. At least this was something Louis hadn't had to endure, thought Amélie, as she sat on her suitcase, his wallet hidden inside her blouse for safe keeping. She stayed close to Jacques and Greta, for the three had promised to stick together throughout their ordeal.

When they finally arrived at their destination a Nazi soldier slid open the door, ordered the prisoners out at gunpoint, confiscated their luggage and told them to stand in line. Men were separated from the women and Greta cried out in protest as Jacques was wrenched away from her. Their fate was decided: women with babies, the elderly, disabled and the sick were sent to their deaths; Greta and Amélie were deemed suitable for forced labour and allowed to live. They were ordered onto a lorry and taken to the camp that was indeed named Auschwitz.

On arrival the prisoners were disinfected and shaved, Amelie's lovely long dark hair falling in ribbons from her head. They were instructed to strip naked and leave their clothing and possessions, ready to collect after their shower, but when Amélie asked for her belongings a soldier laughed at her.

'You have nothing, you are nothing. It is all you deserve, Jewess.'

She flew at him in her nakedness, screaming, 'I am French! I am Catholic! I demand that you return my things!'

The soldier turned his gun on her, threw her a camp uniform and hissed, 'I don't care what you are, that's all you're going to get.'

He pushed her into a line of other prisoners and she shuffled along with them to a desk where her name was taken and a number painfully tattooed on her arm. She found Greta and together they were put into a dormitory where they held each other, glad to have a friend among this hell, their treasured possessions so cruelly taken from them.

'Everything's gone...' Amélie cried, 'Papa's wallet with his wedding ring, the photographs of my mother... I have nothing!'

Greta tried to comfort her, saying, 'remember the photos, remember every single detail, every word, then you will always have them. You have your memory, your mind, your soul. You are your own person. They can't take that away. And you have your son!'

Amélie clung to Greta, and through her tears she thought yes, I still have my son.

CHAPTER 20

Hertfordshire, 1942

Philippe and Yann were in the middle of a wood, rigging up a shelter whilst watching out for the enemy. The October night was cold and they needed the survival techniques they had been taught to endure the long trek through the heaths and woodlands of the Chiltern Hills. They cooked the rabbit they had trapped and skinned, staying near the fire for warmth. As they ate the two discussed what they missed most about France, both of them anxious to get back to their own country despite the dangers, and impatient to finish this training so they could get out and do some real work.

After an uncomfortable night they packed up their kit and headed for their final rendezvous point, looking forward to a hot meal and a proper bed. They were just approaching the edge of the wood when suddenly they were grabbed from behind, a knife at their throats, and dragged down a path to a waiting van. They were gagged, their hands tied behind their backs, and pushed into the back of the van which drove off at speed.

*

Philippe was tied to a chair in a darkened room, disorientated, tired and hungry. An SS officer marched up and down in front of him, demanding information, shouting and threatening violence. Philippe had no idea where he was or how long he had been there. Powerless and intimidated, he clung to what he had been trained to do: to say nothing. Eventually he was taken away and thrown back in his cell where he fell into a deep sleep, only to be awoken a few hours later for the process to be repeated.

After a few days which seemed like weeks, Philippe awoke one morning to be greeted by Hugh Goodwin, the course director, who said, 'you have resisted interrogation for long enough. Well done, Monsieur Swann, you've passed the test! But next time, try not to get caught in the first place…'

*

A celebration dinner was held at the manor house for the trainees. Goodwin announced,

'I am pleased to say that you have all earned your place in the SOE, with flying colours. You will shortly be given details of your assignments and I wish you luck. We will conclude with some words from a senior member of the Security Services.'

The man who rose to make a short speech was none other than Mr Legge. Afterwards, Philippe went and spoke to him.

'I'm very grateful to you, and I can't wait to get over to France. How is your wife? And Angela?'

'Keeping well, thank you. We were lucky, our house survived the bombing. Angela's portrait was undamaged, you'll be pleased to know. I was very sorry to hear about the School of Art.'

'It was a terrible loss. Several of my friends were killed. Do you have any news of Paris?'

'Yes, but not good I'm afraid. The Resistance network we were communicating with was compromised. Somehow the Nazis managed to penetrate it and arrested six of the people involved. They were all shot.'

Philippe gasped. 'That's terrible! So you have no communication now?'

'We've created another network but it's becoming harder to keep it safe. There are many in Paris who prefer to collaborate with the enemy as conditions worsen.'

'And you have no more news of my family?'

'I'm afraid not.'

Another man approached, so, shaking hands, Mr Legge said, 'good luck, Monsieur Swann. I wish you every success.'

Philippe was more concerned than ever about his family. If the members of the Resistance who had been in contact with his mother were dead, how could he find out what had happened to her and his grandfather? The only way for certain was to go to Paris and see for himself, but that would have to wait until the war was over.

Philippe and Yann were told they were going to north-west France to work with the local Resistance in Normandy. It was a difficult mission, requiring the best of the new trainees and the best person to run them - Beatrice Webb. Beatrice, who was delighted to be working with the two men, came to the manor house to prepare her agents for the task ahead. Spreading out a map of Normandy on a table she said, 'you are going to be based in a town called Lisieux which lies on an important rail link between Paris and Cherbourg. The Nazis use it to transport weapons and men, and your role is to gather intelligence about movements of troops, equipment, any unusual build-up of forces, and to gauge the morale of the enemy. You will report to the local Resistance chief who will advise which targets are suitable for sabotage. Tell us in your radio broadcasts what equipment and supplies you need and we will arrange air drops to designated areas. And always use the codewords we have taught you.'

As they took in all this information, Beatrice produced a packet of Gauloises and offered them to her agents.

'My God!' cried Philippe, 'where the hell did you get these?'

She smiled. 'I have my contacts…'

Beatrice briefed the men on their new identities: Philippe was to become Pascal Lejeune and Yann would be Gilles Charpentier, factory workers from Pont l'Eveque in Normandy. These were the names they were to be known as, from now on.

'You must embrace your new selves, learn their backgrounds, what they've done, how they think. You need to adjust psychologically and make some adjustments. So, Pascal: the beard will have to go. And Gilles, you will have your hair cut short.'

Beatrice held her hand up as Pascal protested. 'No objections!' she said, firmly.

In their new guise the men were issued with identity cards and documentation, given genuine French clothes to wear and provided with family snaps to add authenticity to their cover stories. They were each armed with a gun and a knife. Finally they were given a cyanide capsule to hide on their person, their ultimate way out of trouble.

When she and Pascal were alone Beatrice said, confidentially, 'I am going to tell you a special word known only to you and me. If you ever find yourself in grave danger, you must tell SOE. I will know that it can only have come from you, and I will do everything in my power to help you. The word is *Sulis*.'

It sounded familiar.

'I thought it was appropriate for someone from Bath!'

'Of course - Aquae Sulis - the waters of the sun.' Pascal vaguely remembered Clare telling him something about that.

'Thank you, Beatrice. I will not forget it - or you. I am very grateful for everything you have taught me.'

On Pascal's last night at the manor house he was in his room getting ready for bed when there was a knock at the door. He opened it and was surprised to find Beatrice standing there, holding a bottle of cognac and two glasses.

'I thought we should have a toast to your success!'

He invited her in, watched as she poured two generous measures and together they savoured the strong amber liquid. Pascal was intrigued - he suspected she didn't do this with all her agents.

'I wanted you to know that I'm pleased we met. I've enjoyed your company these last weeks.'

'Thank you. You're a fascinating woman, Beatrice.'

She put down her glass. They were the same height and she moved closer, put her hands on his shoulders, looked him straight in the eye and kissed him on the lips. He was surprised, but not displeased. He took off her spectacles, looked into her hazel eyes and put his arms around her. They kissed again, for longer. He suspected it was her first time, but she had clearly decided that this was what she wanted to do, and he had no reason to dissuade her. They removed their clothes and got into bed in their underwear. She was thin, with not much of a figure, not normally his type, but she was certainly willing, sighing with pleasure as he caressed her and removed the rest of her clothes. Finally she was ready and he said, I will be gentle, and he was.

Afterwards she thanked him and he held her in his arms, feeling privileged to have made love to such an extraordinary woman.

'Don't worry, I don't want you to marry me!' she said. 'I just needed to know what it was like. You're the first person that's made me want to do that.'

'I am honoured. And I won't be the last.'

'Mmm — I'm not so sure about that…'

CHAPTER 21

Bath, 1942

Clare was at home with her mother when she suddenly felt a sharp pain across her belly.

'I'll go and fetch the midwife!' cried Mrs Pargetter, running out the door, returning soon afterwards with the same local lady who had delivered Clare herself, twenty-one short years ago.

'Now, don't you worry, my lover!' the midwife said, reassuringly, as Clare let out a scream of agony, 'everything's going to be fine…'

At first Clare thought of Reg, then of Philippe, but soon she thought of nobody at all as her mind became blinded by pain. But she was in good hands and after a four-hour labour gave birth to a healthy boy with wispy, sandy-coloured hair, like his father. Clare cradled her newborn who looked up at her with blue eyes similar to her own.

'What a lovely little chap!' declared the midwife.

'We're going to be very happy together, you and me, aren't we?' said Clare, looking down at him.

Clare's mother was thrilled with her grandson.

'What are you going to call him?'

'Alfred, after your Dad - my Grandad. You know how close I was to him when I was growing up and he was such a lovely man. So, Mum, meet your grandson - Alfred Watkins.'

*

Rosamund's pregnancy was apparent and her friends were surprised but pleased for her, knowing how much she had longed for a child. They relieved her from charity duties, knowing how important it was to rest, at her age. Eileen was excited at the prospect of having a new baby in the house and keen to help in any way she could. Dr Roberts kept a watchful eye on his patient, for although she was a strong, healthy woman, at over forty, one had to be careful.

Rosamund hadn't heard from Mortimer but that wasn't unusual; operations on the North Atlantic convoys were intense and dangerous and, as he'd told her on many occasions, 'there's no post box out in the middle of the sea!' But she longed to know that he had received her news, hoping with all her heart that he would be pleased, and that it would never even occur to him to question whether the expected child was his.

France, 1942

The Lysander aircraft flew low over the pitch-black countryside, then in the distance the pilot spotted a line of flares marking the designated landing area. Three…two….one….they touched down and the pilot slowed the plane, steering it around the field while the door opened and a ladder was let down from the side.

Pascal and Gilles threw down their baggage and disembarked, then the plane turned around and took off into the darkness. A well-built man in his forties ran towards them.

'Swallows in Spring!' he cried - a codeword they recognised. 'Welcome to France!'

In the cold November night the passengers recovered their bags and followed the man across a field to a barn at the back of a nearby farmhouse where he announced, 'my name is André Lazarre, the leader of our Resistance group, and these are my fighters!' He gestured to half a dozen men, aged from twenty to sixty, peace-loving farm workers whose lives had been turned upside down by war, now willing and able to fight the enemy. The men were dressed in their *bleus* - the blue overalls worn by French labourers - and sitting on straw bales. The barn stank of goats.

André said, 'this is my land and I live in the farmhouse with my family. Tonight you will stay here, then tomorrow I'll take you to Lisieux to friends who will accommodate you. But now, you must eat!'

André dished out some bread and cheese and bottles of red wine which the group shared, then the men departed leaving the newcomers to sleep in the barn. Pascal said, 'I can't believe how wonderful that cheese tasted. It's good to be back in France!'

The next day Pascal and Gilles were met by André, driving a horse and cart. The two climbed aboard and trotted through gentle, rolling countryside known as the *bocage*, a patchwork of small fields with high hedges, the home of brie and camembert, and apple orchards producing cider and calvados, the local apple brandy. As they approached the outskirts of Lisieux the roads became busier with lorries, cars and military vehicles, then they arrived at a modest house where they were welcomed by their hosts, Monsieur and Madame Moulin.

The guests were shown up a hidden staircase leading to an attic room where they could safely unpack their kit without interruption or discovery. Over a lunch of potato soup with bread and spicy *saucisson* they rehearsed their story: the two young men were cousins of Monsieur Moulin from Pont l'Eveque who had come to Lisieux to work in his engineering business.

André briefed the arrivals on what supplies his Resistance group needed and established the grid references of suitable drop zones where packages could be landed. That evening in the attic room Pascal opened the case containing the precious miniature radio set and at the agreed hour of seven o'clock, tapped out the encoded requirements on the transmitter.

Pascal and Gilles spent the next few days familiarising themselves with Lisieux, finding it hard to accept the sight of German soldiers on patrol, the ancient, peaceful town defiled by occupation. They walked along the historic streets of half-timbered houses up to the impressive Basilica of St Thérèse with its high archways and large white dome. On its steps they witnessed an argument between an old man who challenged a soldier and was beaten to the ground for his trouble. Pascal moved to help the man but Gilles barred his way, whispering, 'don't! We mustn't draw attention to ourselves!' and they left the poor fellow to fend for himself.

The smell of freshly-baked baguettes filled the street, the cheeses and cooked meats at the market were enticing and Pascal and Gilles found it hard to disguise their pleasure at rediscovering the food they loved. They went into a café and ordered a beer, watching their fellow customers. Two middle-aged women were engrossed in conversation and Pascal and Gilles couldn't help but overhear the snippets of conversation which wafted their way:

'…so when her husband was away she invited the postman in…'

'…and there was me wondering why my delivery was late!'

'…and you'll never believe what she did then…'

They leaned towards each other confidentially, whispering, then both erupted in laughter, crying '*ooh là là là là là,*' raising a hand in front of them, shaking their wrists rapidly as if they'd burnt their fingers. Recognising the typical French gesture, Pascal and Gilles smiled at each other, knowing they were home. They finished their beers, bought some cigarettes from the *tabac*, then stepped back into the street to be stopped abruptly by a German soldier on patrol.

'Your papers!'

He held out his hand and looked the two men up and down suspiciously. Pascal and Gilles tried not to appear nervous while the soldier checked their paperwork, but everything was in order and he let them go on their way.

The shipment was due on Friday night and the agents were in position, sheltering in woods adjacent to a flat piece of farmland with André and his group. Towards eleven they heard an aircraft approaching, heading towards the bonfire lit to mark the way, then the black hulk of the plane came into sight. It flew low overhead and deployed its first parachute with a large wooden crate dangling beneath it. Another followed, then more, until all the cargo had been dropped and the plane headed off, up into the starlit sky.

The men extinguished the fire, recovered the crates and in the shelter of a barn, set about them with a crowbar, revealing a harvest of grenades, guns, explosive materials, boots, clothing and bundles of cash. Pascal and Gilles helped clean and degrease the weapons and distribute them to the Resistance fighters.

Back in his attic room, Pascal sent a message to England: '*airdrop successful. The pigeon is in the loft.*'

At her desk in Bletchley Park, Beatrice read the exchange of messages with her agents in Normandy and smiled. Her protégés were safely in place and ready for action.

CHAPTER 22

Bath, 1942

At The Oaks, Rosamund and Eileen were busy turning one of the spare bedrooms into a nursery. Eileen proved adept with a paintbrush, Rosamund made some curtains with a length of material she found stashed away, she bought a cot, a nursing chair, some soft toys and a table to put the baby on while changing its nappy. She knew little about the practical side of looking after a newborn but was sure that between them, she and Eileen would manage. The two stood at the doorway and surveyed the nursery, pleased with their work. All they needed now was the baby.

In December David Roberts told her, 'I think you have a couple of months to go.'

Rosamund quickly responded, 'end of this month, more like!'

One afternoon she was busying herself at home, sorting out some baby clothes, when the doorbell rang. Eileen was up to her elbows in soapy water, doing the washing, so Rosamund went to answer. A Post Office telegram boy was standing there in his smart blue uniform.

'Telegram for Mrs Mason.'

Rosamund took the telegram and opened it. She looked at the words without understanding them. The telegram boy could tell from her expression it was bad news and wanted to get away as quickly as possible.

'Any reply?'

'No…'

'Thank you. Good day to you.'

Rosamund closed the door, sat down in the drawing room and called to Eileen.

'What is it, Mrs Mason?' she asked, drying her hands on a towel.

Rosamund held the telegram in her fingers.

'It's the Captain. His ship's been blown up. He's lost at sea.'

Eileen gasped. 'I'll go and put the kettle on.'

Rosamund sat, numb, unbelieving. Eileen returned with a pot of strong, sweet tea and poured.

'Have this, it's good for shock. So, what does it mean? Might he still be alive?'

'Maybe…it's what they always tell you when a ship's been sunk…'

She stifled a sob, but no tears came. Mortimer, dead? It was impossible.

Christmas came and went, and Rosamund told her friends the baby was late, very common with a first child apparently, and the doctor assured her all was well. She missed Mortimer more than she had thought possible. Although she was used to him being away there had always been the prospect that he might turn up, unannounced, and breeze in.

Towards the end of January Rosamund was honoured to receive a visit from an Admiral from Royal Navy Command who came to pass on his condolences. He was surprised to see her heavily-pregnant state and apologised for disturbing her.

'The baby's overdue,' said Rosamund, her hand on her swollen belly, 'but don't worry, he or she is quiet at the moment!'

They sat down in the drawing room, Rosamund struggling to get comfortable, and Eileen brought them some tea.

'I didn't know you were expecting. How sad that Mortimer didn't live to see his child. I do hope all goes well for you,' the Admiral said, kindly.

'Thank you.'

'I want you to know that your husband was much admired and held in high esteem. He'll be sorely missed by his colleagues.'

'And there is no doubt that Mortimer is dead?'

'I'm afraid not. The ship was torn in two by a torpedo and nothing could have been done to save her. A handful of survivors were picked up by another ship in the area and they confirmed that Captain Mason stayed on board, urging his men to save themselves. He went down with his ship.'

Rosamund nodded. That is what she would have expected of her husband.

'He was very courageous, devoted to the Royal Navy,' said the Admiral.

Then, looking up at the portrait he said, 'what a fine painting. The artist has captured him perfectly. You must feel as if he's still here.'

Rosamund smiled and tried to hide her emotions. Yes, Mortimer and Michael would always be here.

The following day Rosamund felt a terrible pain which made her stagger and fall. After another wave she knew – at last, it was time. Eileen rang for an ambulance and arriving at the hospital Rosamund was relieved to find that David Roberts was the duty obstetrician. She would be in good hands.

After a six-hour labour Rosamund produced a healthy boy, bellowing lustily. Cradling him in her arms she stared into his blue eyes, gently stroking his fine, fair hair, and for a fleeting moment she could see Michael's face. He was the father, there could be no doubt. The memory of the love she had felt for him that night surged through her and transferred itself to her baby.

Coming back to the present she declared, 'my late arrival! You're a bonny boy!'

The nurse smiled at her, but David knew the baby was of normal weight and size – he wasn't late. But he kept his thoughts to himself.

'You have a fine son. What are you going to call him?'

'Cedric, after Mortimer's father. How I wish Mortimer could see him…'

'Of course,' said David, squeezing her hand, sympathetically.

France, 1943

By day, Pascal and Gilles worked at Monsieur Moulin's engineering workshop where they were accepted without question by their colleagues. By night, with the others of the Resistance group, they carried out acts of sabotage. They quickly notched up a number of successes, disrupting German supply lines by placing large logs on the sleepers of a railway line and setting fire to them, blowing up a signal box and cutting underground communications cables.

André Lazarre, the group leader, conducted his planning meetings in the upstairs room of a café run by his sister and brother-in-law in one of the back streets of Lisieux. Pascal and Gilles had been there several times, assured that the café was a safe location for conducting business and that André and his contacts were trustworthy, although they always carried their guns in case of any trouble. Their meetings invariably ended with a coffee and glass of calvados (*calva*, as they called it), served by Sandrine, André's niece, nineteen years old, a dark-eyed, olive-skinned beauty. When she served Pascal his drinks she always smiled at him and managed to touch his hand or brush her body against his.

At their next meeting André announced their biggest challenge yet: to demolish a metal railway bridge over a river.

'A train comes from Cherbourg with supplies of ammunition for the German army at the same time every week. The plan is to place explosives on the supports of the bridge and to detonate them just as the train approaches. You will need to work quickly and watch out for the soldiers on their rounds - kill them, if necessary.'

The following week Pascal and Gilles were in position. Working in the darkness they fixed the explosives in place and were making their way to their hiding place at a safe distance when two soldiers patrolling the area noticed a movement and came to investigate. The two agents ducked down behind a bush and as the soldiers went past Pascal and Gilles jumped on them, despatching them with a swift, silent blow to the neck as they had been trained to do. They were both shocked by the ease with which they had taken a life but there was no time to reflect: they could hear the train approaching.

As the engine rolled onto the bridge Pascal took cover and initiated the detonator, setting off a mighty explosion and blowing the bridge to pieces, sending the engine and its goods waggons tumbling into the river beneath. Orange flames leapt into the sky and pieces of metal hurtled through the air as the train's deadly cargo ignited. Pascal and Giles ran from the scene, away from the heat of the raging fire and deafening explosions. They reached their rendezvous point where André was waiting for them, jumped into his car and drove quickly away from the spreading blaze.

Later they celebrated upstairs at the café, André raising a glass of *calva* to their success and the brave agents who had carried out the task. They finished the bottle and as Pascal rose to leave, Sandrine took his arm and led him to her bed.

The next day, Gilles was unimpressed.

'I sent a message to England last night to say our mission was successful, while you were having your fun…'

'But I wasn't going to say no, was I? She's quite a girl…!'

Gilles waved his forefinger from side to side in disapproval.

'Seriously, Pascal, you've got to be careful. Remember what we were told, trust no one.'

Pascal sighed. 'I'm sure we can trust Sandrine, she's one of us. But – point taken. I'm sorry.'

CHAPTER 23

Bath, 1943

At the end of April a special service was held in Bath
Abbey to commemorate the first anniversary of the
Bath Blitz. Eileen said she wanted to attend; she rarely
mentioned her parents, but on this occasion she felt
the need to honour them. Rosamund agreed to go with
her - she owed it to Michael and the other art students
who had perished to pay her respects, confident that
no one would make a connection between herself,
Michael and the new baby.

The occasion was sombre and both women
wore black. Rosamund carried baby Cedric in her arms,
hoping he would behave and finding comfort in
cradling his warm, strong little body, wrapped in a
woollen blanket. She looked around at the others in the
congregation, grieving families, many in tears as they
remembered those awful nights a year ago, and held
Eileen's hand as her eyes brimmed. As they rose to sing
a hymn Rosamund spotted David Roberts on the other
side of the aisle, standing between a RAF officer and a
soldier - his sons, she thought, recalling the photo on
his desk. Her heart went out to him at the loss of his
wife.

In his sermon the vicar spoke of forgiveness, but only the staunchest believers seemed convinced - for most, that would take much longer. After another hymn there was a reading in the middle of which Cedric started to cry. Rosamund tried to quieten him but his wails grew louder, so leaving Eileen in the pew she stood up, apologising to those around her, and quickly left the Abbey. As if in sympathy another baby started bawling and Rosamund was soon joined outside by its mother.

The two women stood outside, rocking their babies who settled down, breathing the fresh air.

'How embarrassing!' said Rosamund, 'I'm scared to go back in case he starts again!'

'Me too!' said the younger woman. 'How old is yours?' she asked, coming closer to look at the fair-haired, blue-eyed boy.

'Three months. He's called Cedric.'

'That's a nice name. Mine's Alfred, he's six months. The time goes so quickly, doesn't it. Did you lose anyone close in the raids?'

The young woman, with her kind blue eyes and friendly manner, looked at Rosamund which such empathy that Rosamund forgot the lines she had taught herself to speak. The emotion of the day came upon her, and with the swell of voices singing from inside the Abbey she suddenly found herself in tears.

'Yes - yes, I did...'

'Oh, I'm so sorry.'

She put her arm around the older lady and asked no questions, just held her while her tears flowed. The comfort of strangers reminded Rosamund of the kind Frenchman who had consoled her when she'd wept at Green Park on that awful day, the man who had told her that Michael was dead.

Rosamund calmed herself and dried her eyes. 'I'm so sorry, I don't know what came over me!'

'It's all right - it's the war - we lose those we really love...'

The young woman looked momentarily distant, as a shadow passed across her face.

They realised the service had ended and people were leaving the Abbey. Rosamund saw Eileen coming towards her and took a deep breath to recover her composure.

'I must go, but thank you... it was lovely to meet you. Take care of yourself, and Alfred. My name's Rosamund, by the way.'

'It was nice to meet you, too. I'm Clare.'

Feeling emotional after the service, Clare took Alfred to her mother's and asked her to watch him while she went for a walk, needing to be alone. She found her way to Little Solsbury Hill, climbed to the top and sat down on the grass, enjoying the soft breeze on this pleasant Spring afternoon. The view of Bath had changed since she had come here with Philippe – familiar landmarks and church towers were lost to the bombs and rows of Georgian terraces blown apart. That was the last day of peace before the raids, the day she had made her choice, to stay with Reg, yet now he seemed so far away and it struck her that if it wasn't for Alfred she would feel no connection to her husband at all. By contrast her feelings for Philippe remained strong and she wished that circumstances could have been different. She hoped he was safe, doing whatever it was that kept him in London, and that one day she might see him again.

She heard the plaintive cry of a buzzard and watched it soaring high in the sky on a current of warm air, its fan-tail poised, its straight wings motionless. The mighty bird circled above her, elegantly gliding as it searched for prey, then suddenly swooped down to the ground for the kill, rising again, grasping a bloodied rodent in its talons, and flew away.

*

The School of Art had moved from its temporary home in Bathampton to new premises at Sydney Place in the centre of Bath, a perfect location with light and airy rooms and plenty of space for the students to work. Richard had stayed in touch with Daniel's family and one weekend walked over to pay him a visit. He was welcomed by Mrs Johns who said, 'I'm pleased you've come – there's something I want to show you.'

He followed her into the lounge where Daniel sat, drawing in his sketch book.

'He still hasn't spoken, but he's started drawing these pictures… they're all terribly grim. When he's finished he rips them out of the book and throws them on the floor.' She fetched a pile of paper from the corner and showed Richard drawings of skeletons, bones, corpses and coffins, a macabre set of images which made his flesh creep.

'I think the raids will haunt him forever. Our friends at the Meeting House have told him that when we die, we go to Heaven, but that's not happening to the poor souls in his pictures.'

'It's horrible, and disturbing for you, too, but at least he's expressing himself – he suffered a trauma and needs to get these visions of death out of his system. He'll work his way through it, in time.'

Richard put his hand on Daniel's shoulder in a gesture of reassurance but he didn't respond.

Walking back into the city, Richard's route took him past Locksbrook cemetery which had taken a direct hit during the third bombing raid. The whole area bore the scars of that terrible night and he could still see craters where bombs had fallen on the already dead. He had read about the horrific sight confronting the wardens: corpses blown out of their coffins, human bones scattered across the road. Richard suddenly stopped short, turned on his heel and returned immediately to Mrs Johns who was surprised to see him back so soon.

'I think I understand what Daniel's trying to say. Let me have a word with him.'

With Mrs Johns standing in the background, Richard sat next to Daniel, took his hands in his and spoke to him, gently.

'When you walked home after the raids you were in shock – you'd been through a terrible night and lost your friends. As a Quaker, you are opposed to war, and it must have been terrible for you to experience it, here, at home, in Bath. But when you reached Locksbrook cemetery it got even worse. What you found was horrific, incomprehensible, unforgiveable. This is what you've been trying to tell us with your pictures, isn't it – the things you saw, too horrendous to describe in words.'

Daniel slowly looked up at him.

'It was awful,' he said, haltingly, his voice hoarse after being silent for so long.

Mrs Johns gasped to hear her son speak.

'I couldn't believe that people could die twice. They should have been safely at peace, in the arms of the Lord, but they were scattered all over the road…'

'No wonder you were so distressed, it was a terrible experience. But try and put it behind you now. The people who love you want you back – they need you. Look, your mother is here, she wants to comfort you. Talk to her.'

Richard moved away and Mrs Johns knelt in front of her son.

'Daniel, tell me what you need to say.'

'Mother…'

He began to cry and she took him in her arms, clasping him to her, weeping with him.

Auschwitz, 1943

Amélie and Greta survived their first year of imprisonment, unlike many of the Parisians from Drancy who had perished due to the terrible conditions or been sent to their deaths in the gas chambers. The women grew used to the camp's brutal regime, working from dawn till dusk with only watery soup and bread to eat. Their cruel guards treated them with contempt but Amélie and Greta kept the fight alive in their souls, driven by thoughts of their loved ones, and Greta was heartened by an occasional glimpse of her husband.

Living in their rat-ridden dormitory, the prisoners were terribly thin and stricken with disease, and Amélie's nursing skills counted for little when there were no medical supplies to be had. A tender hand and a word of sympathy were all she could muster. Under cover of secrecy, Jews would gather in small groups to pray and celebrate Shabbat, lighting a candle and saying prayers in Yiddish. Greta persuaded Amélie to join them, saying, 'remember your mother. You are here because of her, but use the faith she had to bring you some solace.'

Sometimes Amélie tried to remember her life before the camp. She mourned her father, lost at Drancy, and prayed that the Nazis would never find her son. She thought of her English husband, the brave Tommy she had nursed back to health in the First war, only to be run over in a Paris street. And then there had been a passionate affair with a doctor which now seemed laughable - how was it possible for two people to be so much in love? She must have been crazy - almost as crazy as she was now, believing, in spite of everything, that somehow, one day, this torture must surely end.

CHAPTER 24

Italy, 1943

When Corporal Reg Watkins received a letter from his wife it was like a message landing from another planet. He was war-weary; the sights he had seen at Dunkirk seemed years ago, and awful as they were, he had experienced a lot worse since. He cut off his emotions entirely; another comrade killed, another enemy shot to pieces, dead women, children, horses - none of it fazed him anymore. The Eighth Army had battled their way through the heat of the North African desert then progressed to Sicily, where Reg had taken part in the Allied bombardment of Messina and earned his promotion to Corporal. In September they had entered mainland Italy and now they were on their way to Rome, driving the Germans northwards.

It was nearly two years since Reg had seen Clare and he felt as if they were strangers. She had written to tell him about the Bath Blitz and how the city was recovering, starting to re-build and get back to normal, but he no longer had any concept of what 'normal' was. Most of her news concerned little Alfred, who had just had his first birthday. She delighted in him and told Reg about every smile, every tooth, his first word, and wrote, 'I talk to him about you all the time, telling him about his brave Daddy.'

He looked at a photo Clare had sent him, holding Alfred in her arms. She told him the child had sandy-coloured hair, like his. Reg stared at the photo, trying to make a connection, but couldn't, so he dropped it on the ground and lit a cigarette. His sergeant, Roy Baker, a short, sly, man with a thin moustache, was watching him and came over.

'Bad news?'

'What? - no, just - you know...' Reg sighed. 'It's so long since I've seen her - and now there's a baby...'

Roy picked up the photo and looked at it.

'Well the kid certainly looks like you! That's something to be thankful for. And your wife, good-looking girl, isn't she...' he said, lasciviously.

'She is...but I can't see me going back to ordinary life with her and the kiddie, not after what we've seen and done out here.'

'Best not to tell her - she wouldn't believe you anyway. Make a new start is my advice - somewhere new to live, a new job. You're from Bath, aren't you?'

'Yes.'

'Well, I'm from Bristol, and I've got some ideas for a business after the war. I'm going to need people to work for me - people who know what I want, how I operate, if you know what I mean...'

He knocked his finger on the side of his nose.

'I could help you out, if you like...'

Reg perked up. 'Sounds good...'

'Look, write to her, tell her you miss her, say you can't wait to see her again and meet your son. She's worth hanging onto. If you make it back, all well and good, and if you don't, you'll be the big hero. You've got to play the game.'

Reg wasn't entirely convinced, but he'd give it a go. It didn't matter anyway, he thought, throwing away the butt end of his cigarette, he'd probably be dead tomorrow.

France, 1943

Pascal, Gilles and the Resistance group were waiting in a field for an airdrop. Sandrine was with them, and she and Pascal had become lovers. In the darkness she whispered to him to follow her into the nearby woods where, out of earshot of the others, she drew him towards her and kissed him. Their passion was instant, they pulled their clothes aside, he pinned her against a tree, lifted her up and she clung to him, her thighs clasping his hips, her mouth seeking his. Their brief encounter ended when they heard the awaited aircraft approaching. Hurriedly adjusting their clothes, they returned to the field where the others guessed what had happened but chose to ignore it.

The aircraft dropped its crates of weapons, ammunition and explosives which the fighters quickly collected together and took to André's barn for distribution. The next evening at the café André spread out a plan on the table and unveiled details of their next target.

'The German Army stores fuel for its vehicles at this depot. It's three miles from the town and surrounded by a high, chained fence. This is where the guards start their patrol,' he said, indicating a spot near the main entrance, 'and this is the route they follow. My men have watched them for weeks, and they never vary. At midnight the guards change over, here and here.' He pointed to two small gates in the fence at the east and west sides ends of the depot. 'They enter and leave by these gates – it's quicker and easier for them than going back through the main entrance. They always stop for a smoke and relax for a few minutes, and that's when we're going to strike.'

'What do you propose?' asked Gilles.

'We have a team of four waiting at each gate, hiding in the bushes. Two men will take out the guards while the other two run towards the fuel tanks and place explosives next to them. They will have five minutes to get clear.'

Pascal stroked his chin while he considered the plan. He still missed his beard.

'And what if we're caught?'

'We will fight. Having two teams attacking from opposite ends of the depot, the enemy's defence will be split. And we have the advantage of surprise.'

'We need a dark, dry night.'

'Yes. There's a new moon on Sunday and the forecast is good.'

'Very well. Brief your men, and I'll inform England that we're going ahead.'

It was Sunday night and the men of the Resistance were in position. André was right: the weather was ideal, the night pitch black. Pascal was taking cover in bushes at the east gate, with Gilles at the west, waiting for the moment. At midnight the relief guard arrived, exchanged pleasantries with his colleague, and Pascal gave the order to go. Two of his men ran swiftly and soundlessly to the gate which the guard had left ajar, entered the depot and attacked both guards from behind, slitting their throats. Pascal and his partner quickly made their way to the fuel tanks and fixed plastic explosive in place with a timing device, but as they sprinted back an alarm sounded, the depot was floodlit and soldiers began firing at them.

Dodging bullets, the men charged out of the depot, taking shelter at a safe distance behind some bushes. Pascal set off the timer, blowing the depot sky-high. The men thew themselves to the ground, covering their heads to protect themselves from flying debris while a second explosion erupted on the west side and a massive fireball rose above them. They waited for the backdraft from the explosions to pass then made their retreat through the smoke and heat, hiding from Nazi soldiers heading in the other direction.

It took hours to get back to the safety of the Moulin's house where André was waiting, looking ashen.

'What's wrong?'

'It's Gilles. He didn't get out in time and was caught in the explosion. He's dead.'

Pascal felt his stomach lurch.

'I don't believe it.'

'I'm afraid it's true. I'm very sorry.'

'I must tell England. I'll send a message straightaway.'

He went up to the attic where, alone, he shed a tear for his friend and comrade and in doing so remembered Michael, blown to pieces on the roof of Green Park by Nazi bombs. How many more friends would he lose in this terrible war?

He wiped his eyes and got a grip on himself. He had to do his job, and in spite of Gilles' death the mission had been successful. With great sadness, he transmitted:

'The heron is home but its blue feather is lost.'

Bletchley Park, 1943

Beatrice was shocked to learn that Gilles had perished, mourning the loss of an excellent agent and one of her own. At the same time she was relieved that Pascal, her erstwhile lover, had survived.

Gilles' death was tragic, but there were other pressing matters to attend to. The staff at Bletchley had been briefed about plans for the Allied invasion of France the following year and Beatrice was immersed in her job, gathering every bit of intelligence regarding the position of German forces and preparing instructions to give her Resistance units. The invasion was to take the form of amphibious landings with air support along the coast of Normandy, and Bletchley's role in cracking the Enigma code and decrypting enemy messages would be fundamental to the operation's success.

The pressure of work was intense and Beatrice was cheered to know that a friend of hers, Tilly Harrison, was about to join the team. The two women had been recruited by the security services during their last year at Cambridge, chosen for their excellent language skills and the fact that being from 'good families' they could be relied upon to keep their mouths shut.

As instructed, Tilly arrived at Bletchley station late at night. Standing on the deserted platform as the red tail lights of the train disappeared into the murky distance, she was reassured to hear a familiar voice in the darkness.

'Hello Tilly! Welcome to Bletchley.'

'Beatrice! I'm pleased you're here!'

'Take my arm and I'll lead you up to the house.'

Beatrice escorted her friend up the shadowy, narrow pathway to the main house and took her to an office where an Army Colonel was sitting behind a desk, smoking a pipe, a black Labrador at his feet.

'Miss Harrison,' said Beatrice, and withdrew.

The Colonel stood up to shake hands.

'Delighted to meet you, Miss Harrison. As you well know, secrecy is paramount if we are to win this war. You are to discuss nothing of what you see and learn here. My secretary will show you to your room for the night, then tomorrow you will report to Hut H. Any questions? Good, that is all.'

None the wiser, Tilly spent the night in an uncomfortable bed in an attic room and the next morning Beatrice came to meet her.

'The gardens look lovely,' said Tilly as they left the main house, passing some flower beds and a lake, 'it's better in daylight!'

They walked towards a group of wooden outbuildings known as the Huts, built to accommodate the many hundreds of people now working at Bletchley. In Hut H a Royal Navy Commander was briefing the staff about future operations. Afterwards he approached Tilly and introduced himself.

'Pleased to have you on board, Miss Harrison. Miss Webb will show you to your desk.'

The two women left the room, an odd couple, thought the Commander, Beatrice so plain and Tilly so pretty, a tall, blue-eyed blonde, aged twenty-two. But there was more to his new member of staff than her looks. His colleagues at the War Office had noticed Tilly's special skill, her uncanny ability to think herself into the enemy's mind, to anticipate their actions, to know what they were going to do before they knew themselves. That was why she was here.

Beatrice found Tilly a room in the same house she shared with others from Bletchley Park. Some of the best brains in the land were billeted in the town, but in the wartime conditions the locals showed little interest in the Bright Young Things who appeared from time to time in the pubs and cafés, laughing and joking together and falling in love, like any other group of young people. Beatrice and Tilly joined in, Tilly attracting men like bees to a honey pot.

At the end of one evening Tilly went to Beatrice's room for a nightcap. It was good to relax away from the constant pressure of their jobs, and as she poured some cognac Beatrice said, 'that fellow Piers has his eye on you!'

'Not just his eye!' replied Tilly.

They giggled like a couple of schoolgirls.

'Do you like him?'

'He's all right…but not really my type.'

'What happened to that chap you were sweet on at Cambridge - Benedict?'

'Oh, him - yes, I was keen on him for a bit, but then he went off with that foreign girl - do you remember? Eva something…'

'His loss.'

'And what about you, Beatrice - have you had any romantic moments?'

'What, me?! Don't be silly, dear!'

But as she said it, Beatrice touched the back of her neck and reddened, ever so slightly, and Tilly noticed.

CHAPTER 25

Bletchley Park, 1944

While other staff at Bletchley were attempting to crack the Enigma code, Tilly was immersed in feeding misinformation to the enemy. In the south-east of England agents were setting up fake infrastructure and equipment, dummy tanks, airfields and landing craft, an elaborate ploy to convince German High Command that Calais, where the English Channel is at its narrowest, was the likely site of the landings.

Tilly took to the task of fabricating false intelligence like a duck to water. A routine signal she sent about the need for additional warehouse capacity in Dover was leaked through diplomatic channels to German intelligence and shortly afterwards, Bletchley intercepted a message speculating as to the reason for this. Tilly led them along, teasing them like a fly fisherman tempting a trout, and to her delight, the enemy accepted the flow of fake information. She and her colleagues discreetly wove a web of deceit, a small but important part of the deception strategy which resulted in German forces being diverted from the Normandy coast, committing the bulk of their military forces to the wrong place.

As the day neared the BBC French service in London broadcast a series of codewords - snippets of poetry, nursery rhymes and quotations - to prepare Resistance groups to carry out plans as instructed by the SOE. The increase in radio activity alerted German intelligence that an invasion was imminent, but because of the barrage of previous misinformation, the warnings were ignored. By the beginning of June an invasion was expected but nobody knew exactly when or where it would be.

France, 1944

On 6th June, D-Day, some 156,000 American, British and Canadian forces stormed ashore at five beaches along a 50-mile stretch of the Normandy coast, the largest seaborne invasion in history. The long, gruelling campaign to liberate North-West Europe from German occupation had begun.

In Lisieux, Pascal and the Resistance group were gathered around the wireless, waiting for their codeword. At last they heard '*the owl and the pussycat went to sea*', gave a cheer and sprang into action. Their orders were to sabotage the railway through Lisieux to prevent German reinforcements reaching their battle lines. Pascal worked with Sandrine and together they laid explosives and blew up a signal box, while others cut rail lines and destroyed locomotives in a train shed. Their mission was successful, but with gunfire in the distance and Allied planes flying overhead it was clear the invasion had begun and fighting broke out on the streets.

As they tried to get back to their base at the café the group found themselves in the centre of a battle with Nazi soldiers opening fire, aiming at anyone in their path, desperate to cling to power. The comrades took cover behind a makeshift barricade and fired back, Pascal aiming his gun at a soldier running towards them and shooting him dead. Sandrine was by his side, shooting soldiers in her turn, maintaining her position as others of the group were injured and one fell dead at her feet, but then her luck ran out and she took a bullet in her neck. Pascal turned to her, dropped his gun and held her in his arms, calling her name, but she was beyond saving.

Pascal stayed behind the barricade until the fighting moved to another part of the town, then carried Sandrine's body to the café where her distraught parents were waiting. Pascal was a wreck, weeping for his lost lover, his clothes filthy and stained with her blood, overwhelmed by the violence unleashed on the streets, littered with the wounded and the dead. He and André ran out to recover others who had perished and buried them, with Sandrine, in a mass grave at the back of the café, finding a priest who gave what comfort he could to the bereaved.

That night the Allies launched a massive bombardment on Lisieux to drive out the enemy and the comrades realised, in horror, that in order for the Allies to liberate the town, first they had to flatten it. Taking shelter with the others in the cellar of the café as planes flew overhead, Pascal was reminded of the raids over Bath, but these were more intense and prolonged, made worse by the knowledge that it was the Allies who were carrying them out. By day the citizens surfaced, slowly, onto the streets to see what damage had been done, to be confronted by Nazi soldiers intent on killing them. They learned that the Allies had seized the ports of Cherbourg and Caen but also heard terrible stories of the blood-filled waves at Normandy and the countless bodies lying on the beaches. The price of freedom was high.

The enemy began to flee as the Allied bombardment took hold, continuing for one week, and another, then the café received a direct hit, the walls of the cellar shook and the ceiling collapsed on them.

'We can't stay here any longer,' declared André, 'we must go to the Basilica.'

They salvaged what they could and decamped to the Basilica which was already crammed with hundreds of refugees, seeking shelter with the religious communities who lived there. They stayed in the crypt amongst the already dead while the raids continued relentlessly. Conditions were appalling, the stench sickening, there was little food and water, but they had no alternative. At last, in mid-August, Allied tanks and British troops reached Lisieux and after two days of fierce fighting the Germans finally surrendered.

The citizens emerged from the Basilica, one of the few buildings that was largely unharmed, and into the light. They were filthy, stinking and starving, gratefully taking the food dished up to them by the British Army. The town was ravaged, its ancient streets destroyed and over eight hundred people killed.

When he re-gained his strength, Pascal, washed, clothed and fed by the Army, went in search of Monsieur and Madame Moulin. He picked his way through the wreckage of the flattened town to the ruins of their house, but there was no trace of its occupants, and his own belongings and the precious radio transmitter had been blasted away. It was heartbreaking; he had come to know and respect this town and its people and to see it in ruins was beyond comprehension. It was a strange victory.

Pascal returned to the Basilica with hundreds of other homeless people who had nowhere else to go and found André, exhausted by the raids and years of fighting. They sat together and André said, 'we have lost many of our comrades and loved ones, but we will always be grateful to you and the SOE. The Nazis have been driven out and our town is in French hands once more. But our work is finished and now you must go.'

'I will never forget you and your family, especially Sandrine. She was a brave and beautiful woman. It has been my privilege to fight alongside you and our comrades.'

The two shook hands.

'If there is anything I can do for you in the future, let me know,' said André.

'Thank you, I will remember that. But you're right: I must go now. I need to get to Paris.'

Pascal was sitting in the back of a lorry with some American soldiers, travelling slowly over the blasted roads in the wake of Allied troops driving the German army eastwards. He had spotted the convoy as it travelled through Lisieux, and with the gift of a bottle of *calva* he'd saved from the ruins of the café, he hitched a ride. It was a slow and difficult journey as the convoy bumped its way across the Normandy countryside, still a battle zone with guns firing all around them, roads blasted with pot holes and aircraft soaring noisily overhead. They lumbered on, the men slept, smoked, shared rations. It was the slowest, most perilous hundred miles to Paris. As they drove through towns and villages people saw the American flag and cheered them, the saviours bringing freedom, heartening the soldiers who waved back.

Pascal thought of Sandrine, Gilles and the other friends he had lost, and of the changes war had wrought in himself, the willingness to face the enemy and kill them. He didn't think of himself as brave; it was a job that needed to be done, which he'd been trained to do. He had taken the lives of many men, but they were the enemy, and it was either them or him. But he did wonder how he could ever reconcile his past with his future. When this war was finally over, what would he do? How could he go back to his old life, painting pictures?

Finally the convoy reached Porte d'Italie on the southern boundary of Paris and halted, awaiting orders to enter the city. The battle for liberation was raging there and the situation was highly dangerous.

As Pascal jumped out the lorry an American sergeant said, 'be careful - the fighting's still going on. You can come back here if you've nowhere else to go.'

'Thanks, I'll bear that in mind. But first I've got to try and find someone.'

CHAPTER 26

Paris, 1944

Pascal arrived in Paris in the middle of an uprising with Resistance forces erecting barricades in the streets and organising themselves to sustain a siege. He made his way towards the Seine passing wrecked cars, burnt-out buildings, smoking fires, and dead bodies sprawled on the ground. He reached the Gare d'Austerlitz and crossed over the river, the mighty cathedral of Notre Dame on the Ile de la Cité rising above the city like a beacon of hope. He trod the familiar streets, his pulse racing, then there it was - his old apartment block. His eyes went to their window on the first floor - was his mother there? So many times he had tried to imagine her living under the occupation, wondering how she was coping, and at long last he was about to find out. And his grandfather - was he still alive, even? He neared the block with trepidation, a warning bell ringing inside his head. Trust no one, don't let your guard slip.

Pascal entered the building which was basically unchanged, but shabby and unkempt. He ran up the staircase, two steps at a time, found his apartment and banged on the door, his heart thumping out of his chest.

'All right, all right!' shouted a male voice.

An unshaven man wearing a vest, with a cigarette dangling from his mouth, opened the door.

'What's all the fuss?'

Pascal was shocked.

'I'm looking for Madame Swann - is she here?'

'No, she's not. Who's asking?' he said, looking suspiciously at this stranger.

The warning bell rang again.

'My name is Pascal Lejeune. I'm a friend of the family.'

The man's wife came to see what was going on.

'He's looking for a woman called Swann,' he said, turning to his wife.

She shook her head. 'We've lived here for six months. I've never heard of her. Are you sure you've got the right address?'

'Yes, of course!' shouted Pascal, growing impatient and increasingly anxious.

The next-door neighbour heard the raised voices and came out onto the landing to see what was going on.

'Here, see if you can help him,' said the man, and slammed the door in the stranger's face.

Pascal turned to the neighbour.

'I'm looking for Madame Swann, she used to live here…'

The woman shrugged. 'I don't know her. I moved here in '43 to look after my sister, Madame Duclos, then after she died I stayed here.'

Pascal vaguely remembered Madame Duclos, a sneaky, miserable woman.

Then she added, 'perhaps she was taken away in '42 in the round-up.'

'What?'

'When they rounded up the Jews. My sister told me her neighbour was taken, and quite right too. Yes… now I think of it, I remember her talking about Madame Swann, a Jewess.'

'No, you must be mistaken. She's not Jewish!'

The woman spread her arms with her palms up and raised her shoulders.

'*Bof* ! Whatever, they took her away. And the old man too, I think my sister told me… Anyway, who are you?'

Pascal shook his head in disbelief at what he was hearing.

'It doesn't matter,' he said, and ran down the stairs and out of the building.

To calm himself he went to the café on the corner that he used to frequent. All the familiar faces had gone, making him realise just how much had changed in the four years since he'd left Paris. He ordered a coffee and a *calva*, and lit a cigarette to aid his thinking. The drinks warmed him and as he smoked his second cigarette his mind became clearer. The old woman was talking rubbish - of course Amélie wasn't Jewish! On the other hand, she certainly didn't live in their old apartment any more, nor did her father. He needed information about what had happened to them from a trustworthy source, then he thought: the hospital.

He left the café, and on his way to St Antoine racked his brains to remember the names of his mother's colleagues, people she'd spoken about. He could only remember one.

When he arrived at the hospital he went straight to the orthopaedic department and asked a young nurse at the reception desk, 'I would like to speak to Dr Fournier.'

The nurse looked blank. 'We have no one here by that name.'

'But he worked here, before the war…'

'I'll just ask.'

She returned with a severe-looking woman who said, 'may I help you?'

'I'm looking for Dr Fournier.'

'And you are...?'

'My name is Pascal Lejeune.'

The woman frowned and pursed her lips.

'I'm afraid Dr Fournier is no longer with us.'

'Oh… Do you know Nurse Swann? Amélie Swann?'

The woman froze.

'She, also, is no longer with us.'

The woman looked him straight in the eye.

'It is better if you do not ask these questions. Good day to you.'

She stood, holding her ground. Pascal moved away from the desk and sat down. He didn't understand. What had happened to them? And what could he do now? At a loss, he got up and was walking out of the hospital when a ward sister ran up behind him and touched his arm.

'I heard you asking for Nurse Swann,' she said, looking around to make sure no one could hear.

He stopped in his tracks.

'Yes! Do you know anything? I am Pascal Lejeune, a family friend.'

'She was rounded up in '42 and sent to Drancy. I saw her there - it was terrible. Dr Fournier was shot, with five others of the Resistance.'

Pascal gasped, trying to take in the awful news.

'So what happened to her?'

'The same as happened to all the Jews at Drancy - she was taken to Auschwitz.'

His knees buckled beneath him.

'But why? She's not Jewish!'

'They said she was, because of her mother.'

She looked around, anxiously.

'I must go - I have said too much.'

She squeezed his arm and quickly walked away.

Meanwhile, the severe-looking woman was with Dr Moreau, repeating the young man's question.

'So – someone is interested in the fate of Dr Fournier and Nurse Swann. And his name was...?'

'Pascal Lejeune – or so he said...'

Dr Moreau sat back in his chair and considered the matter.

'Thank you, Madame, you can leave this with me.'

He reached for the telephone on his desk and dialled a number.

'Good afternoon, Oberleutnant Engel. I have some information which you may find of interest...'

*

Pascal returned to the American convoy and stayed there for the night. He couldn't believe what he had learned. His mother - a Jewess? He tried to remember what she had told him about his grandmother - how, as a child, Raisa had fled from East Prussia with her parents and made a new home in Paris. Was that why they fled - because they were Jewish? Growing up, raised as a Catholic, it had never occurred to him, and his family had never spoken about it. He remembered the jewellery box his mother raided when they needed extra money - she used to take pieces to a trader in the Marais - but that was the only connection with Jews that he could recall. If it was true, she had kept her secret well. How had anyone found out?

Then it finally dawned on him - that was why Amélie had sent him to England. She had heard what the Nazis had done to the Jews in Eastern Europe, she knew how they came after Jews and the descendants of Jews… she had feared for his safety. Now, at last, he understood, and he wept at the realisation. It was his duty to find out for sure what had happened to her.

Over the next days Pascal returned to his old district, dodging along back roads to avoid the crossfire between the remaining German forces and Parisians fighting to reclaim their city. He went to the café near his old home, watched and listened, and befriended the owner, whom he suspected was a member of the Resistance. When business was quiet he approached him and said, confidentially, 'my name is Pascal Lejeune. I've been working in Normandy but I came to Paris to find someone. Can you tell me anything about Drancy?'

The man shrugged his shoulders.

'Very little. They rounded up Jews from round here in '41 and '42, thousands of them, and took them to Drancy. They shipped them off to Auschwitz, and when there was room at Drancy they rounded up some more. Many perished. Who are you looking for?'

'Madame Swann – a family friend - and her father.'

'Very well. If I hear anything I'll let you know.'

Pascal left the café, satisfied that he had done all he could for the moment. But, lost in his thoughts, he had let his guard down and failed to notice a man lingering on the corner, watching him.

When Pascal next went to the café the owner said, discreetly, 'Monsieur Lejeune, I have a message for you,' handing him a piece of paper which Pascal unfolded and read:

I have news of Madame Swann. Meet me at Café Bleu near Opéra Garnier tonight at 8pm.
A friend.'

Pascal was suspicious, but at the same time curious. He couldn't pass up the chance to find out what had happened to his mother, so that evening he headed to the rendezvous, his loaded gun reassuringly in its holster.

Café Bleu was in a quiet street round the back of the opera house. As Pascal entered he noticed a stout, middle-aged man sitting alone, smoking a cigar. He looked up from his newspaper and gestured to his guest to sit opposite him. Pascal's back was to the door, but there was a mirror on the wall and he could see what was going on behind him. The two shook hands.

'My name is Dr Moreau. I worked with Nurse Swann at the Hospital St Antoine. I understand you have been asking after her.'

He beckoned to the waiter who brought two beers. Dr Moreau slipped him a tip and looked at him meaningfully.

'Yes. I'm Pascal Lejeune, a family friend. Do you have any news of her?'

Dr Moreau didn't believe for one minute that the young man was just a friend. He was certain he was Philippe, the missing son.

'Yes… I'm afraid she was taken to Drancy with the other Jews. I take it this comes as a surprise to you. Madame Swann hid her secret well - her mother was a Jewess from Eastern Prussia. She was arrested because she had Jewish blood.'

Pascal started at hearing these words spoken in such a matter-of-fact way. He also realised that the waiter had disappeared and they were alone.

'She would have been taken to Auschwitz to settle in the East, start a new life with her fellow Jews… it was for the best.'

Dr Moreau took a puff on his cigar and his gaze shifted as the door of the café opened.

Pascal glanced in the mirror and switched to full alert as a Nazi soldier entered.

Dr Moreau stood up and said, 'here is someone I would like you to meet. Oberleutnant Engel, may I present Pascal Lejeune - better known, I believe, as Philippe Swann.'

Dr Moreau stood back, grinning, as the Oberleutnant took a pistol from the inside pocket of his jacket but Pascal was too quick for him and dived to one side, catching a bullet in his upper left arm but still able to fire his own gun at Engel. The German fell backwards, reeling from a fatal shot to the chest, his shirt covered in blood. Pascal pulled himself up from the floor, pushed a chair out the way and charged out of the café.

Moreau froze for a moment, then shouted, 'murder! Murder! Police!'

Pascal ran and ran, pushing his way past people on the pavement, holding his arm which was bleeding profusely. He stole into a dark alleyway, hiding in the shadows as two gendarmes ran past, and tried to recover his breath, the pain worsening. He ripped a piece from his shirt to use as a tourniquet and, holding the material in his teeth, tied it around his arm. He was losing blood and getting weaker but had to keep moving so he took a deep breath and ran again, down the back streets until he found himself in the Rue du Faubourg St Honoré. And that was when he had an idea. Summoning his strength he dragged himself along the road, leaving a trail of blood, until he came to the British Embassy. He banged on the door and when it opened he threw himself inside the building, collapsing at the feet of an astounded guard.

'My name is Philippe Swann,' he gasped. 'I work for the SOE. Tell them…tell them…*Sulis*'.

PART THREE

CHAPTER 27

Paris, 1944

On 25th August, General de Gaulle triumphantly entered Paris and the occupying German forces surrendered. Victory parades followed and the streets were lined with citizens cheering the Allied troops, overjoyed to be back in control of their damaged but beautiful, liberated city. The light had returned.

While the celebrations were taking place, arrangements were being made by officials at the British Embassy to re-patriate a wounded SOE agent.

Hertfordshire, 1944

The agent was resting at a country house in Hertfordshire used as a safe place for recuperation. He was sitting in a sunny lounge, his left arm in a sling. Today he had a special visitor.

'Beatrice! It's so good to see you!'

He made to get up from his chair but she waved him down, and shook his right hand. She was relieved to see him alive and well, careworn from his experiences but still handsome. Her attraction to him was as strong as ever, but she put her feelings to one side and kept matters on a professional basis.

'How are you?'

'Recovering. The doctor said there's no permanent damage but I've lost a lot of strength in my arm. Thank you for getting me out.'

'You gave me a fright there - but you did exactly the right thing. I'm pleased they managed to get you back here so quickly.'

'The Embassy staff did a terrific job - mostly because of you, I think!'

She smiled. 'So, Paris…?'

'Yes - I went to find my mother, but…'

He paused, not ready to talk about her yet, and changed the subject. 'The bombardment at Lisieux, it was terrible, so many dead. Why did the Allies have to destroy it?'

'It's war. We had to. Without the bombing it would have taken too long to capture the town and many more would have died.'

'But there was hardly anything of it left!'

'It will be re-built, when the war ends. The Americans will pay for it.'

He shook his head, struggling to understand.

'And what about this deception strategy that people here are telling me about? We didn't see much sign of it!'

'You may not have thought so, but it made a huge difference, believe me. That's why so many German units were in the wrong place. If they'd all been waiting for us on the Normandy coast - well, we'd still be fighting there now.'

He took a while to digest this information, trying to imagine how the situation could have possibly been worse.

Beatrice said, 'tell me about your mother.'

'It's horrific - I found out that she was rounded up and taken to Drancy with the Jews, then sent to Auschwitz. I think my grandfather went with her.'

'Oh God, that's awful… I didn't know your mother was Jewish.'

'She's not – she's Catholic! But her mother was a Jewess, and that was good enough reason for the Nazis to arrest her. When I was growing up they told me very little about my grandmother - I knew she'd fled from East Prussia as a child, but that was all. I suppose they thought what I didn't know couldn't harm me.'

'And your mother sent you to your Aunt in Bath to protect you. She had your best interests at heart - she must love you very much.'

He sighed. 'I wonder if she's still alive? I must find out what's happened to her, and my grandfather. What can I do, Beatrice?'

'Nothing, for the moment. When the war ends the camps will be liberated and you may be able to find out something - there is always hope - but I must warn you, from what we hear the situation is absolutely dire. Don't expect to find out anything soon.'

He understood, accepting that this was going to be difficult. Then he said, 'I'm so sorry about Gilles - it was when we blew up the fuel depot - he didn't get out in time and was caught by the explosion.'

'Yes, I was sorry to learn that. He was an excellent agent. When hostilities are over we'll send his family some compensation - but the loss of a son is a terrible thing.'

His mind went to Sandrine and the other comrades he had lost.

'So what happens now?'

'Our troops are heading towards the Rhine but there's a lot of fighting to come yet. In France it's all about recriminations. They're tracking down collaborators, seeking out Nazis who committed war crimes - and this is where you can help us. We won't send you back there, but you have information that could be very useful. When you've recovered you'll be de-briefed by the team. They'll want to know every detail of your time in France - it will help us in these final stages.'

'Of course, I'll pass on everything I know. So, I'm still a member of the SOE?'

'Yes - and secrecy is more important than ever. You are not to make contact with anyone outside the organisation, not friends or family – don't send any letters. You'll work with us for the duration.'

'All right. Now, tell me, am I still Pascal Lejeune? Or am I Philippe Swann?'

'Sadly, Pascal Lejeune was killed in the crossfire in Paris – that's the story we're putting around. You are Philippe Swann.'

'Good!'

Then he added, 'can I grow my beard again?'

Auschwitz, 1945

On a freezing January day, Russian soldiers were ordered to enter the camp. Even outside the stench was terrible and they had to cover their faces to stop from retching.

When the defeat of Nazi Germany by the Allied forces seemed certain, the Auschwitz commandants had received orders to abandon the camp and destroy evidence of the horrors that had taken place there, blowing up buildings and burning records. Nazi guards force-marched tens of thousands of prisoners to other concentration camps and countless died on their journey. The Russian soldiers were about to discover the thousands that remained.

The camp was the size of a small town, with rough roads leading to accommodation huts and in the distance a group of buildings with soot-blackened chimneys. At first everything seemed quiet, deserted, but then prisoners who were still able to walk gradually emerged from the huts, shouting with joy and falling at the feet of their liberators, crying with relief that their years of hell were over. As the soldiers ventured further into the camp they discovered mounds of corpses, warehouses crammed with tens of thousands of pieces of clothing and pairs of shoes, personal belongings, and tons of human hair, shaved from detainees before they were gassed. Over a million people had been killed here.

Young Private Ivanov was ordered by his sergeant to go into one of the huts to round-up any survivors and collect the deceased. He took a deep breath and entered, his heart thumping with fear for what he might find. He could not believe this vision of hell, the appalling stench of so many dead bodies. And yet, here and there, he found some who, against all the odds, were still alive and he shouted for the medics to bring stretchers to take them away.

In one room he found an emaciated woman in a corner, sitting propped up, her eyes closed. He thought she was dead but approached her to make sure. He prodded her with his rifle and jumped back in shock when she opened one eye and stared at him. Her hair was matted, she was filthy, and thin as a bag of bones. She held out her trembling hand to him and said, in a voice scarcely above a whisper, 'I shouldn't be here. I am French. I am Catholic.'

Bath, 1945

At the Beau Nash cinema Clare watched the newsreels in horror, unable to comprehend man's inhumanity to man. She knew there were Jewish refugees living in Bath and wondered how they must feel, looking at these pictures of starving, skeletal people, people they may even have known back in their home countries. It didn't bear thinking about. She prayed that this was so terrible it could never happen again. Surely, in his lifetime, Alfred would never have to witness suffering on this scale or watch such appalling images on a screen.

After the report of the liberation of Auschwitz came the more cheering news of the Eighth Army's progress through Italy. The Allies had advanced beyond Rome, taken Florence and survived a terrible Winter. Clare resented the way people were calling the troops in Italy 'D-Day dodgers', knowing that her husband Reg was equally brave and had encountered many horrors in fighting his way through Italy. She felt so distant from him, and although she wrote regularly she struggled for things to say, beyond telling him about Alfred. She had received a nice letter from him before Christmas but not much else, just the odd postcard charting his journey, including one from Rome with a picture of the Colosseum. '*Rome is an interesting city,*' he'd written, '*one day I'll bring you and Alfred here to see it.*' This had surprised her; it was the first time he had mentioned anything about the future and the thought heartened her.

Clare had resumed her job at the railway station, leaving Alfred with her mother while she worked her shift. She was pleased to be back - much as she loved looking after her son she missed adult company and the money was useful. Moreover, she had a plan. She was thinking about where to live when Reg came back - her parents' house wasn't big enough for all of them and they'd need their own home. Reg had hinted at the possibility of a job in Bristol with his sergeant which sounded promising. She started to look around at places to rent, somewhere in a nice area, and was pleasantly surprised to find that, with her savings and the money Reg was earning as a Corporal, they should be able to afford something reasonable. Please, she thought to herself, please let this war end soon, before anyone else gets hurt, so we can all get on with our lives.

Rosamund also watched the news reports, appalled at the dreadful treatment of people in the Nazi concentration camps. If anything justified going to war, losing loved ones, then this was it. She missed her husband dreadfully but was proud of what he had achieved in his Naval service. Then she thought of her son, Cedric. He would join the Royal Navy, there was no doubt about that: it was the only suitable career for Mortimer's son. Her own father had been an Admiral so Cedric clearly had a seafaring heritage. She didn't want him to have to go to war, but if needs be she would support it. Someone had to stand up and fight these terrible dictators, these cold-blooded murderers. Great Britain prided itself on its seapower and she had visions of her handsome, blonde son standing on the bridge of a warship, leading his men to victory. He was only two but she'd already put his name down for the best Prep school in Bath, knowing that was what Mortimer would have expected; a good education was what mattered, offering him the best possible start in life.

Back at home, Eileen greeted her with a cup of tea and said to Cedric, 'show Mummy what we've been doing this afternoon!'

The little boy grinned and ran to the kitchen, returning with sheets of paper scrawled with crayon.

'He loves drawing!' said Eileen, as the delighted child presented his mother with a picture of a large round face with strands of yellow hair scribbled over the top.

'Mummy!' said the boy, pointing to the picture.

Rosamund's heat sank, art being the last thing she wanted her son to be good at, but the boy looked at her so appealingly that she forgave him, pulled him onto her lap and said, 'that's very good, darling. Now, let's read a book, shall we? What about this one - *My First Book of Ships* - ?'

Richard paid one of his regular visits to Weston to see Daniel and was delighted to find him in good spirits with Emma, his girlfriend, by his side. The two were looking at some sketches of her that Daniel had drawn.

'These are excellent!' Richard declared, 'you're certainly getting your old skills back.'

He didn't want to put any pressure on him, so said, 'there's always a place at the School for you, you know, when you're ready.'

'Thank you, I will come back, one day.'

'Daniel and I are going to walk to Victoria Park this afternoon,' said Emma, 'the cherry blossom is out and it looks so lovely.'

'What a good idea. The park is beautiful at this time of year.'

Daniel squeezed Emma's hand and said, 'she's helping me to see the good things.'

CHAPTER 28

Hertfordshire, 1945

On the 8th May, SOE agents were gathered at the
manor house to mark Victory in Europe Day. After
nearly six years of fighting, the war in Europe was at
an end. The Eighth Army had successfully driven
enemy forces out of Italy, the Allies had reached Berlin,
Hitler was dead in his bunker and the Germans had
surrendered. The agents listened to Winston
Churchill's speech on the wireless and now they were
celebrating in style with a special meal, champagne, and
dancing to music from a gramophone. The only snag
was that they were out of a job.

Philippe was struggling with what to do after
the war. After his dramatic departure from Paris he had
no wish to return there, but what could he do in
England? The skills the SOE had taught him wouldn't
help him find a job in peacetime, he had no trade, no
aptitude for business, and couldn't imagine himself
working in an office, having to answer to a boss. Art
was all he knew, and he decided to resume painting,
using his experience of war to develop new styles and
subjects. But would that be enough to earn a living, and

where should he base himself? Mr Legge was at the celebrations and Philippe told him his dilemma.

'You could always come back to Bath,' said Mr Legge. 'My wife has a list as long as your arm of friends who were impressed with Angela's portrait and want one of their own children. Art's a worthy profession, it's what you're good at and you know people there who can help you, Richard Cross, for example.'

'That's true…I suppose if there is a demand for my work, it would be a good place to start.'

'And once you've established yourself you'll have the freedom to develop new ideas.'

The prospect of returning to the familiarity of Bath was appealing, and Philippe wanted to see Aunt Mary and Derek again. He told himself it had nothing to do with the chance of seeing Clare, or his fervent hope that somewhere in Italy, Reg Watkins lay dead and buried.

Beatrice came to join the party, bringing a friend with her. She spotted Philippe, delighted to see him in good health, and said, 'there's someone I'd like you to meet - my friend and colleague, Tilly Harrison.'

They shook hands, Philippe impressed by the attractive blonde who struck him as being both empathetic and sharp as a razor.

'Philippe was an operative in Normandy.'

'You must have seen some terrible things,' said Tilly, looking at Philippe with an understanding air whilst admiring his handsome features.

'Yes… I lost several comrades and friends. The bombardment was horrific.'

'A necessary evil.'

'I wouldn't be here now without Beatrice's help.'

'Really?'

Tilly looked at Beatrice who blushed slightly and said, 'it was nothing… All that matters is that we survived. Let's celebrate, shall we?'

They toasted each other with champagne, then Philippe asked his colleagues what they were going to do next.

'I'm going to the Foreign Office in London, then I'll be posted to an Embassy,' said Beatrice.

Tilly said, 'I'll go to my parents' in Berkshire - my mother wants me back home! I'll probably help out in the family business for a bit. I'm looking forward to seeing my brother, Peter - he was a POW and has just been released. He's in the RAF and his plane was shot down, it must have been beastly for him. What about you, Philippe?'

'I'm thinking of going back to Bath and taking up Art again. My Aunt lives there and it's as close as I've got to home. There's nothing for me in France.'

'Let me know how you get on – I'd like to stay in touch,' said Beatrice.

'What she means, Philippe, is that once you've worked for the Security Services you can never leave! You'll always be waiting for that telegram…'

He gave a Gallic shrug. 'I wouldn't mind. I would be pleased to serve our countries. And one day I hope to find out what happened to my mother.'

Beatrice looked at him, sympathetically. 'If ever I'm in a position to help you, I will.'

Tilly observed their exchange, aware of an understanding between the two of them. Then, looking around the room wistfully, she said, 'it has been a very special time for us all. I will miss everyone.'

They knew they would never be able to share their unique experience with anyone else.

Bath, 1945

On a bright Summer day Philippe was driving along the A4 with a road map on the seat beside him, heading towards Box, where Derek's sister lived. He had been pleasantly surprised to find that his back-pay from the SOE was sufficient to buy a second-hand Austin 7 and to put a deposit on a room that would double as a studio. Thanks to Mrs Legge he had several commissions for portraits and a future in Bath was looking promising.

Philippe stopped to ask an old man for the address he was looking for, having to listen carefully to understand his strong Wiltshire accent. He found the cottage, stopped the car and knocked on the door.

'My name is Philippe Swann – Mary Stevens' nephew. You may remember, we met at Mary and Derek's house in Larkhall at Christmas, before the raids. Do they still live here with you?'

The woman was surprised to see the handsome foreigner with his charming accent on her doorstep and looked at him, intrigued.

'Yes, I remember! You're the artist. Mary and Derek aren't here, they moved back to Bath a while ago, to another house in Larkhall.'

'I see. Could you give me their address please?'

She returned with a scrap of paper.

'Here you are,' she said, 'give them my best, won't you.'

'I will. Thank you, Madame.'

Philippe smiled and waved as he drove away and the woman stood, watching until her exotic visitor disappeared out of sight.

It felt strange to be navigating his way around the busy streets of Bath in his own car, taking in all the changes from the last three years. Philippe found his Aunt's new home, an end of terrace house about a mile from their old one. He knocked on the door and waited until Mary answered. She caught her breath.

'Philippe!'

'Mary! I'm so pleased to see you!'

He went inside, hugged her tightly and lifted her off her feet. She hugged him back, noticing how strong his body felt – he'd put on some muscle and looked very fit, but when she touched his upper left arm he winced.

'Sorry! I didn't mean to hurt you.'

'It's all right - I injured my arm, but it's getting better.'

'Right… well, come in, tell me what you've been up to…oh, this is so exciting!'

Mary explained that their old house and others in the terrace had been declared unsafe and had to be demolished, but with their savings they'd managed to put a deposit on their new home. 'It's better than renting, a good investment for our old age. It was kind of Derek's sister to put us up for so long, but it's lovely to be back in Larkhall.'

Philippe looked around the room which was similar to the old place, even down to the canary in a cage, and he spoke to the bird which began to sing.

'He's new,' said Mary. 'Poor old Dickie died and I missed him so much, Derek said 'for God's sake get another one!' So I did. He's called Sunny.'

'Because he's yellow!' laughed Philippe, realising how much he'd missed his Aunt and her funny ways. He was pleased to see his painting of Pulteney bridge hanging on the wall above the fireplace.

'We managed to salvage it from the old house, with some odd bits of furniture. We were lucky to survive, you know.'

'Yes, we were...' Philippe remembered with horror the raids on Bath and the weeks he had spent sheltering in the Basilica in Lisieux.

Mary noticed Philippe's car and concluded that he must have been earning decent money. 'You'll find it quiet down here after being in London. How have you been?'

He lowered his voice, for effect. 'It was interesting - very busy! I was working for the Government and I'm afraid I can't talk about it.'

'Oh! Goodness!'

She didn't know what else to say, so he continued, 'but I have decided to move back to Bath. I'm going to look for somewhere to live and use as a studio.'

'Well you're welcome to stay here until you're settled - we have a spare room.'

'Thank you, that would be wonderful!'

Later, Mary asked whether there was news of Amélie.

'I…I found out that she was taken to Auschwitz, with my grandfather.'

Mary gasped. 'But that's awful! I didn't realise she was…'

'No, she's not! She's Catholic. But her mother was a Jewess and that was enough for the Nazis to imprison her.'

'Goodness! I'm so sorry, what a terrible shock. I suppose that was why Amélie was so keen for you to come to Bath, she was protecting you. I don't suppose Jack ever knew anything about it.'

'No, I'm sure he didn't. It was a secret, but somehow, someone found out…'

He suddenly remembered the self-satisfied grin on Dr Moreau's face in the café. His face darkened and Mary knew not to ask any more.

Derek came home from Stothert's, surprised but pleased to see Philippe again. He shook his hand vigorously and they talked about the war, its impact on Bath and their relief that the bombers hadn't returned.

Philippe asked, 'have you seen anything of Clare Watkins?'

Mary had been waiting for that question.

'Not so much, now - when her husband came home from Italy they moved over to Lower Weston, they found a nice new flat there. They have a little boy, Alfred - he must be nearly three. Clare's father died recently - it was his bronchitis - so her mother's on her own now. She didn't want Clare to leave, but Reg insisted that they get their own place.'

Philippe absorbed this new information with a dull thud in his heart. He hoped Clare was happy now she had what she wanted.

The next day Philippe went to an estate agent who provided him with a selection of suitable properties for rent. He went to a café, ordered a coffee and sat going through the details, remembering how awful English coffee tasted and missing his glass of *calva*. He whittled his selection down to the top three and spent the afternoon visiting them, settling upon a bed-sitting room at the top of a Georgian terrace on Lansdown Hill with a magnificent view over the city. It was quite a climb up the stairs but that would keep him fit, and the room was large enough to be divided to create a painting studio. With a bed in one corner, cooking and washing facilities in another, a couple of chairs and a table, it was all he needed. He agreed terms with the landlord, paid the deposit and arranged to move in the following week.

Philippe bought some essentials and re-equipped his art supplies. On moving day he said goodbye to Mary and Derek, promising to see them soon, and drove to Lansdown Hill. After several trips up the stairs he looked around his new home, light and airy, just right, with its wonderful view over Bath. He finally believed that the war was over; he was safely back in England and ready to make a new start.

Germany, 1945

The nurse at the Red Cross resettlement camp in Germany was kind, dressing her patient's wounds with care, treating her broken body as delicately as handling a piece of porcelain. The woman had gained a few pounds in weight, slowly, because they found that if patients ate too much too quickly their bodies couldn't process the food and they would be sick. The sores on her face were beginning to heal and her hair was growing in white clumps. She hadn't spoken and although she had a number tattooed on her arm they had no idea who she was, or what nationality.

Occasionally the woman would cry out and cover her face with her hands, then lapse back into sleep. The nurse would do her best to comfort her, aware of the unimaginable horrors she had faced, then turn her attention to the hundreds of others who needed her care.

CHAPTER 29

Bath, 1945

Philippe contacted Richard and paid a visit to the School of Art at Sydney Place where he was greeted like a member of the family. Richard proudly showed him around then said, 'in fact the School's expanding. We've been offered some rooms at Corsham Court, ten miles east of Bath. It's a tremendous opportunity and a fantastic place, so inspiring - the gardens are stunning, there's a lake, ancient yew trees and even some peacocks!'

'Sounds impressive!'

'It is. We hope to start there next year and develop some new courses on Art and Design, and to train Art teachers. And I'll tell you who's going to join us - Daniel! He's ready to come back now and I'm sure he'll make a marvellous teacher. You should go and see him.'

'Yes, I will.'

'It's good to have you back. If you need any help from the School of Art, just let us know.'

Philippe spent the next weeks organising his studio and working his way through requests for portraits of children from well-off families, friends of Mrs Legge. He sketched his subjects in their homes, finding something of interest to talk about to help them relax, and completed the paintings in his studio. Word spread and the demand for commissions grew.

Taking a break from work, Philippe arranged to visit Daniel. To save petrol he decided to walk over to Lower Weston, buttoning up his coat against the chilly Autumn wind. Daniel greeted him at the door with a firm handshake and a big smile and showed him to the back of the house where his father had created an Art room. Philippe was relieved to find Daniel much like his old self, if a little older and more reflective.

'You've been busy!' said Philippe, looking around at a number of canvases and sketches. A half-finished portrait of a young woman was on the easel. Philippe examined it closely, admiring Daniel's brushwork.

'I think I recognise her!'

Daniel smiled. 'Emma - yes, she came to our Summer exhibition in '41. We're engaged and plan to get married next year.'

'Congratulations! I'm pleased for you.'

'Thank you. She's a wonderful girl - she was there all the time for me, when I was ill.' Then more quietly he said, 'I still think of Michael from time to time - he saved my life that night.'

'I know. And I was so horrible to him, the last time I saw him - I still can't forgive myself.'

'You mustn't say that - so many dreadful things happened…anyway, tell me what you've been doing.'

'I was in London - I found some office work.'

'Really? Could have fooled me!'

Daniel had noticed Philippe's muscular physique and a new confidence about himself. Philippe shrugged and turned the conversation to the present, while Mrs Johns brought some tea.

'Richard was telling me about Corsham Court.'

'Yes - it's very exciting. I'm training to be an Art teacher and when we're married Emma and I will move to Corsham.'

'Sounds like you've got it all worked out!'

'I hope so - and we both have faith in the Lord.'

At the end of the afternoon Philippe took his leave and the two promised to stay in touch. Philippe began his walk back into the city, remembering the aftermath of the raids and his grief at losing Michael. He was pleased Daniel was in good spirits, but aware that underneath the bonhomie he was still fragile.

As Philippe approached Victoria Park he saw a woman and a small boy walking towards him and noticed something familiar about her. She was wearing an oversized winter coat and a headscarf knotted tightly around her chin, and as they grew nearer he realised it was Clare and her son. In the same moment she noticed him and they stopped in their tracks.

'Philippe! I'd heard you were back.'

'Clare! And this must be Alfred!' he said, squatting down and smiling at the little boy who hid behind his mother.

'It's all right, Alfred, this is Philippe, an old friend of mine.'

The boy emerged and smiled shyly at him. He instantly liked this man with the kind brown eyes and the neat brown beard. Philippe stood up and he and Clare looked at each other, noticing the changes in their faces, Philippe more rugged-looking and Clare who had a weariness about her.

'How are you?' they both said, at the same time, and laughed.

'Very well,' he replied, 'and you?'

'I'm fine.'

She smiled and he could see a glimmer of the old Clare, underneath.

'We've just been to the park, on the swings, haven't we, Alfred?'

The boy looked up and nodded, holding his mother's hand tightly.

Philippe told Clare he was living on Lansdown Hill, then said, 'I was sorry to hear about your father.'

'Thank you. I miss him, and Mum's devastated.'

'You've had a hard few years.'

'I suppose I have - but the war was hard for all of us. What about you? Mrs Stevens told me you were living in London.'

'Yes… I was quite busy there, but I'm pleased to be back in Bath. I've just been to Lower Weston to see Daniel Johns, a friend of mine from the School of Art – you might remember him.'

'I think I do. That's where we live, too - we moved when Reg came back from Italy.'

'Yes, Mary told me.'

'Actually I come over to see Mum on Saturday afternoons when Reg is at the football. Perhaps I could meet you at your Aunt's one day? It would be nice to catch up with you.'

Although he had promised himself not to get involved with Clare again, he found himself replying, 'all right - I'd like that.'

'I'd better go – it's getting dark and Reg will be home soon.'

They said goodbye and went on their way, Philippe pleased to have seen her but concerned that the beautiful, vibrant woman he had known and loved had lost her sparkle and become so dowdy. Looking after a family was bound to take its toll, but he felt that something wasn't right.

Clare and Alfred walked home, her mind reeling. Philippe was like a breath of fresh air and he looked so well, more mature and self-assured - being in London must have suited him. Her suggestion to meet at his Aunt's had just slipped out, as a gesture of friendship - she hadn't intended it as any more than that. And yet, seeing him stirred her old feelings…

She let herself into the ground floor flat, part of a small block built on the site of two Victorian villas destroyed in the Blitz. It was comfortable and they'd been lucky to get it, one of the first new-build properties available for rent after the war. She sent Alfred to play in his room, then took off her coat and hung it up. Looking in the hallstand mirror she removed her headscarf, turned her head to one side and pushed back her hair to inspect the bruise on the side of her face. It was pale yellowy-grey, fading fast, almost forgotten.

A few moments later, Reg returned.

'Hello, babe. What's for tea?'

Germany, 1945

The patient, Amélie Swann, propped herself up in bed and asked the nurse for writing paper and a pen. With a shaking hand she wrote a short note to her son, telling him she loved him, explaining as simply as she could what had happened to her and her father. She concluded,

'So now I am in hospital at a resettlement camp in Germany. I will stay here until I am fit enough to look after myself. Please write to let me know how you are. I long to hear from you. Your loving mother…'

Amélie wrote the envelope to Monsieur Philippe Swann at the address in Bath where she had written previously, and asked the nurse to post it. She waited anxiously for a response, but a month later the letter was returned, unopened, marked *'name and address unknown. Return to sender'.*

Amélie didn't understand. Her son, his Aunt and her house couldn't have disappeared. But if he wasn't there, where was he, and how on earth was she going to find him?

CHAPTER 30

Bath, 1945

When Reg returned from Italy he had taken up the offer of a job with Roy Baker, his Army sergeant, in his new business venture in Bristol, buying and selling Army surplus goods. In fact one of the reasons Reg had chosen their new home was so he could catch the train to Bristol from Weston station, an easy commute. He set off every morning in his pin-striped, double-breasted de-mob suit and trilby hat with a self-confident air, an ex-serviceman adapting successfully to civilian life. With his thin moustache Clare thought he looked like a spiv, but she kept it to herself.

While Reg was at work Clare spent her days looking after Alfred, cleaning the flat, shopping and trying out new recipes to make the rations go round. She missed her job and the company of her colleagues at Green Park, but Reg had insisted on her giving up work, believing his wife's place was in the home. She didn't argue because Reg was earning enough to pay the rent and they lived in a pleasant road, but she felt lonely.

To entertain herself she took an interest in the neighbours' comings and goings, particularly Dr Roberts who lived opposite in Eagle House which he shared with a family of Jewish refugees. She felt sorry for him because he'd lost his wife in the Bath Blitz. She learnt that his elder son Henry was a RAF officer and his younger son Anthony was in hospital, having fallen ill on his return from fighting in Italy.

One dark evening in October, shortly after Clare had seen Philippe, she was cooking the tea when Reg came home in a bad mood.

'The bloody train was late again!' he cussed, angrily ripping off his tie and going into the bedroom to change. He had an important darts match that night and didn't want to miss it.

'Hurry up, will you, I'm starving!'

'Yes – won't be a minute!'

Alfred, who had just had his third birthday, ran into the room playing with a toy aeroplane. Reg shouted at him to be quiet, raising the back of his hand to him, and the boy ran to his mother in tears. Clare wiped his eyes, saying, 'don't worry, Daddy didn't mean to shout. Sit down and I'll bring you your tea.'

Alfred hated the rough stranger called 'Daddy' who had come to live with him and his mother. He was scared of his temper and had much preferred it before, when he and his mother were living happily with his grandparents in Larkhall.

They began to eat but after one mouthful Reg cried out in disgust, 'what the hell's this?', flinging down his knife and fork and pushing his plate away. 'It's revolting!'

'It's called snoek, they're encouraging us to eat it because there's not much else! It's a fish.'

'Tastes like dog food to me!'

Angrily, he got up from the table.

'I'm going down the pub, practise my darts.'

'But you'll be hungry!'

'I'll get some chips on the way home.'

He slammed the door and left, and Clare and Alfred looked at each other. Clare pushed the grey, rubbery compound around her plate.

'I must say, it doesn't taste very nice! What if I make us some cheese on toast?'

She gave Alfred a hug and he grinned up at her.

One Saturday when Bath City were playing at home, Clare waved Reg goodbye as he went off to Twerton Park with his pals and she and Alfred caught the bus to Larkhall. Her mother was delighted to see them and they chatted for a while, then Clare said, 'I'll just pop down and see Mrs Stevens and you can have Alfred all to yourself. I shan't be long.' Clare's mother had no objection; she enjoyed looking after her grandson and giving her daughter a break.

When Clare got to Mary Stevens' house, Philippe was waiting in the back parlour room, hoping she would come. Mary discreetly left the pair alone while they talked, old friends catching up on more than three years of news. Philippe was relieved to see that without the frumpy coat and headscarf Clare looked more as he remembered, still with a good figure, her breasts accentuated under her tight-fitting jumper. She was wearing lipstick, her fair hair curled around her shoulders and she looked brighter than when he'd seen her at the park; maybe she'd just been having a bad day. He asked about her family, watching her face as she spoke animatedly about Alfred, whom she clearly adored, but her eyes clouded when Philippe mentioned her husband.

'He's got a good job, and we've got a nice flat. But…'

She sighed and changed the subject.

'Tell me what you've been up to!'

Philippe wanted to avoid talking about what he had done after the Bath Blitz so he glossed over the intervening years and spoke mostly about art, his new home and the commissions he was undertaking.

'You're so talented, Philippe. We had such fun when you were working at the railway station, didn't we! I'm pleased we can be friends again.'

Her voice betrayed an underlying regret that they couldn't be more. Their eyes met, and they knew their attraction was still there, ready to be re-awakened.

Philippe suddenly remembered Gilles warning him not to trust Sandrine, but Sandrine had died, bravely, for the Resistance. Clare, on the other hand, was potentially more dangerous. Philippe knew he should get out, now, and never see her again, but he couldn't help himself. He touched her hand and said, 'I'm pleased we're friends, too.'

Reckoning she'd left the pair alone for long enough, Mary came to join them, then Clare looked at her watch and said, 'I'd better get back to Mum's and pick up Alfred. If the tea's not ready by the time Reg gets home I'll be in trouble!'

Mary said goodbye and Philippe saw Clare to the door.

'This has been lovely,' she said. 'Can we meet again, here?'

'Yes, I would like that.'

He watched as she walked away, knowing his feelings for her were still strong, and equally sure that underneath her act of being the devoted wife and mother, she was unhappy.

Clare said nothing to her husband about her reunion with Philippe, knowing it would make him angry, but Philippe was an old friend, and why shouldn't she see him if she wanted to?

*

At The Oaks, Rosamund, Cedric and Eileen were expecting an important visitor. Rosamund's elder sister, Eunice, had returned from the Far East with her husband, Algernon, an Army Colonel, and had written to Rosamund to tell her she was coming to visit.

Eunice arrived by taxi with suitcases in tow and the sisters greeted each other with a kiss. They hadn't seen each other since before the war when the Army had posted the couple to Singapore. Eunice still regarded The Oaks as home and needed no encouragement to pass judgement on the changes Rosamund had made in her absence. She was impressed by the portrait of Mortimer, saying how sorry she was to hear of his death.

'And now you have a son, what a fine boy!' she said, as Cedric looked at her, wide-eyed.

Eileen served tea while they talked about their experiences of the war.

'We were lucky,' said Eunice, 'we got out of Singapore before the Japanese invasion, but several of our friends didn't. Some of them ended up in Changi Prison… horrible.' She shivered. 'It was dreadful, dear, the stories we heard...'

Rosamund understood. She had seen the newsreels and knew how cruelly the Japanese had treated prisoners of war.

'We spent the rest of the war in India. Algernon was so brave, and we survived – that's all that matters. He's been posted to Aldershot but no doubt we'll be off abroad again soon.'

'How are your boys?'

'Very well. They'll go straight from boarding school to Sandhurst, like their father. It's for the best - we move around so often it would have been far too disruptive to have them living with us.'

Eileen took Cedric out to play, leaving the sisters alone to talk.

'So, you and Mortimer finally managed to have a child.'

'Yes… it took a long time, but my obstetrician told me never to give up hope.'

'He's a delightful boy. So sad that Mortimer didn't live to see him.'

Eunice walked around the room, looking at the collection of framed family photographs. Seeing one of their parents she picked it up and said, 'it all seems so long ago - irrelevant, really. Since Singapore I've changed my views. I try and focus on the future now, not the past.'

Looking at other pictures of Mortimer she observed, 'Cedric doesn't look like him at all, does he,' then, fixing Rosamund with a look, 'you weren't unfaithful to him, were you?'

The directness of the accusation made Rosamund blush.

'Of course not!'

'Mmm… I'm quite broad-minded nowadays, dear – I've seen things in the Far East you would never believe. Mortimer was good to you, but I was never sure he gave you the warmth and love you needed. If somebody else could, I wouldn't blame you.'

Rosamund was too shocked to respond, just managing to say, 'my dear sister, you couldn't be more wrong. Of course Mortimer is Cedric's father and I don't want any more said about it.'

After Eunice had left, Rosamund looked around at the family photos taken over many years and grew concerned that other people may notice Cedric's lack of resemblance to Mortimer. She said to Eileen, 'could you help me with a job, please? I need a large cardboard box. I want to put all these old photographs up into the loft.'

'Oh! Don't you want them any more?'

'Well, they belong to the past, and I've changed my views. I want to focus on the future.'

'Very well – there's a grocery box in the kitchen, that should do.'

'Thank you, Eileen.'

Together they packed up all the photographs and Eileen stowed them away. Afterwards, sipping her tea in the drawing room, Rosamund looked up at Mortimer's portrait, the one image of him that remained. She had no intention of ever parting with *that*.

Germany, 1945

Amélie left hospital and was convalescing at the resettlement camp until she was fully fit and able to look after herself. Amid the hundreds of displaced persons she was overjoyed when Greta came to visit her. They had been separated when the Russians had liberated the camp, but Greta had recovered more quickly and managed to track her down. They hugged and cried, overjoyed to see each other among the survivors.

'But where is Jacques?' asked Amélie.

Greta's eyes filled with tears.

'He died…' she said, sorrowfully. 'I heard from one of the people who used to pass messages for us. It was just before liberation. The malnutrition, the hard labour - his body gave out.'

'I'm so sorry…'

The women hugged again, mourning the loss of a good, honest man. Then Amélie asked, 'what will you do now?'

'I have no wish to return to Paris, there is no one there for me and my old life is gone. I've decided to go back to my roots, Amélie – I'm going to Poland, to see the town my parents came from. I doubt I have any relatives because not many Jews would have survived, but the hills and lakes are beautiful. I hope I may find solace there.'

'I will miss you. You're the best friend I've ever had.'

'I will miss you too, Amélie. And what about you, where will you go?'

'I want to go back to Paris, to see my home city again. I'm worried about Philippe, though. I haven't been able to contact him in Bath and I don't know where he is.'

Greta took her hands in hers.

'You will find him, Amélie, one day, I am sure of it. Keep praying and God will bring him to you.'

CHAPTER 31

Bath, 1945

Philippe spent Christmas with Mary and Derek, thankful to be celebrating the occasion together for the first time since the end of the war. Rationing was still in place, but Mary managed to cook a good chicken dinner and make some mince pies. Clare invited her mother over for a family celebration, knowing it would force Reg to be on his best behaviour and giving Granny the chance to spoil Alfred rotten.

In the new year Philippe and Clare met at Mary's house on Saturdays when Reg was out with his friends. He showed little interest in how his wife spent her time and had no cause for suspicion. Sometimes Clare brought Alfred with her to Mary's and during the Winter months they stayed indoors playing board games, Philippe finding to his surprise that he enjoyed the family atmosphere, and Mary loved having them all there, keeping her company while Derek was out tending his allotment.

Reg started socializing in Bristol after work and occasionally stayed over with Roy Baker and his wife.

Clare didn't miss him, in fact she preferred it when her husband wasn't at home. She had hoped for a decent future with him, but as the months wore on she realised it was never going to happen. Since he'd returned from Italy he had changed so much, becoming aggressive and uncommunicative, shouting at her and Alfred, and her dreams had turned to dust. One evening after Reg came home from the pub he lashed out at her, for no reason at all. Clare was relieved that Alfred was in bed and didn't witness it, but the mark on her cheek where her husband slapped her was painful, and she looked at him in shock and disbelief. Reg stood back, caught his breath, then stepping towards her, said, 'I'm sorry, babe, I didn't mean it. I promise I won't do it again.'

That's what you said last time, she thought.

One warm Saturday in early Spring, Clare and Philippe went for a walk together and she found herself telling him about Reg's outbursts of temper which were becoming more frequent, and how she had to be careful what she said for risk of setting him off. It was clearly weighing her down.

'I'm lucky to have you to talk to, you're very understanding.'

'I try!' he said, although his patience was wearing thin. He struggled to understand why she chose to stay with this heartless man.

'He did suffer during the war, you know,' she said, responding to his unspoken thoughts. 'He still gets nightmares about Dunkirk, waking up shouting about blood in the sea and men drowning, it's horrible.

And I don't think Italy was much better - he must have seen some dreadful things out there. I think that's why he likes being with his boss - his old Army sergeant - I suppose they understand each other, what they've been through.'

'Yes, but he shouldn't take it out on you and Alfred.'

'I suppose not.'

They found themselves walking towards Little Solsbury Hill and remembered their picnic there, that last day of peace before Bath was blitzed. Wanting to put away thoughts of her unhappy marriage and to connect with Philippe, she asked, 'what did you really do, after the raids? Mrs Stevens told me you were in London, but you haven't said much about it.'

'I was working for the Government. I'm sorry, I can't tell you anything more.'

'Oh!' she exclaimed, not sure she understood, but recognising she would always be excluded from that part of his life.

'I missed you,' she said.

'I missed you, too.'

They were walking along a pathway and became aware that they were alone. He put his arm around her, she turned to him and they looked at each other. They kissed, on the mouth, a slow, lingering kiss, the kiss they had resisted but which wouldn't wait any longer. It was a kiss of tenderness, caring, closeness, and as they embraced, any pretence that they were just friends fell away. They knew that the feelings they'd had before were still there, growing stronger, and that very soon, they would have to do something about it.

While out shopping, Clare spotted a notice in a window advertising a local club for pre-school children and thought it would be suitable for Alfred. With no siblings to play with he needed to make some friends, so she took him along the following Wednesday afternoon and he loved it. She told Reg, saying, 'it's good for Alfred to be with other children, and it will give me a chance to catch up with the housework!' to which Reg gave a grunt and returned to his newspaper.

On her next visit to Larkhall she mentioned the club to Mary and Philippe, and Mary said, 'what a good idea! Alfred will benefit, and you'll have some time to yourself.'

Philippe and Clare exchanged a glance, and this time, housework was the last thing on her mind. When he walked her to the door he whispered, 'now you have a free afternoon, would you like to come to my place?'

He looked deep into her eyes.

'Yes, I'd love to.'

The following Wednesday Clare took Alfred to the club then caught the bus into Bath. It was a day of April showers, and sitting alongside housewives and pensioners going about their business, Clare watched the raindrops trickling down the window as they drove past the familiar sights. But whereas the other passengers looked glum, Clare felt excited, knowing that today was special; she had made her decision. She knew she was taking a huge risk and that if Reg ever found out she would be in deep trouble, but her feelings were too strong to resist.

She got off the bus and walked quickly up Lansdown Hill through the rain, and by the time she reached the top of the staircase leading to Philippe's room she was out of breath. He welcomed her in and hung up her wet coat.

'I don't know whether those stairs will keep you fit or wear you out!' she exclaimed, as he threw her a towel to dry herself off. While he went over to the stove to make some tea she looked around the room and behind the screen which divided his living area from the studio. A portrait of an attractive young woman was on the easel.

'She's the wife of a local solicitor,' said Philippe. 'I go to their house to do my preliminary sketches, then I come back here and paint. The sitters are usually more comfortable in their own homes.'

'So she hasn't been here, then,' Clare said, with a hint of jealousy.

'No!' he laughed, 'you're my one and only visitor!'

Clare noticed a postcard from Portugal, propped up on the mantelpiece. She picked it up, glanced at the back and read:

'Lisbon is a fascinating city, beautiful art work, you'd love it! Hope you are keeping well. B.'

'Who's 'B'?'

'Oh – a friend I met in London.'

'A woman?'

'Yes. She works abroad and sends me postcards from time to time.'

'I see...'

'Don't worry, she's no threat to you! In fact, some people say she bats for the other side...'

Together they went over to the window to admire the view of the city. The rain had cleared and sunlight was glinting off the slate rooftops.

'It's spectacular, and look, the trees are coming into leaf,' said Clare.

'It's wonderful - the main reason I chose to live here.'

Philippe stood behind her, placed his hands on her shoulders and she felt a shiver of pleasure as he kissed the side of her neck. Gently, he turned her to face him.

'I love you.'

'I love you, too.'

He kissed her on the mouth, her face, her eyes, he undid her blouse and caressed her breasts, desperate to kiss them, to see her naked. She ran her hands through his hair, pulling him towards her, longing to feel her body against his, skin on skin. She unbuttoned his shirt, but when she pushed it off his shoulders she noticed the scar on his upper left arm and caught her breath.

'I was wounded, but it doesn't hurt.'

They kissed again, taking off their clothes and fell onto the bed, delighting in each other, overjoyed to show their true feelings, to surrender to the bliss of loving and being loved. In their ecstasy the world went away and all that mattered was the two of them, together, in this room, taking pleasure in each other's bodies and souls as they had yearned to do for so long, fitting together perfectly like two halves of the same whole.

Afterwards he held her in his arms and they slept for a while, *le petit mort*, the little death that followed their climax. She awoke and caressed his chest, then asked, 'how did you get that scar?'

'I had an accident.'

'Mmm – a nasty accident!'

Then she kissed him on the lips and said, 'it's all right – I realise there are certain things you will never tell me about. I must stop asking.'

He glanced at the clock.

'You'd better go.'

Reluctantly she extracted herself from his embrace and got dressed. He lay and watched her.

'This is the best day of my life.'

'And mine.'

She sat on the side of the bed and they kissed again, hating to part, sure of their love for each other. He watched as she walked down the stairs, knowing that she was all he wanted, and his fate was sealed.

CHAPTER 32

Bath, 1946

On a beautiful June day, Daniel and Emma were married. The ceremony was conducted at the Quaker Meeting House and among the guests were Richard and Ann, and Philippe, who felt privileged to be invited to this unusual wedding. They sat with the other guests in a circle and settled down quietly, then Daniel and Emma arrived together, in silence, he in a smart suit with a waistcoat, she in a white lace bridal gown, carrying a bouquet of roses and freesias. The couple stood and said their vows before God, their hearts brimming with joy, their eyes shining with the love they felt for each other and the Lord.

The registrar read the traditional Quaker marriage certificate aloud and the couple signed it. Everyone was seated, in stillness, then a woman stood up and congratulated Daniel and Emma, sharing words of support, and sat down. After a period of reflection, others did the same, until the ceremony was deemed to come to an end and the registrar invited all the guests to sign the large marriage certificate as witnesses to the important occasion.

After the ceremony the guests were invited to Daniel's parents' to celebrate. Having congratulated the newly-weds and meeting Emma's parents, Philippe sought out Richard and asked him how things were going for the School of Art in Corsham Court.

'Very well, we're settling in nicely. I divide my time between there and Sydney Place. We're expecting a large intake of new students in September, a post-war boom! Daniel's doing well, he's going to make an excellent teacher.'

'Yes, I'm sure he will.'

Philippe found Daniel, wanting to wish him every happiness, knowing the trauma he had suffered after the raids and how Emma had supported him when he had been at his lowest.

Daniel asked, 'and what about you? No romance on the horizon?'

'Well…I have been seeing Clare again.'

A wave of disapproval passed over Daniel's face. 'The married one? I thought you'd left her behind when you disappeared off to London.'

'Yes, I did – but I keep coming back to her.'

Daniel raised his eyebrows. 'Well, I hope you know what you're doing…'

Philippe wasn't sure that he did, but to deflect the conversation said, 'I wish Michael could have been here today – he'd be so happy for you.'

'Yes… let's have a toast.'

They clinked glasses and said, 'to absent friends.'

*

238

Walking up Lansdown Hill one afternoon, Philippe passed a smartly-dressed woman in her mid-forties coming the other way. She looked familiar and he smiled at her, then she turned and spoke to a young boy a few yards behind her, saying, 'stop dawdling, Cedric, we'll be late!' Philippe looked at the fair-haired, blue-eyed boy, about the same age as Alfred, who had stopped to stare at a bumblebee buzzing from flower to flower in a garden. Philippe winked at the boy who gave him a broad smile, then ran ahead to join his mother. The boy had a mischievous look in his eye and vaguely reminded him of someone. It was only later that Philippe remembered where he'd seen the woman before: she was Mrs Mason, the woman he'd held in his arms as she sobbed at Green Park after the Blitz, mourning the loss of Michael.

*

When Clare next came to Philippe's he noticed some bruising on her shoulders and said, angrily, 'you can't stay with him, he's dangerous! You should report him to the police.'

'That wouldn't be any good – they don't interfere between husband and wife.'

'Then leave him! Get a divorce!'

'Come on, divorce isn't for people like me! We couldn't afford it, for a start! And if I go to Mum's he'll only come and find me and take me back and it will be worse.'

'Don't tell me you still love him!'

'I don't – not how I love you. But he is Alfred's father, and I'm sure it's himself he's angry at, not me.'

'Perhaps, but it's you and Alfred that he's hurting!' Philippe shook his head in frustration.

'I'm sorry, I love you, but I can't see a way out. After this last time he swore never to hurt me again.'

'And you believe him?'

'I have to.'

*

Philippe had a commission to paint the portrait of a local businessman, Mr Hoffmann, who happened to be Jewish. He was a friendly type who liked to chat and while discussing the war he mentioned the Holocaust, the term being used for the Nazi genocide of Jews.

'My uncles, aunts, and grandparents were taken to Bergen-Belsen,' he said, sorrowfully. 'The stories are horrific. I don't know whether any of them survived. I was lucky because my parents came to England before the First war, and I was born here, but the rest of our family stayed in Germany.'

Philippe listened intently, sympathised, then told him about the situation with his own mother.

'How can I find out whether she is still alive?'

'It's too early yet. In time we will learn more, but there are so many changes happening over there and it is still very dangerous.'

Then he added, 'you should pay a visit to Mr Greenstein's hotel – it's where the Jewish community in Bath worship on Shabbat. You may find some comfort there. I'll tell the Rabbi to expect you.'

Philippe considered this and the next Saturday he went along, standing at the back of the congregation and feeling alien. After the service with its strange Yiddish chanting the Rabbi approached him.

'You must be Monsieur Swann, the artist - my friend Mr Hoffmann told me to expect you.'

'I'm pleased to meet you.'

'Your mother was not of the faith?'

'No, but my grandmother was - she fled from East Prussia with her parents and they settled in Paris, but my mother was Catholic. But for the Nazis that was good enough to arrest her.'

'It has been a harrowing time. All the people who come to this service have relatives they left behind.'

'How can we know who lived and who died?'

'We can't, yet – it's too complex. Put your trust in God. I will pray for you that it is a good outcome. If you want to learn more about our faith, let me know.'

'Thank you, but I am Catholic, like my mother.'

'I understand. Well, our community is here if you ever need us. God bless you, Monsieur Swann.'

Philippe left Mr Greenstein's hotel deep in thought. He walked through the city, its busy streets full of Saturday shoppers, but not seeing them. He needed to be alone and headed towards Beechen Cliff, the wooded hillside to the south of the river, and climbed the steep hill to Alexandra Park. He walked past families and couples enjoying the Summer sunshine until he found a quiet spot where he sat on a bench under a beech tree.

He looked at the panoramic view of the city, scarred by the raids, its stone terraces and crescents blackened from the fierce fires that had blazed. It was a year since he had returned to Bath and although his artistic career was thriving he couldn't shift the dissatisfaction that was gnawing at him. The Rabbi was kind and well-meaning, but Philippe was no longer sure he had faith in a God who had allowed his chosen people to undergo such a terrible fate – in fact the more he thought about it, the angrier he became. He wondered how his mother had coped at Auschwitz, a Catholic amongst the Jews, and whether she resented her mother for being the cause of her incarceration. He wouldn't be able to rest until he had found out Amélie's fate, even if it took years. It would be kinder to think she was dead, her suffering at an end, and yet, deep inside, he clung onto the hope that somewhere, somehow, she was still alive. He should go to Mass tomorrow, to pray for her, but in his present mood he saw little point in going through the Catholic rituals if he no longer believed in them.

Then his thoughts turned to Clare. He loved her, deeply, and wanted her for his own. He failed to understand why she stayed with Reg, a violent bully, showing him a loyalty which he didn't deserve, and he was concerned for her and Alfred's safety. He hated Reg with a passion, and if he couldn't persuade Clare to leave him he resolved to take matters into his own hands, for all their sakes.

CHAPTER 33

Bath, 1946

In July, Reg came home with some news.

'We're going to a posh dinner dance in Bristol. Roy Baker, my boss, has invited us - his wife will be there too. It's in a hotel with local business types and it's a good chance to make contacts. You'll need a new dress, babe, and I'll hire a dinner suit!'

Clare wasn't sure what to make of this and told Philippe about it.

'I'd rather go to a dance with *you*!' she said.

'Me too! But you must go, or he'll think it odd. You may even enjoy it!'

Clare had her doubts but decided to make the best of it. She didn't have enough coupons for a new dress but in a second-hand shop she found an elegant, low-necked, black gown which fitted her perfectly.

The anticipated evening came, and Reg said to Clare, 'you look lovely, babe. Now, don't forget, this is an important night for me – Roy's got me lined up for some extra work which means extra money. Be nice to him, won't you.'

'Of course I will.'

Leaving Alfred with a babysitter they caught the train to Bristol and were amongst the first to arrive at the hotel, along with Roy and his wife, Elsie. As Roy shook hands with Clare he stared down her cleavage and said to Reg, 'you've been keeping her quiet!'

Reg laughed and put his arm around his wife. 'I know!'

'If I can have a quick word before we begin…'

Roy led Reg away, leaving Clare with Elsie.

'Don't worry, he's like that with all the girls!' Elsie said, resignedly. 'Let's sit down, shall we?'

The two women sat at a table and Elsie offered Clare a cigarette, which she took.

'God knows what they get up to all day but it keeps the money coming in.'

'I thought it was buying and selling Army surplus?'

Elsie exhaled, blowing smoke out of her nostrils. 'Yes… and the rest… a bit of this, a bit of that, no questions asked… But who cares about that tonight? Let's get sloshed and enjoy ourselves, eh?'

They ate their meal, there were some speeches, then the band struck up and the dancing began. Reg and Clare shuffled around the floor together for a couple of numbers then went back to their table. As the night wore on the men were smoking and laughing, making lewd remarks and reminiscing about their Army days in Italy.

'Remember that prozzie in Rome, eh?' said Roy, digging Reg with his elbow, 'the one with the big…'

There were loud guffaws, making Clare feel distinctly uncomfortable. She remembered with a pang of regret the postcard Reg had sent her from Rome, saying they may visit there one day, knowing it was all a lie. As she watched Reg and Roy in a haze of cigar smoke she knew with certainty that she no longer loved her husband; she didn't even like him. The more the men drank, the louder they got, and she said, 'let's dance, Reg,' just to get him away, but after a spin around the dancefloor Roy came over and pushed in between them, saying, 'my turn, I think.' Roy held Clare close - too close for her liking - and he reeked of beer. He led her around, pushing himself against her, then he whispered in her ear, 'your Reg is a lucky man. I wouldn't mind coming home to this every night –' and with one hand he squeezed her breast and with the other, pinched her bottom.

Clare pushed him away, crying, 'get off me, you horrible little man!', and slapped him across the face. The other dancers stopped to see what was going on while Roy stepped back, holding a hand against his reddening cheek, saying, 'only a bit of fun, love!'

Reg stormed towards them, saying, 'sorry, Roy, don't know what got into her!' He grasped Clare by the wrist and yanked her away.

'You've got a wild one there,' called Roy after them. 'You need to teach her a lesson!'

'What the hell do you think you're doing?' Reg hissed in Clare's ear, 'I'll be lucky to have a job if you carry on like that!'

'I don't care! He groped me! I don't like him!'

Reg turned angry. 'It doesn't matter whether you like him. He's really helped me - us - since the war. And you've got no idea what we went through together, him and me, in Italy, nearly getting blown to pieces!'

'Oh, I'm sorry, I thought you spent all your time with prostitutes!'

'Don't you dare speak to me like that! We're going home, *now!*'

They travelled home on the train in silence, paid the babysitter then resumed their row.

'It was horrible, him touching me like that. You should have defended me!'

'There's you on your high horse! You can handle yourself, don't expect me to do it for you.'

She went to the bedroom and took off her dress and he followed her.

'Roy's right, it's time I taught you a lesson!'

He took off his suit and shirt, grabbed her by the shoulders, threw her onto the bed, pulled off her underwear and forced himself on her. She tried to push him away but he was too heavy and in spite of her protests he carried on, shouting, 'you're my wife and I'll do what I want!'

He finished with a self-satisfied grunt, then rolled over and slept, while she lay beside him, sobbing silently.

In his bedroom next door, Alfred was also in tears, having been woken by his parents arguing. The three-year old didn't understand what was going on but knew that Daddy was hurting his mother, and he hated him with all his heart.

Paris, 1946

Amélie looked out the train window as they approached the Gare de l'Est. Even under the Summer skies the city looked drab, recovering from the ravages of war, and signs of fighting in the final months before liberation were still visible. But above it all the Eiffel Tower stood in the distance, watching over the city as defiantly as ever.

It was a strange homecoming with nobody to come home to.

When Amélie had been declared fit enough to leave the resettlement camp the Red Cross had supplied her with new identification papers and given her the train fare to go home to Paris, with a little spending money too. She felt tired after her long train journey - she was thin, her bones were weakened, her white hair was cropped and grew in odd patches, but she was here, she had survived. She was not yet fifty but looked and felt twenty years older.

Carrying the battered suitcase she'd been given she walked towards the Place de la Bastille but stopped short of her old apartment block, not wanting to go there - it would be full of strangers and she had no wish to remember the horror of when she and her father had left. She felt anxious, aware that people were staring at her. A woman passing by spat at her and cussed, and Amélie heard the word 'collaborator'. Of all the insults in the world that was the worst, and Amélie turned angrily to answer back but the woman had walked on and the moment was lost. Amélie checked into a cheap hotel then went to a café on the corner for something to eat, trying to adjust to being in the outside world again, free to do as she chose without guards shouting at her. It was good to remember what freedom was like; this was the reason the war had been fought.

The next morning she went to the Catholic church to pray, kneeling and weeping for all she had lost. The priest was kind and listened to her confession, and she left the church feeling renewed and stronger. Next she walked to the hospital at St Antoine, the only place she could think of where she might find someone she knew, and where she would feel safe. Perhaps they may even have a job for her. At the orthopaedic unit the receptionist looked at her blankly, and Amélie protested, 'but I used to work here! There must be someone who remembers me!' Then she thought of the nurse she had seen at Drancy and asked for her.

'You mean Sister Lacroix? I'll fetch her.'

Sister Lacroix approached the old woman.

'Can I help you?'

'It's me, Sylvie - Amélie Swann.'

She gasped in horror. 'I'm sorry…I didn't recognise you!'

'It's all right, I know I've changed! Can we talk?'

The Sister looked at her watch and said, 'I have a break in ten minutes. Why don't you sit outside in the gardens and I'll join you.'

Sitting together on a seat in the hospital grounds, Sylvie Lacroix was in shock at seeing Amélie again. Sylvie told her what she remembered of that horrific time when Jean-Pierre Fournier had been arrested with other Resistance members and shot, then she said, 'but the war is over now. Dr Moreau was arrested as a collaborator, and his secretary too.'

'I'm very pleased to hear that.'

'You must have suffered so much, Amélie.'

'I nearly died at Auschwitz. They kept me at the resettlement camp in Germany until I could look after myself. But I wanted to come back to Paris, and now I need a job. Is there anything for me here?'

Sylvie shifted awkwardly, saying, 'we're not taking on anyone at the moment - money is short. And you really don't look fit enough to work, Amélie...'

Amélie felt her words like a blow, knowing that her appearance was indeed likely to put off any employer. She was disconsolate, and in view of her distress, and to change the subject, Sylvie said, 'a man came looking for you just before liberation. He said he was a family friend - Pascal Lejeune.'

Amélie shrugged. 'I know no one by that name.'

'I told him you'd been taken to Drancy and then to Auschwitz and he was terribly shocked. He asked about Dr Fournier too.'

Amélie had a strange thought. 'What did he look like, this Pascal Lejeune?'

As Sylvie described him Amélie wondered, might it have been Philippe? She couldn't think of anyone else who would come looking for her. But what was he doing in France, and why would he have changed his name?

'Do you know where I can find him?'

'I'm afraid he's dead - we heard that he'd been caught in the crossfire when the Allies came.'

Amélie's hopes sunk as quickly as they had been raised.

'How do you know? Who told you?'

'I can't remember - there were so many rumours going around at that time, but I'm sure I heard someone say he was shot.'

Sylvie had to return to her shift, so Amélie thanked her and walked back towards her hotel. She stopped at the café and as she drank her coffee she thought about what Sylvie had told her. Who was this man who had been so keen to find her? Thinking back to her days with Jean-Pierre, it struck her that his Resistance colleagues must have been in contact with someone in England who knew Philippe. Had they persuaded Philippe to join the Resistance? He may have come to France to fight, under another name. It seemed incredible, but maybe? She sat at her table, deep in thought, the only customer, and the café owner came over to ask if she was all right.

'Yes, thank you,' she replied, then on a whim she asked, 'did you ever know someone called Pascal Lejeune?'

The man thought for a moment then said, 'yes, he came here just before liberation. He was looking for someone… a Madame Swann.'

Amélie's heart beat faster.

'He told me he'd been working in Normandy. Came here for a few days, then he disappeared. I heard later that he'd been shot in the crossfire.'

Amélie's heart sank, again. 'So he is dead.'

'I'm sorry.'

Amélie left the café, dying inside. She wandered through the streets, trying to come to terms with what she had learnt from two separate sources. She convinced herself that Pascal was really Philippe, that he had come to Paris to find her and been killed in the process. The one light that had sustained her through the horrors of Auschwitz had been cruelly extinguished. Now she had nothing.

She walked for the rest of the day and into the night. All those years in the camp she had fought to stay alive, and for what? Everything had changed, there was no prospect of a job and those she loved were dead. Paris meant nothing to her any more. What was the point of going on? She was exhausted with the effort of clinging on to hope, and her well of courage had run dry.

In the early hours of the morning she stood on the Pont d'Austerlitz, staring into the deep, dark waters of the Seine flowing beneath, feeling lower than she had ever felt, even at the camp. There was a simple end to this misery. She hauled herself up onto the balustrade and looked around; no one was there. She said a prayer to the Holy Mother, made the sign of the cross, took a deep breath and stepped into the void.

CHAPTER 34

Bath, 1946

Rosamund was standing at the school gates, waiting to collect Cedric. She chatted companionably to the other mothers, a decent set of people, as only those with money could afford to send their children to Bath's best Prep school. Cedric being so bright, she had started him there early, aware that as an only child he would benefit from mixing with others from good families, and he had quickly made friends. The children emerged in their smart, expensive uniforms and Cedric ran up to his mother, proudly holding a picture he'd painted of a boat on the water.

'Very good, darling!' she proclaimed, pleased to see that at last he was showing some interest in the sea.

A woman Rosamund didn't know admired the painting and spoke to Cedric.

'What a lovely picture! Your Granny must be very proud of you!', smiling at Rosamund.

Rosamund's face turned to thunder and she said, firmly, 'I am *not* his Granny. I am his *mother*!'

She grasped Cedric's hand and led him away, leaving the embarrassed woman staring after them.

*

Clare began to feel unwell and was sick in the mornings. She didn't tell anyone but made an appointment to see a doctor for tests, and when she returned a week later he said, 'congratulations, Mrs Watkins - you are pregnant!'

She was speechless.

'I hope this is good news. You have a son, don't you. Hopefully it will be a girl this time and you'll be able to complete your family.'

'Yes…'

Clare left the surgery, her head spinning. She and Philippe were always so careful, but what if one of those damned condoms had failed? Then she thought of that horrible night after the dance when Reg had forced himself on her - the timing was right. But how could she be sure which of them was the father?

Clare was too vexed to tell anyone about her pregnancy. Reg had been home during the Summer holidays and she hadn't had the chance to see Philippe, which was just as well, she thought, as she wouldn't have been able to hide the truth from him.

Reg returned to work, and one evening in September he came home in a temper, having been told by Roy that he was cutting back on his hours and pay, 'and guess whose fault that is?' he shouted in Clare's face, 'he doesn't trust me now, not after your outburst on the dancefloor!'

'I'm sorry, Reg, but I wasn't going to put up with him behaving like that…'

'Stuck up cow!'

Reg stomped into the bedroom to change out of his work clothes. They sat and ate their tea in silence,

Alfred looking anxiously at his parents, knowing they had had another row and hoping it wasn't because of anything he had done. After tea Clare washed the dishes and Reg moodily read his newspaper, while Alfred amused himself playing tiddly winks.

'What are you doing?' Reg asked him, irritated.

'You have to flick all the little discs into the cup. It's good fun. Philippe showed me how to do it.'

'Who?'

'Philippe, Mummy's friend. He's from France.'

Reg erupted. He went into the kitchen and dragged Clare by the hair into the living room where Alfred stood, frightened out of his wits.

Reg put his face menacingly close to hers.

'Have you been seeing that Frenchman? I knew you were sweet on him when he painted your picture, but what's he doing back here now?'

'Let me go, Reg! I can explain! But not in front of Alfred! Let me get him to bed first…'

'No! If he hadn't mentioned it I wouldn't have known! How long has this been going on?'

Clare was shaking. 'I've only seen him a few times - he came to see his Aunt in Larkhall and I bumped into him.'

'Oh yes?'

'He's only a friend, Reg.'

'You expect me to believe that, do you?'

He suddenly thought of those Saturdays when she'd come home from her mother's while he'd been at the football - that preoccupied look, her face flushed…

His anger and jealousy were uncontainable. Alfred ran to his room in fear while Reg tore into Clare, slapping her hard across the face then punching her in the stomach. She tried to fight back but he was stronger than her, so she held her arms up defensively, trying to avoid his blows, but that final punch sent her to the floor. She felt a sharp pain and cried out in agony while a stream of blood flowed onto the carpet.

He stood over her, his fist clenched, and she screamed out, 'stop hurting me, Reg! I'm pregnant!'

He jumped back in shock and his anger rose.

'And is it mine? Or is it *Philippe's*?'

'Of course it's yours! But I'm scared, Reg, I think I'm losing it... You must call an ambulance - please...'

She passed out and he ran to the phone box on the corner to ring 999.

The next morning, in hospital, Clare realised that the obstetrician caring for her was Dr Roberts, her neighbour who lived opposite, and he recognised her too. He sat down at the side of the bed and asked, gently, 'how are you feeling, Mrs Watkins?'

She felt groggy from the anaesthetic they'd given her the night before, and whispered, 'my baby?'

'I'm afraid you lost her. I'm so very sorry. Your internal organs were badly damaged and we had to operate. I regret to tell you that you will be unable to have any more children.'

She caught her breath as she tried to take in the news and the doctor gently put a comforting hand on her shoulder.

'I noticed bruising on your abdomen, and on other parts of your body. Your husband told us you'd fallen off a stepladder at home, is that right?'

She hesitated for a moment then said, 'yes…I was reaching into a cupboard and lost my balance…'

Dr Roberts looked at her, concerned - he had seen too many cases like this.

'Very well. But be careful! And think about what sort of a life you want. I live opposite you, so promise me that if you ever feel you are in danger, or need any help, come and knock on the door.'

It was such a kind offer her eyes filled with tears and she said, 'thank you, Dr Roberts, I promise.'

Reg came in, full of mock distress, taking Clare's hand in his and saying, 'I'm so sorry, babe.'

Dr Roberts got up and said, sternly, 'take care of your wife, Mr Watkins, she's been badly hurt,' and fixed him with a look.

The doctor left the couple together and Reg said, 'what's up with him? You'll be all right, babe. The sooner I get you home the better.'

When she had recovered and Reg was at work, Clare went to see Philippe and told him what had happened. He hit the roof, pacing around the room, cussing Reg and threatening to kill him with his bare hands. When Clare pleaded with him to calm down he embraced her, saying, 'I'm only angry because I love you and can't bear to see you hurt. And the baby you lost - she could have been mine!'

'She could…and I can't have any more.'

'That man is a monster! You can't stay with him any longer. Come here and bring Alfred with you, I can take care of you.'

She broke down in tears. 'We can't, there's not enough room for us all! But what can I do? I'm scared to stay, especially now he knows I've been seeing you, but I'm too frightened to leave, he'll just come looking for me and then it will be even worse. I wish he would just…disappear…'

'We could go to France! Reg would never find us there. We can start a new life together where nobody knows us. You'd love it – and so would Alfred!'

'But I can't just up and go! I can't leave Mum - and I can't even speak French!'

'We'd get over that. You can't stay with him, I won't let you.'

He held her as she sobbed, and in his mind he saw things very clearly. He thought back to his days with the SOE when the decision was simple: when an enemy was in your path, you destroyed him. And Reg was undoubtedly the enemy.

'He's got to go, otherwise you'll live the rest of your life in fear of him. As I see it, we've only got one choice…'

*

Philippe formed a plan and turned it over in his mind, thinking it through in detail as if it were a Resistance operation. He checked out the practicalities, then when he was sure and ready, told Clare.

'We can do this - you and I - for our future, and for Alfred.'

She had her doubts.

'I do want him gone, more than anything. I want to be with you, of course I do, but it sounds so dangerous. Reg really scares me, but what you're proposing is scaring me too! You're talking about *murder*, Philippe - we could hang!'

'Only if we're found out - and we won't be.'

CHAPTER 35

Bath, 1946

One Monday evening in November, Reg and Clare were at home listening to the wireless, Clare trying to hide her nerves. Towards eleven o'clock there was a knock on their door, and the two looked at each other.

'Who's that, at this time of night?' said Reg, getting up to answer.

He opened the door and before he knew what was happening Philippe forced his way inside. Reg was totally caught by surprise and didn't stand a chance. In the textbook SOE move he had practised many times, Philippe lay his right hand flat and forcefully struck the side of Reg's throat, two inches below the ear, feeling the crunch and collapse of the windpipe, the airway demolished by the force of the blow, then he placed the same hand on Reg's shoulder and drove his knee hard into his groin. Reg dropped to his knees, thrashing around on the floor, his bloodshot eyes protruding from their sockets, and Philippe uttered, 'that's for hurting your wife,' pressing down on his neck to hasten the process, until Reg lay still.

Clare slowly emerged from the lounge.

'It's done,' said Philippe.

She looked at her husband, dead on the floor of the hallway, saw his bulging eyes and retched.

'He won't hurt you again.'

'But it's horrible!' she cried, turning away.

'Don't look at him. Fetch a sheet and I'll cover him up,' said Philippe, calmly.

Shaking, Clare went to the airing cupboard and returned with a sheet that was as white as her face. She stood, frozen, as Philippe laid the sheet like a shroud over Reg's body. Seeing she was in shock he ushered her back into the lounge and held her, saying quietly, 'I know it's horrible, but remember how horrible he was to you. He's never going to hurt you again, ever. He's gone. Now, try to stay calm and remember what we planned. We've got to get this right.'

He looked at her, intently, and she looked back at him and said, 'yes, I know.'

'Now, why don't you go and check on Alfred to make sure he's asleep, then go and pack Reg's bag, as we agreed.'

She went to Alfred's room, relieved to find him sleeping peacefully, oblivious to the violent act that had taken place just a few feet away. In her own bedroom she emptied the wardrobe of Reg's clothes and, quivering with nerves, packed them into his old army kitbag while Philippe removed Reg's wristwatch.

Ready for the next part of the plan, Philippe glanced outside to check that all was quiet.

'I'll lift him by the shoulders, you take his feet.'

Eleven stone of dead weight wasn't easy to manoeuvre, and Philippe's left arm was weak, but between them they dragged Reg's shrouded body outside and into the street. It was almost midnight and not a soul was in sight. They carried the shroud to Philippe's car, laid it on the back seat and covered it with a rug. Clare went back indoors, glanced into Alfred's room and prayed that he would stay asleep for the next half hour, then she picked up the kitbag and joined Philippe. He started the engine and carefully drove the mile through the deserted streets to their destination.

They got out the car and Philippe found what he was looking for: the trapdoor in the wall where coal used to be delivered, but which was no longer in service. He tugged at the door which was stiff from lack of use and propped open the flap. With Clare's help he dragged the shroud out of the car, unwrapped Reg's body and with a deep breath they heaved it through the opening and pushed it down the shute, hearing it land with a satisfying thud. Philippe closed the trapdoor, put the sheet in the back of the car then they drove carefully back to Clare's. Still, nobody was around; Bath was dead on a Monday night.

Clare dashed inside to find Alfred, asleep, and sighed with relief. She and Philippe embraced, their emotions in turmoil, then he said, 'I love you. We won't be able to see each other for a while, but you know what you have to do. Don't contact me until you're sure it's safe.'

He left and she heard the car drive away.

Clare went to bed, unable to believe what they had done. She kept seeing Reg, lying in the hall, and began to shake uncontrollably. She was shocked at how quickly and efficiently Philippe had despatched him, and knew he must have killed before. Is this what he had learnt during those missing years, after the Bath Blitz? She wondered how many other lives he had taken – but that had been war. This time, Philippe had acted to protect her and Alfred, and she had played her part in it. It was too late for any regrets, and for all her distress one thing was certain: Reg would never harm her or Alfred again because he was lying, dead, in the vaults at Green Park station.

*

That same night David Roberts was in bed, reading. Just before eleven he heard an Austin 7 pulling up in the street outside Eagle House. He recognised the noise of the engine, having owned one himself. After a while he heard the car leave, only to return about half an hour later. Curious, he got out of bed and opened the curtain slightly to see a man and a woman entering the block of flats opposite. A light went on in a room on the ground floor and he realised it must be Mrs Watkins; he didn't recognise the man she was with but it certainly wasn't her husband. Shortly afterwards the man returned to his car and drove away. Puzzled, David went back to bed and resumed his book, thinking about his dear wife whom he missed so much.

*

The next morning, Tuesday, Clare was still in a state of shock but tried to get a grip on herself for Alfred's sake. As she served her son his breakfast in the kitchen he asked, 'where's Daddy?'

'He had to leave early to go to work.'

Seeing his father wasn't there to tell him off, he said, 'Mummy, please may I have some jam on my toast?'

Clare smiled at him. 'Of course you can!'

That morning Philippe drove to the woods on Claverton Down, knowing exactly where he was going as he'd already checked out the spot. He parked his car up a secluded pathway, took Reg's kitbag and the sheet from the boot and walked into the woods, shuffling though a carpet of Autumn leaves, until he came to a small clearing where he gathered some twigs and lit a small fire. Not a soul was around. As the fire gathered pace he burned the sheet, the kitbag and its contents, smashed Reg's wristwatch with a stone and added the pieces to the flames. He watched until the fire burnt out, leaving a pile of ashes which he covered with earth and leaves. He took one final look to check that he had left no trace behind; the SOE had trained him well.

Philippe drove into Bath, back to his room where he had a stiff cognac to calm himself. He went through his mental check-list: Reg's body was entombed in the vault which he knew, from Clare, was sealed up and had not been used since the war. His possessions were destroyed. Reg was gone and there was no reason to think he would ever be found. Now, it was up to Clare.

On Wednesday it was time to enact the rest of the plan. Clare rehearsed the words she had prepared, went to the telephone box on the corner, took a deep breath and dialled the number. A gruff voice answered and, trying to sound cheerful, she said, 'Mr Baker – Roy – it's Clare Watkins, Reg's wife.'

'Oh! Good morning!'

'Er – first, Roy, can I just say, I'm sorry we didn't get off on the right foot at the dance. I do apologise for my behaviour. I think I had too much to drink!'

His voice warmed to her. 'That's all right, love – we'll make up for it next time! What can I do for you? And where's that husband of yours?'

'Oh! I was rather hoping you would be able to tell me! He didn't come home last night and I wondered whether he'd stayed over at yours.'

'No, I haven't seen him since he went home on Monday.'

'Really? I wonder where he is, then?'

'Oh, I shouldn't worry, he's probably visiting a client… he'll turn up when he's good and ready.'

'I see… well, hopefully he'll come home tonight. Thank you, Roy.'

'All right, love – and I'll look forward to seeing you again at the next dance!' he said, with a filthy laugh.

On Thursday Clare called Roy again but this time she was in hysterics and could hardly get her words out.

'Calm down, dear! Tell me what's happened.'

'After I spoke to you yesterday I spent the day at my mother's and when I came home, all Reg's clothes have gone! The wardrobe's empty! All his shirts, his suit and hat – and his kitbag's gone too. Oh Roy, what's going on?'

Roy was shocked. 'Sounds like he's cleared out – but he hasn't come here, I haven't seen him. Leave it with me, I'll ask around, see if anyone knows anything. Ring me back tomorrow. And try not to worry, dear.'

That evening Clare told Alfred that his father had gone away for a while.

'I hope he never comes back!' said the boy.

On Friday, Clare made one final call to Roy.

'Can't help you, I'm afraid, love. One of my chaps thought Reg might have a lady friend, but he'd be daft to leave you, wouldn't he? He'll come crawling back with his tail between his legs, you'll see. I should leave it for a few days, then if you don't hear anything, tell the police.'

The following week Clare went to the police station to report her missing husband, but they weren't really interested. They took his description, said they would ring round the local hospitals and speak to Roy Baker, and told her not to worry. Later, a policeman came to the flat, inspected the empty wardrobe, asked Clare for a recent photograph of Reg and spoke to some neighbours but no one reported anything untoward. The officer sat down with Clare and asked, as kindly as he could, 'Mrs Watkins, was everything all right with your marriage?'

She feigned shock.

'We had our moments, but we got along…Are you trying to tell me he might have another woman?'

'Well, it has been known…'

Clare took out a handkerchief and wiped her eyes.

'I don't believe it - he wouldn't leave me and our little Alfred, and with Christmas coming…'

She stifled a sob and the embarrassed policeman said, 'it's only a possibility… I'm sorry I had to ask. Does he have any relatives? Is there anywhere he might go?'

'No - he lost his close family in the war. But he always wanted to go to Scotland - I don't know why…'

'All right. We'll put out an alert and let you know if we hear anything. These things happen, and people usually turn up.'

In the post Clare received a final pay cheque from Roy with a short note saying,

'… *I'm sure Reg will come home soon but I'm afraid it's no work, no pay so this is it, love.*'

Clare took Alfred to see her mother, acting the betrayed wife, but her mother knew Clare had suffered at Reg's hands and was pleased he had gone. Clare told Mary, whose reaction was similar. When Mary passed on the news to Philippe he responded, 'good, I'm pleased. He doesn't deserve her.'

Mary looked at him, enquiringly, and he continued, 'Clare and me? Yes, I did like her, but we've run our course. We had an argument and I'm not seeing her any more.'

David Roberts heard the local gossip that Mrs Watkins' husband had left home and was thankful for it. He had been very concerned about her injuries and only felt sorry for the other woman that Reg had apparently taken up with. Something niggled at the back of his mind about the car he'd heard late the other night, but he was so busy with his work at the hospital he thought no more about it.

Clare kept up the pretence over Christmas, spending a quiet few days with Alfred at her mother's in Larkhall, being careful not to have any contact with Philippe who was at Mary and Derek's. The lovers waited until the new year to be reunited, meeting at Philippe's place where at last they embraced, relieved to see each other again. Clare told him about the false trail she had laid.

'Excellent! I'm so proud of you, I know how difficult it's been. How's Alfred?'

'He's fine – I've taught him to tell everyone he misses his Daddy, but in truth he's pleased he's gone!'

Philippe smiled and held her close. 'Now we have to stay quiet and wait. You can come here, but we must be discreet.'

'Yes, we don't want to start any rumours. I've missed you so much, Philippe! I've been scared at night – I have these awful nightmares. I keep seeing Reg's body, on the floor… and his eyes…!'

He held her tighter. 'You'll forget it in time, my love. The main thing is, that man is never going to hurt you or Alfred again.'

CHAPTER 36

Bath, 1947

The Winter of 1946 to 1947 was the worst in living memory. The terrible weather made travelling around Bath almost impossible, with snow piled high along the roadsides and the steep hills too hazardous to drive up or walk down. With the shortage of fuel it was cold everywhere and Philippe was grateful for his room at the top which was relatively cosy. With her savings running low Clare decided to leave her flat and when the weather improved she moved back to her mother's. She took a part-time job at a grocer's in Larkhall to earn some money, a deserted wife who had to make her own living, while her mother minded Alfred.

Clare visited Philippe as often as possible, but they couldn't be seen together for fear of arousing suspicion. She continued to pay regular visits to the police station to ask about Reg, and in May, six months after his disappearance, she spoke to an officer who dusted off the file and said, 'I'm sorry Mrs Watkins, we're still no further forward. A couple of months ago one of our men in Edinburgh reported a possible sighting but it was a false alarm. We'll keep looking, but

I'd say he's determined not to be found. You may have to accept that he won't come back.'

'Thank you,' she said sadly, dabbing her eye with her handkerchief as she left.

Later, as Clare lay entwined around Philippe in his bed, he said, 'I think we've waited long enough. It's time for us to move to France and start afresh.'

'It sounds exciting, but I'm worried about leaving Mum – she's not well. Do we really have to go? Can't we stay here in Bath?'

'No, it's too risky. We wouldn't be able to get married for at least seven years, and then you'd have to go to court to prove Reg was no longer alive. I'm convinced that the only way we'll be able to live as a proper family is if we move to France.'

'It's a huge step for me and Alfred, leaving everything we know…'

'Of course – but if we want to be together we can't stay here.'

'So what shall we do?'

'I'll go ahead and find us somewhere to live, and you and Alfred can join me when you're ready.'

'But won't we need papers or something?'

He smiled.

'You can leave that to me.'

Before Philippe left Bath he went to Sydney Place to say goodbye to Richard and Ann, then drove to Corsham to see Daniel. Passing through Box he thought of when he called on Derek's sister, after the war, and here he was, two years, a love affair and a murder later, about to return to France.

Philippe found Daniel's house where he was warmly welcomed.

'I've decided to go back to France,' he announced.

'So, you've run out of people to paint in Bath?'

'Ha! No, I feel it's time to return. And I want to try and find my mother – I might stand a better chance, being over there. I'll miss my Aunt, though, she's done so much for me.'

'And Clare?'

'I've given up on her – women are just too complicated…'

'Right. Well, I'll miss you, old pal – take care of yourself, won't you.'

'Thank you, I will. How's the School?'

'Marvellous – teaching's great and Corsham Court is so inspiring. We love it here and it's a great place to raise a family.'

As if on cue, Emma came in, cradling their new baby girl, a cutie with dark wavy hair like her father.

'She's lovely!' said Philippe.

'We have been blessed,' said Daniel, smiling at Emma and taking her hand.

Philippe said goodbye to Aunt Mary.

'I'll miss you– you've grown to be like a son to me,' she said, tearfully, 'and Derek will miss you too. I know you intend to stay in France, but if you ever want to come back, or need anything at all, you only have to ask. And I do hope you'll find your mother, one day.'

She looked at him in such a way that he wondered if she knew more than she let on. He hugged her and said, 'thank you, for everything. I will write to you with my new address, when I have one.'

Philippe sold his beloved Austin 7 and pocketed the cash, knowing he would need every penny to support his new venture. He and Clare met in his room for one final time and made love, remembering the happy times they had spent there together.

'We've been through a lot,' said Clare.

'Yes... and now we have the best to come. It's the only way – if we stay around here we'll aways be worried that someone might get suspicious. We're going to have such a happy life in France, the three of us. Join me as soon as you can, won't you?'

'Yes, I promise.'

They embraced, hating to part, not knowing when they would see each other again, but Philippe reassured her, saying, 'I love you, I will wait for you, but you've got to be sure - once you leave you'll never be able to come back.'

Paris, 1947

The woman helped the frail old man to drink from a cup, gently propping up his head, and gave him some pain killers.

'Thank you, nurse,' he said.

'I'm just a volunteer.'

He looked her in the eye and said, 'whoever you are, thank you.'

The woman went to the kitchen to help prepare the evening meal for the next intake of vagrants and lost souls. While she was peeling a mountain of potatoes another volunteer came up and said, 'you've got a lot to do, Amélie, let me help you.'

She smiled at him and said, 'thank you Charles, I could do with a hand!'

The two worked companionably together, preparing the dish of *hachis parmentier* that was on this evening's menu at the hostel for the homeless. Amélie owed her life to Charles who had fished her out of the Seine that Summer night, a year ago. Despite her intention to end it all, Amélie's instinct to survive had prevailed and as soon as she hit the water she began swimming, struggling in the deep-flowing river, gasping to stay afloat. Charles, who was conducting his patrol of the homeless along the banks of the Seine, spotted her, threw her a lifebelt and swum out to drag her to shore. She was weak and cold, gulping for breath, and he called his colleagues to help him carry her to the hostel. He noticed the number tattooed on her arm, and when she was able to speak he asked if she was Jewish. She replied, 'no. I am French, I am Catholic.'

As she recovered she stayed at the hostel and worked as a volunteer, finding a purpose in helping others out of their suffering. She didn't reveal much about her life and people didn't ask - everyone had secrets and privacy was respected. Amélie was happy there and over the past year her health had much improved. Her white hair was growing less erratically and one of the women gave her a smart, short haircut which suited her. She put on a little weight and got stronger, accepted clothes from charity donations, and regained her inner strength. She saved some money from doing odd jobs and cleaning, and knew the time had come for her to leave.

Charles was the only person she confided in.

'Where will you go?' he asked.

'I've lost my son. My home was here in Paris, but it is no longer. The people and places I used to love have gone. But there remains one special person I dearly wish to see again…'

CHAPTER 37

France, 1947

Philippe caught the boat train to Paris, observing how the city had changed since he had last been there in the days prior to liberation. He didn't have time to linger, however; he had business to attend to and headed west, taking the train to Lisieux. As he travelled deep into the Normandy countryside he looked out at the familiar landscape of the *bocage*, now mercifully without military vehicles and signs of Nazi occupation, aware of the irony that this was the same railway line he and his colleagues had sabotaged so many times. He recalled the bombardment of Lisieux and the terrible suffering its people had endured as their town was flattened by Allied bombing in the wake of the D-Day landings. He arrived to find new buildings emerging from the ashes, funded largely by American money, and the Basilica standing firm, watching over the people it had protected during those terrifying nights.

Philippe made his way towards a newly-built café on the main square and to his delight found André Lazarre standing behind the gleaming zinc counter, his white apron tied around his middle, polishing a glass, for all the world as if the war had never happened. André looked at him in disbelief.

'Pascal! I thought you were dead!'

The men kissed each other on both cheeks, shook hands vigorously and the visitor said, 'Pascal is dead, but Philippe Swann is alive and well. It's so good to see you, André! How is everyone?'

André poured glasses of *calva* and toasted Philippe's return.

'My son runs the farm now,' said André, 'it was too much for me. I work here with my sister. She and her husband bought this new café after the old one was blown up.'

They lit cigarettes, reminisced about their lost loved ones and listened to each other's news, then André asked, 'so what brings you here?'

Philippe looked around to make sure they were not being overheard, and said, 'I want to move back to France, but there is a problem. I am going to need papers…'

'And this 'problem', does she have a name?'

Philippe laughed. 'Yes, she does – Clare. And she has a young son, Alfred. We want to live in France as man and wife.'

'But for reasons you do not need to explain, you cannot get married in England… I understand. Give me the details and leave it with me.'

'Thank you, André. I will pay you well.'

'It's the least I can do for an old comrade. Now, more *calva*!'

Philippe's next train was to La Rochelle on the Atlantic coast. He had pleasant memories of spending holidays there with his mother and grandfather years ago, and it struck him as a good place for a family to settle. He watched the countryside go by as the train steamed along, noticing the change from the *ardoises*, the grey slate roofs of Normandy, to the *tuiles canals*, the terracotta tiles of the houses as they crossed the Loire and travelled south, a sure sign of the warmer climate in this part of France.

La Rochelle had stayed in his mind as a quaint old city by the sea. The reality was, of course, different: the ancient port, which had served as a German submarine base during the war, had been under siege by the Allies and much of the city had been destroyed. Philippe explored what remained and it was clear that it would take years to restore the place to its former glory. And yet, sitting at a café on the quayside in the early Summer sunshine with a chilled glass of rosé, watching the fishing boats with their catch, Philippe felt a sense of optimism, that life went on. He was sure Clare and Alfred would love it here, and it was the kind of place an artist could make a reasonable living. He booked into a hotel and looked around for a place to rent, finally settling on a small house along the coast. He paid the deposit and wrote to Clare, telling her all about it:

'...I have found us a lovely little house with a view of the sea... you and Alfred will adore it. I've arranged the papers we will need. We can live as man and wife, and I can adopt

Alfred – if that is what you want. We can be a proper family. Please come and join me as soon as you can. I love and miss you, Philippe'

He wrote to his Aunt, saying how happy he was to be back in France, alone. Finally he wrote to Beatrice via the Foreign Office, telling her about his decision to return to his beloved homeland where he could pursue his artistic career in peace.

Bath, 1947

Clare missed Philippe dreadfully and looked forward to receiving his letters, which she kept private. The house Philippe had found sounded delightful, but as the months went by she found it harder to imagine taking the final step of leaving Bath and all she had known to go and join him for good. During the day she kept busy caring for Alfred, her increasingly frail mother and working at the grocer's, but at night all her demons were let loose. Without Philippe there to reassure her she suffered terrible nightmares, seeing Reg, dead in the hallway, and would wake up drowning in sweat. The events of that extraordinary night seemed unreal and she remained shocked that Philippe, the kind, gentle artist she had fallen for, had proved himself capable of murdering a man in cold blood. But for all of it, Clare was relieved her violent husband was gone. She loved Philippe, he was her future, and she had to put her trust in him.

In October it was Alfred's fifth birthday and Clare and her mother organised a party for him at home, inviting some friends from his new school.

Saving up the sugar ration Clare produced a cake and the children had a marvellous time, playing games, making a lot of noise and wolfing down the food. By the evening Clare's mother was exhausted and went to bed early.

The next morning Clare went to wake her, but when she touched her cold face it was clear that she had passed away during the night. She kissed her and knelt by her bed as her tears flowed, devastated at her mother's parting but consoled by the thought that she had gone, peacefully, after a joyful day with her family. Clare broke the news to Alfred that his beloved Granny was dead, and sought out Mary who comforted them as best she could.

After the funeral, sitting with Alfred in the strangely empty house, Clare mourned her mother, and knew the time had come to make a decision. She could stay here, live out her life in Bath, fearing suspicion, haunted by Reg's ghost, or she could move to France to live with the man she loved, and who loved her.

So she wrote and told Philippe:

'...I'm so sad about Mum... I've got loads to do, sorting out the house and all her things, but once that's settled Alfred and I will come and join you. There's nothing to keep us in Bath now.'

Over the next weeks Clare dealt with her mother's affairs and sold her possessions - she was her only heir and the small legacy would be useful. She gave her notice at the grocer's and told Alfred's teacher they were moving to London to start a new life, and he wouldn't be coming back to school after Christmas.

She quietly obtained a passport, asking an old friend of her father's to countersign her application with no questions asked.

On her last night in Bath, Clare had her recurring nightmare but this time when she awoke she faced it with defiance, determined not to let Reg intimidate her from the grave, convincing herself that what she and Philippe had done was justified.

In a state of nervous excitement, mother and son finally turned their backs on Bath. It was only on the train to London that Clare told Alfred they were going to take the boat across the Channel to Paris where Philippe would meet them.

'You like Philippe, don't you?' she asked.

'Yes, he taught me lots of games.'

Suddenly a look of trepidation crossed his face. 'Are we going to see Daddy?'

Clare smiled and put her arm around him. 'No, darling – we're never going to see Daddy, ever again.'

'Good!' he said, breathing a sigh of relief.

Reaching London they made their way to Victoria station where they passed through passport control without incident and boarded the boat train to Dover. Standing together on the deck of the ferry, bracing themselves against the cold December wind, they watched as the white cliffs receded into the distance, waving goodbye to England and their old lives, excited by the prospect of going somewhere strange and foreign.

After a choppy crossing the ferry arrived at the wide beaches of Dunkirk, forcing Clare to remember Reg and the horrors he had suffered there. But that was his life, and this was hers. Now, it was peacetime, Reg had gone forever, and she and Alfred were looking ahead to a whole new future.

From Dunkirk they took the train to Paris and when they finally disembarked at the Gare du Nord, Philippe was waiting for them. They ran towards his open arms and he held Clare, tightly, and kissed her on the lips, overjoyed to see her after their months apart. They brought Alfred into their embrace and Philippe stooped down and ruffled his hair, saying, 'hello Alfred, it's so good to see you!' and the boy smiled up at him. With his arms around them, kissing them and brimming with joy, Philippe said, 'welcome, both of you! Welcome to France!'

PART FOUR

CHAPTER 38

France, 1955

Clare was at the market, buying a chicken and vegetables for supper and trying to work out the price – after eight years she still struggled with francs and French numbers. But as she left with a full shopping basket the trader smiled and said, '*merci*, Madame Swann.' She was well-known, the English woman who had moved to La Rochelle with her husband, the artist, and her son by her previous marriage, her first husband having died due to an illness. She walked back home where Philippe was painting in his studio and he welcomed her with a kiss.

'I'm making *coq au vin* tonight,' she said.

'Wonderful!'

Clare had been taught how to cook the French way by their neighbour, an elderly widow, who knew how to conjure up healthy meals to feed a family. She taught Clare to tear lettuce, not cut it; to dress salad with olive oil, wine vinegar and lemon juice; to make *potage* from leftover vegetables; and how to use garlic and all manner of herbs and spices. Clare began to appreciate the French obsession with cheese, learning to savour the depth of taste and the varieties, and how it made sense to serve cheese after the main course of a meal, before dessert, to cleanse the palette and finish the red wine. The only thing she wasn't keen on was cognac, which she found too strong, and she preferred to drink her after-dinner coffee on its own.

Clare and Philippe shared a fresh baguette and some camembert for lunch, chatting about their day, then he returned to his studio while she prepared their supper. As she divided the chicken into pieces and chopped the vegetables she looked out the kitchen window to the view of the sea. It was a gusty day and she watched the sailing boats with their billowing sails bobbing up and down on the waves, following the same route along the coast as she, Philippe and Alfred had taken in the dinghy they'd hired the previous Summer. It made her smile, thinking of the fun they'd had. Clare browned the chicken, added herbs and wine and put the casserole to simmer on the top of the stove. Drawn by the delicious aroma Philippe came into the kitchen, touched her shoulders and turned her towards him. They kissed, lingeringly, he checked his watch and said, 'we have an hour before Alfred gets home…'

Philippe led her to their bed and the couple made love, joyously, delighting in each other as much as when they were first together in Philippe's room on Lansdown Hill. Sex grew better as they became used to one another's wants and needs and they revelled in the freedom to enjoy their physical relationship. They lay in each other's arms, briefly, as the sensuous early Summer breeze wafted over them through the open window, then reluctantly got up and dressed.

At four o'clock twelve-year-old Alfred returned from school, charging in and dropping his bag on the kitchen floor. He scoffed his *goûter* – the traditional snack of bread and jam that French schoolchildren are fed on their return home – then ran up to his bedroom to change out of his uniform, eager to get down to the beach and meet his friends.

'Make sure you're back by seven!' Clare called to him as he disappeared out the door.

Tall, thin and with sandy-coloured hair, Alfred resembled Reg when he was young but had grown like Philippe, copying his mannerisms and appearing more French than English. Alfred had swiftly picked up the language and grown close to his stepfather, calling him 'Papa', delighting Philippe who loved him dearly. They had told Alfred early on that his father was dead and they had married, in secret, with a marriage certificate to prove it, along with papers confirming Alfred as Philippe's adopted son.

At seven, as bidden, Alfred returned and they sat down together to eat their supper. Philippe inhaled the fragrant scent of herbs and wine from the casserole, put the tips of his fingers to his lips and kissed them, proclaiming, '*délicieux*!' with a theatrical flourish, making Clare and Alfred laugh. They ate the *coq au vin* appreciatively, washed down with a bottle of red Bordeaux, Alfred's diluted with a little water, and scraped up the juices on their plates with chunks of baguette. Afterwards the three relaxed outside on the porch, reading and watching the sea birds soaring and swooping into the sky as the sun set on another perfect day in the life of the Swann family.

It had taken Philippe some years to establish himself amongst the artistic community in La Rochelle, but gradually he became known for his colourful paintings of local scenes which proved popular with the growing number of tourists visiting the area. A local gallery owner showed some interest and helped promote Philippe's work, drawing the attention of a Parisian art dealer who was on holiday. When he offered to show Philippe's work at his gallery he leapt at the chance, thrilled to have found a wealthy sponsor, the stuff of dreams for an artist. After some successful sales the owner suggested that they hold an exhibition, and now, having prepared a representative range of his work, the artist was ready.

Leaving his wife and stepson at home Philippe caught the train to Paris, returning for the first time since he had met Clare and Alfred at the Gare du Nord. He was here primarily because of his exhibition, but he had another reason: to meet Beatrice, who had written to tell him she had taken up an appointment at the Embassy in Paris. He went straight to the Rue du Faubourg St Honoré and waited for her in the lobby, wincing at the memory of the last time he had been there, collapsing with a bullet wound to his arm.

When Beatrice appeared they greeted each other with a kiss on both cheeks, then stood back to see how they had been treated by the passing years. She was unchanged: self-contained, confident, tall, thin, plain, wearing a dogtooth tweed suit and flat, lace-up shoes. He looked mature, attractive, with the odd fleck of grey in his beard, and her heart missed a beat at the sight of him.

'I thought we could have lunch at Maxim's, it's close by,' she said, maintaining her poise. 'Don't worry, my treat – I know you're a penniless artist...'

They fell into step together, chatting easily, and the ten years since they had last met faded to naught. 'I spent three years in Lisbon,' said Beatrice, 'then I was in Rome for a while, but Paris is the best.' At the restaurant Beatrice ordered two *filets mignons* and over a decent bottle of Burgundy, Philippe told her about his decision to move to France and his marriage to Clare.

'I'm pleased for you - you have a ready-made family. And your paintings are selling well?'

'Yes! My exhibition opens tomorrow evening – you must come.'

'I'd love to.'

After the meal, sipping their *digestifs*, Philippe ventured, 'do you know any more about the records from the camps? I am still desperate to know what happened to my mother. Being in Paris is bringing it all back to me...'

'No, I'm afraid not. The trials of some German war criminals have taken place – you'll have seen the reports about Nuremberg – but too many of them have got away with it. Many ex-Nazis fled to South America to escape punishment, would you believe.'

She sighed in despair.

'I fear it will take some years yet before the full records are released. But rest assured, I promise that as soon as I can do anything, I will.'

After lunch Philippe escorted Beatrice back to the Embassy and made his way to the gallery in the Rue de Rivoli to meet the owner. They spent the rest of the day putting the final touches to the exhibition, then Philippe retired to his hotel for an early night.

That same night, alone in her bed, Beatrice allowed her thoughts to wander to Philippe, remembering when he had made love to her, before he went to France to fight with the Resistance. All her adult life she had strived to maintain her image as the calm, capable diplomat, intellectual, incisive, and when required, ruthless. But she was only human, and seeing Philippe again she knew her feelings for him were as strong as ever, but must remain known only to her. In the darkness her hand crept beneath her winceyette nightie, finding the spot which gave her pleasure as she whispered her lover's name into the night.

Philippe spent the next day re-acquainting himself with his beloved city, pleased to find its essential heart and soul unchanged. It had regained its *joie de vivre*, bustling with tourists, traders, thriving cafés and shops, streets packed with cars parked bumper to bumper and new buildings under construction. The only signs of occupation were the occasional wall riddled with bullet-holes and commemorative plaques marking the spots where members of the Resistance had been shot dead.

Drawn towards his old quarter, Philippe stood on the Pont d'Austerlitz, looking down into the deep, murky green waters of the Seine flowing beneath, then shifted his gaze across to the Ile Saint Louis and the Ile de la Cité, the two small islands in the centre of the river, the ancient heart of Paris. He suddenly felt a strong connection to his mother, hoping against hope that, somewhere, she was still alive, and that one day he may see her again.

He sent a postcard to Aunt Mary, telling her about the exhibition and how pleased he was to be back in Paris. He liked to stay in touch and wrote to her regularly about his life in La Rochelle, but omitting to say that Clare and Alfred were with him.

In the evening Philippe's exhibition opened to moderate success. The full range of his work was on display, from seascapes and landscapes to portraiture and abstract works, a new field for Philippe which enabled him to express his post-war reflections and grief for the dead. Buyers were intrigued by the new artist who had trained in Paris and Bath, and reviewers agreed that his work showed promise. He was pleased when Beatrice arrived, taking in his work with a critical but friendly eye. She stopped in front of a portrait of an attractive woman with shoulder-length fair hair and clear blue eyes.

'Is this your wife?'

'Yes, that's Clare.'

'She's very pretty,' she said, without a hint of jealousy.

'Yes, she is,' he said, proudly.

The evening ended with several pictures marked with red dots to show they had been sold, and the gallery owner disappeared with his cronies, leaving Philippe and Beatrice together.

'My turn,' he said, and took her to a Bistro for a late supper. Afterwards he walked her back to her apartment and she invited him in. As they relaxed over a bottle of cognac, Beatrice, curious about Clare and her ex-husband, probed Philippe on the subject, sure there was more to this than he had let on. By now Philippe's tongue was loose.

'I hated him. He was violent - he hurt her when she was pregnant and she lost her baby.'

'How awful!'

'I was so angry, but she refused to leave him!'

'And then he died...?'

Philippe shook his head. He couldn't lie, not to Beatrice – she was the one person who could see through him, and the one person he could trust with the truth.

'I killed him.'

Beatrice looked at him, impassively, and waited for him to continue.

'I killed him and we disposed of the body and his clothes. He'll never be found. The SOE trained me well.'

She considered this for a moment.

'I understand. I'm not here to judge. You had your reasons and the means to carry it out. And now I know why you paid a visit to André Lazarre...'

'You miss nothing!'

'It's my job.'

Then she added, 'I hope it was worth the risk.'

'Definitely. We are very happy together and that man is never going to hurt Clare or Alfred again.'

After another glass Philippe said, wearily, 'I ought to go back to my hotel...'

'But it's late, and you've had too much to drink. Why don't you stay here?'

'All right, if you're sure.'

'You can have the sofa.'

The next morning Philippe awoke to the aroma of coffee and toast. Beatrice breezed into the lounge where her visitor lay prone, covered with a blanket.

'Good morning! Come and have breakfast.'

As they ate she watched him with a degree of amusement, his hair unkempt, still groggy from the night before, but she was pleased to have him there, enjoying his presence, his masculinity. She got ready for the office and they left her apartment together.

'Goodbye, Philippe, it's been lovely to see you. Let me know when you're in Paris again.'

'I will.'

He gave her a kiss on the cheek, and they parted.

CHAPTER 39

France, 1958

At home in La Rochelle, Philippe and Clare's interests expanded in line with those of their son. Alfred developed a passion for fossil hunting and over successive Summer holidays he and Philippe spent hours exploring the coastline, combing the cliffs and shores at the Pointe du Chay, discovering marine fossils amongst the layers of rocks and sand where dinosaurs had once roamed. Alfred loved all things scientific and developed an interest in geology, reading all the books he could lay his hands on to find out how planet Earth was formed and how geologists used fossils to determine the age of rocks, his interest becoming an obsession. Clare tolerated the accumulation of rocks he brought home, tapping at them with his geologist's hammer, his treasured possession, in order to split the rocks and reveal precious fossils hidden within.

Clare was happy that Philippe and Alfred got on so well, sometimes spending so much time together she almost felt jealous. Alfred had quickly adopted French ways, and sometimes she felt left out when they were speaking to each other using *argot* – slang – which she didn't understand. Such as: when Philippe came home and announced that he had bought a *bagnole*, Alfred was delighted, rushing outside to look, while Clare stood in the kitchen, wondering what on earth they were talking about. Philippe grinned and put his arm around her.

'It's a car!' he said. 'Come and see it.'

The ancient, blue Citroën 2CV was parked outside, and not wanting to wait, Philippe said, 'leave the cooking, Clare – let's go for a drive!'

They piled into the car which jerked and spluttered but finally got moving and carried them along to the sea and back.

'I understand now!' shouted Clare over the noise of the engine, 'it means 'an old banger'!'

They had many trips in the car which Philippe managed to keep going, using the maintenance skills he had learned from his grandfather and brushed up on while in the SOE. They travelled north to the Vendée coast, enjoying the wide beaches of Les Sables-d'Olonne, fringed with pine trees, watching the waves rolling in off the Atlantic and eating oysters farmed along the coastline. Other times they headed east to the Venise Verte, the green waterways of the Marais Poitevin, indulging in the local gastronomy of goats' cheeses and pâtés. The only thing Clare couldn't stomach was a type of sausage called *andouillette* which Philippe and Alfred loved, but she thought smelt foul and had the texture of elastic bands. There were certain French foods she would never learn to appreciate.

Philippe paid regular visits to Paris and as word spread about his artistic skills there was an increasing demand for his work. He usually met up with Beatrice and together they visited the Louvre and explored the cafés of the Left Bank where the intelligentsia of Paris held court, espousing their revolutionary social and political ideas. They found each other's company stimulating and always had plenty to discuss, so it was with sadness that, having a *petit café* at the Café de Flore, she told him she was leaving Paris.

'My tour's coming to an end and they want me in London. I'll miss seeing you, but I'll be back soon.'

'I'm sorry you're leaving – I've enjoyed discovering Paris again, with you.'

'Likewise.'

She smiled at him and took his hands in hers.

'You're a good friend, Philippe.'

'And so are you. I'll miss you, a lot. Paris won't be the same without you.'

France, 1960

By the time Alfred was eighteen he was an expert on the Jurassic period and set on his career path, gaining a place at the Sorbonne to study Science. Philippe and Clare took him to the railway station at La Rochelle to see him off on the train to Paris, unable to believe how quickly the years had gone. On the platform Clare was in tears, hugging her big son while he hugged her back, promising to eat properly, and to write. As the engine gathered steam and the whistle blew, Alfred prised himself away from his mother and gave Philippe a final hug, saying '*au revoir*, Papa,' and got into the carriage. Philippe put a consoling arm around Clare's shoulders as they watched the train disappear into the distance.

'He'll be fine, don't worry, *chérie*,' he said, reassuringly. 'We've taught him to look after himself and he'll have a great time, all his future before him.'

For a wistful moment Philippe recalled his happy years at the Ecole des Beaux-Arts, cut short by the war.

'Come on, let's go home and have a quiet night in – just the two of us.'

He kissed the top of her head, breathing in the scent of her hair, aware of how much he loved her. Nearing forty she was as attractive as ever, even with the odd grey hair and an extra few pounds gained from indulging in her favourite *pâtisseries*. He gave her his handkerchief and she wiped her eyes.

'Thank you, darling, that sounds lovely.'

Clare was sad her son was leaving home, but as Philippe had told her, 'better for him to be at university than in the Army.' Algeria's war of independence from colonialist France was raging and Alfred had been fortunate to escape conscription, much to Clare's relief. She remembered how war had affected Reg at a similar age and didn't want Alfred to have to suffer the same trauma, especially in a conflict she struggled to understand and which had already taken many lives. Compared to other mothers of her acquaintance she felt lucky to know that her son was safely in Paris.

Bath, 1960

Rosamund was thrilled: Cedric had gained his place at Dartmouth and was about to follow his father and grandfather into the Royal Navy. She looked proudly at her six-foot, blonde, blue-eyed son in the uniform of a Naval cadet. Eileen stood with her, tearful, and gave him a hug.

'I'll miss you, Master Cedric!'

'I'll miss you too!'

He turned to his mother and kissed her. 'Goodbye, Mummy. I'll write to you, I promise!'

Rosamund watched as he walked down the driveway of The Oaks, carrying his kitbag, his tall, slim, youthful figure reminding her of someone else, a long time ago. He turned and waved one last time, then he was gone.

Back indoors, Eileen made some tea to settle their nerves and they sat and drank it at the kitchen table.

'I can't believe it, Master Cedric, grown up and gone!' said Eileen.

'Oh, but he'll be back! I feel as if I've been waiting for this day for years.'

'What shall we do now? It will seem awfully quiet without him.'

Rosamund sighed. 'I haven't really thought about that. Perhaps I'll start my charity work again. It would be hard, though - I'm not sure whether I can face those awful people…'

Paris, 1961

The Swann family had the opportunity to be together again at a major exhibition of Philippe's paintings in Paris. He had undertaken several commissions for portraits of well-known people in the capital and his reputation was growing. Clare and Alfred were proud to support Philippe at the *vernissage* with the chance to meet some famous faces from the higher end of the Paris social circle, and Philippe was equally pleased to have his family there with him.

Beatrice was back at the Embassy for a short tour and made a special effort to attend the exhibition. She introduced Philippe to the Ambassador and his wife who had come along to meet the artist.

'I'd love you to paint my husband's portrait when you can fit him in,' said the Ambassador's wife.

'Of course! It would be an honour.'

'Good! I'm sure Beatrice can make the arrangements.'

Beatrice smiled, then turned to Philippe who introduced Clare. The two women shook hands and Clare said, 'I'm so pleased to meet you at last - the mysterious 'B'!'

'The postcards...' said Philippe.

'Indeed!' said Beatrice, all charm, 'it's a good way to stay in touch with old colleagues, especially when you travel around as much as I do.'

'You worked with Philippe during the war, in London, didn't you?'

'Yes, that's right – a long time ago now.'

Clare introduced Alfred, and Beatrice shook the young man's hand, struck by how different he was, physically, from Philippe, yet how alike they were in their mannerisms; he certainly seemed more French than English and she could see how close the two were.

A photographer was there to record the event and interviewed Philippe for an article in *France-Soir*, the Paris newspaper, and a French Arts magazine. Beatrice went on her way, leaving Philippe with his family, pleased that her efforts to publicise his work and gain him new commissions were bearing fruit. She was more than happy to do a favour for her old SOE comrade, friend and one-time lover.

The exhibition closed for the evening and Philippe took Clare and Alfred out to dinner, enjoying the chance to hear about Alfred's studies and student life – he had grown up quickly in the year he had been away from home. They discussed the people they had met at the gallery and Clare said, 'Beatrice is quite something, isn't she – so plain, but formidable!'

'*Une lesbienne!*' said Alfred.

'She's a woman of many talents,' said Philippe, coming to her defence, but to humour Clare he added, 'I told you she was no threat!'

CHAPTER 40

Bath, 1963

In Bath, modern buildings, car parks, houses and shops were springing up across the city, leaving the austerity and greyness of the post-war years behind. Terraces blackened by soot from wartime fires were being cleaned, revealing the beauty of their original honey-coloured Bath stone, and there was a spirit of renewal about the place. The city had become popular for fashion shoots, especially since the re-opening of the Assembly Rooms with its new Museum of Costume, and was awash with the latest styles with girls in mini-skirts and young men in slick suits and narrow ties.

On the music scene the Pavilion hosted all the best pop groups including one called The Beatles, creating memorable nights for those who were lucky enough to get tickets.

At sixty, Rosamund didn't approve of the new fashion trends or pop music, preferring to spend her evenings quietly in the drawing room at The Oaks, reading and re-reading letters from Cedric. He had completed his first tour as a Midshipman on a destroyer patrolling the Far East and while in

Singapore had visited his Aunt Eunice. She and her husband had retired there, having grown accustomed to the climate and way of life, not wanting to chill their bones in the English Winter.

'...it was good to see Aunt Eunice,' Cedric had written. 'She kept looking at me and telling me how proud my father would be to see me in the Royal Navy.'

Rosamund smiled to herself, understanding her sister's pointed comment.

Following the patrol Cedric had returned to the UK and come home to Bath for a spell of leave. Rosamund's only disappointment was his choice of girlfriend: he'd introduced her to someone called Wendy Fowler, a rather common girl in a ridiculously short shift dress who was no match for him, and she hoped he would soon forget her. In any case he was now back at Dartmouth preparing for his next deployment to the East coast of the USA, so had other things on his mind. Rosamund stared up at Mortimer's portrait, knowing how proud he would have been of Cedric's achievements. She had consigned thoughts of Michael to the back of her mind some years ago, and had almost reached the point of believing her own lie.

*

In Larkhall, Mary was trying to get used to Derek being at home: after fifty years of working, man and boy, he had retired. She was worried that he'd get under her feet, but they came to a happy compromise where he spent some mornings at his allotment and other times they had days out together. They took coach trips to Weston-super-Mare and the south coast, visited Derek's sister and even started ballroom dancing lessons at the Forum. It was a happy period of Mary's life and her only regret was not seeing her nephew. She missed him since he had gone back to France and wished he wasn't alone – he had a lot to offer and would have made a wonderful father. Then she thought, men do have their secrets and he doesn't have to tell me everything. He sounded cheerful enough in his letters, anyway.

France, 1963

Philippe and Clare proudly attended Alfred's graduation at the Sorbonne, having gained his first class degree in science. He was going to stay on for another year to study for his Masters, specialising in Geology, the science of the rocks. After the ceremony Alfred joined his parents, giving them a hug. Clare stood back to look at him in his robes and said, 'I wonder what your father would have made of it all!'

Alfred's face turned to thunder.

'My father is *here*,' he said, emphatically, looking at Philippe. 'How dare you mention *that man* on a day like this?'

Clare's face fell.

'I'm sorry, Alfred - it just…slipped out. I didn't mean to upset you.'

'Of course not,' said Philippe, stepping in between the two, not wanting an argument to spoil the day, although he was also offended by Clare's reference to Reg. 'Come on, let's go and eat – I booked the restaurant for one o'clock.'

The three had a subdued lunch together, then Alfred left them to continue celebrating with his friends. Alone with Philippe, Clare said, 'I'm sorry I spoilt the moment – but for all of it, Reg was his father.'

Philippe tried to contain his anger.

'Biologically, yes. But all Reg ever did for Alfred was frighten him and threaten him with violence, you know that. He'll never forget witnessing what he did to you. It's taken him years to push it to the back of his mind – don't force him to remember.'

Clare touched Philippe's hand.

'You're right. It's thanks to *you* that we have made such a successful life here, the three of us. I won't mention him again.'

*

The next time Philippe saw Beatrice in Paris he could tell that underneath her usual calm exterior she was excited about something. They walked together to the Parc de Monceau and sat on a bench in a quiet corner where they could speak without being overheard.

'I'm taking up a new post, but you must keep it to yourself,' she said, confidentially. 'It's sensitive, because I'm going behind the Iron Curtain, to Poland. We won't be able to correspond directly but we can stay in touch via the Foreign Office. It should be interesting…'

Philippe was impressed. The Cold War was raging and a posting to the Eastern Bloc would be fraught with difficulty and danger.

'I'm sure you're up to the challenge! How's your Polish?'

'Not the easiest of languages! I'm going to the diplomatic language school for a year to do a crash course before they'll let me loose!'

'Well I wish you the best of luck. And I'll miss you.'

'You too, Philippe.'

*

After Alfred gained his Masters degree he took up the offer of a job in the south of France to research the geology of the area around Aix-en-Provence. He was thrilled: it was just the opportunity he had been looking for from a scientific viewpoint, and it was a wonderful place to live. Based at Aix University, he spent his time in the surrounding hills taking soil and rock samples and analysing them in the laboratory. He surveyed how the rocks channelled the hot springs which emerged at various points in the city, notably at a fountain covered in thick moss where people would drink the steaming water in the belief that it cured all manner of ailments. Alfred quickly made his home among the sun-dappled, fountain-splashed squares and narrow streets, and fell in love with a local girl, long-legged, olive-skinned Bernadette.

His parents joined him for a holiday, renting a typical honey-coloured stone house with a terracotta tiled roof in the city centre. Clare missed Alfred and was glad to spend some time with him, enjoying his company and having someone to chat to in English -

as good as Philippe's English was, it was never quite the same as talking to someone in their mother tongue.

It may have been because of missing her son that some aspects of life in France had begun to jar. Although Clare had made some friends she always felt like the outsider, missing out on in-jokes and little asides, which, when she asked her friends to explain, never seemed quite so funny. For all that she loved the French food and scenery, there were aspects of life in her adopted country that she found frustrating – the bureaucracy, standing in a queue in the heat while a laconic bank clerk took hours to sort out a simple query, an inertia which made her wonder how anything ever got done.

However, Clare was determined to enjoy her holiday and putting her reservations about France and the French to one side, she loved Aix. She spent hours in the warm sunshine, browsing the market stalls laden with succulent Provençal olives and almonds, preparing simple meals on the nights they ate in. Alfred took his parents around the local sights, pleased to show off his new home, and introduced them to Bernadette.

'The weather is lovely now, but you have to beware of the *Mistral*,' she told them. 'It's a very strong wind which blows from the north in the Winter and the Spring. People call it *'un vent à décorner les boeufs!'*'

Clare looked blank, and Alfred explained – 'it can take the horns off a cow!'

Philippe and Clare travelled around in their new car, discovering the glorious technicolour countryside, driving down long, straight roads bordered by poplar trees then emerging next to fields of bright sunflowers and vineyards with row upon row of ripening grapes. They drove past acres of purple lavender stretching to the horizon, breathing in the perfume, and explored the coastline, brimming with creeks and coves with magical views over the azure Mediterranean Sea. Philippe was inspired by the warm colours and luminosity, feeling an artist's bond with Van Gough and Cézanne who had captured the beauty and ambience of the area so vividly.

After the holidays Philippe and Clare reluctantly said goodbye to Alfred and returned to La Rochelle, refreshed, Philippe bursting with ideas for future art works. Clare was delighted to see her son and husband so happy, accepting that, if things weren't always easy for her, moving to France was the best and only thing they could have done.

CHAPTER 41

Poland, 1964

After an interminable train journey across the bleak plains of Eastern Europe, Beatrice arrived in the Polish People's Republic, ready to take up her new post at the British Embassy in Warsaw. The war had left the Polish capital a smoking ruin and now the country was ruled by a Communist government under Moscow-imposed martial law. A massive rebuilding programme had filled the city with large apartment blocks, soulless, concrete boxes, devoid of colour. It was Autumn, but in the absence of trees or nature in any form, there was no visible sign of it. Her first impressions were of an austere, highly-controlled society with police on every corner watching for any sign of dissent, and the people on the street appeared joyless.

The British Embassy was housed in an older, more characterful building, one of the few spared by the war, together with other countries' embassies, the diplomatic heartbeat of Warsaw. The Ambassador told her what to expect.

'No frills, no luxuries, being watched wherever you go – welcome to the Eastern Bloc! Newspapers and TV are controlled by the Party, religion is suppressed, your phone will be tapped. Never forget, the Soviets are in control here and will monitor your every move. Our job is to monitor theirs.'

Beatrice was allocated an apartment in an austere block but cheered it up as best she could with photographs and books from home. She made contact with agents from other countries and Polish spies, local people who were working against the Soviets, and began to establish herself in her job. The social centre of the Embassy was the bar which was just like a proper English pub complete with plaid carpet and a TV in the corner. It was dingy and smelt of stale beer but it was a good place to get to know her colleagues and have a few shots of Polish vodka.

The long Polish Winter seemed endless but suddenly the weather brightened, the sun broke through and her colleagues began talking about the Summer holidays.

'The Winters are so long here, it's only the thought of Summer that makes the place bearable,' said Annette, a friend she'd made.

'What do you usually do?'

'We go to the Mazury region in the north-east – they call it 'the land of a thousand lakes', although there's nearer twice that many! There are some cabins there and we make a block booking. Half the team go in July and the other in August. Want to come along?'

When July came Beatrice joined the group of around a dozen from the Embassy with their families and took the train to the north-east.

'You're in for a treat,' one of the wives told her. 'Mazury is Poland's hidden treasure and the scenery is superb. Even the police keep a low profile.'

Beatrice looked out the window as they left the city, looking forward to the break. Gradually the severe urban architecture of Warsaw was replaced by smaller towns with older-style buildings and she spotted pairs of storks, perched on their nests on the rooftops. They steamed on through gentle, rolling hills and farmland, and after a four hour journey arrived at Gizycko in the heart of the lake district.

Beatrice stepped off the train, looked at the green hills beyond and took a deep breath, savouring the fresh air and warm sunshine. She was going to enjoy this.

She spent the holiday hiking, exploring the forests and learning to sail, but the team couldn't totally switch off from work and one evening after dinner she overheard the archivist for the military attaché talking about Auschwitz.

'They've started to release the records of who was imprisoned there, very sobering. Just think – one million lives, ended…people's mothers, fathers, sons, daughters…'

Beatrice pricked up her ears and said, 'the mother of a friend of mine was at Auschwitz. How can we find out whether she survived?'

'You're welcome to come and look through the records if you like. I'll warn you, though – there are thousands…'

'Thank you – I will.'

This was the development Beatrice had been hoping for. She would never have a better opportunity to fulfil her promise to Philippe: to find out what had happened to his mother, Amélie Swann.

The days grew short, and back in Warsaw Beatrice began her long trawl through the records from Auschwitz. She examined the ledgers meticulously, line by line, incredulous at the endless list of names, so much suffering endured, so many lives lost. She found an entry recording a group admitted from Drancy in Paris in October 1942, taking a sharp breath when she saw the name 'Amélie Swann' among them, although there was no trace of her father, Louis Duvalier. Beatrice concluded that he must have died at Drancy.

Late one evening a colleague saw her at her desk working in the light of an angle-poised lamp.

'Goodnight, Beatrice. It's late, you should go home.'

Beatrice took off her spectacles and stretched.

'It's either this or stay in my apartment doing my knitting! But your right. I'll just go through one more page…'

'Very well – I'll leave you to continue your labour of love.'

Beatrice smiled – yes, that's what it was – her labour of love.

Bath, 1965

At Corsham Court, during his morning break from teaching, Daniel was skimming through a selection of Arts magazines when an article suddenly caught his attention – an extract translated from French about an exhibition in Paris of paintings by a critically acclaimed artist called Philippe Swann, accompanied by photographs of his work. Daniel showed the article to Richard who said, 'goodness! Philippe is doing well!'

'He certainly is!'

Then Daniel said, 'in fact, thinking about Philippe and our old times at Green Park - do you remember that we stored some canvases in the vaults at the railway station?'

'Yes – of course! And thank goodness we did, or they'd have been lost to the bombs like all the others.'

'Indeed! Well, I read in the local paper the other day that the station's due to close – they're going to stop running passenger trains from there next year.'

'Those Beeching cuts, I suppose…'

'Exactly. I thought we should fetch our paintings before they get mislaid. We've got plenty of room to store them here.'

'Good idea – do go ahead.'

Daniel hired a van and drove to Bath with Gordon, one of his students, to help with the heavy lifting. They spoke to one of the station staff who checked the records, identified where boxes containing canvases from the School of Art were stored and took the visitors underground to the vaults. Daniel found the place most unpleasant – it was cold, there was a musty odour and a ghostly feel about the place which made him shiver. He remembered Philippe taking the canvases down there with the help of Clare Watkins who had been working at the station at the time, and he didn't envy them their task.

In the light of a gas lamp Daniel and Gordon set to work, carrying the boxes to the surface and loading them into the van. They worked as quickly as they could, not wanting to stay below ground for any longer than necessary. Suddenly, down in the vaults, a loud noise like thunder crashed above their heads, the whole place shook and Daniel froze. Gordon noticed and said, 'don't worry, it's only a train leaving the station.'

Daniel took some deep breaths and apologised, saying, 'for a minute there I thought the bombs were going to drop again! You're too young to remember, but it brought it all back…'

Their task complete, they returned to Corsham Court and stacked the boxes safely in a storage room, to be unpacked and examined in due course. That evening, with the memory of the raids in his mind, and thinking of Michael and Philippe, Daniel re-read the article from Paris in the Arts magazine. He looked again at the photographs, noticing in one of them a woman in the background that he hadn't spotted before. His mind must be muddled by the events of the day because he could have sworn that she was Clare Watkins.

Poland, 1965

After weeks of searching, Beatrice reached the ledgers of January 1945 which showed that when Auschwitz was liberated, Amélie Swann was taken to a Red Cross resettlement camp in Germany. Relieved to know that Amélie had survived the terrible ordeal of Auschwitz itself, Beatrice tracked the records to find that, after a period in the camp hospital, Amélie convalesced until she was discharged in August 1947 when she had taken a train home to Paris. Beatrice got straight onto the phone to ask a friend at the Embassy in Paris to try and trace her, but after an extensive search she could find nothing. Amélie Swann seemed to have disappeared into thin air.

Devastated at having got so far only to be thwarted, Beatrice decided to change tack. Putting to one side the worst scenario - that Amélie was dead – Beatrice conjectured as to what might have happened to her. She may have found Paris unbearable without those she had loved, but where might she have gone? Was there a friend, perhaps – someone Amélie had met at the camp – that she'd grown close to? With this theory in mind Beatrice re-visited the ledgers, thinking, come on Beatrice, this is why you were employed at Bletchley, because you're good at noticing patterns, making connections…

She noted the names of the people who were sent from Drancy to Auschwitz at the same time as Amélie and were still alive when the camp was liberated. The numbers whittled down until very few were left, and one in particular stood out: Greta Blum.

Her husband Jacques had died just before liberation and Greta had been sent to the same resettlement camp as Amélie. The two must have known each other. Beatrice followed Greta's movements to find that when she left the camp she had taken a train to a place called Elk, in Poland. It was possible that Greta had stayed in contact with Amélie, and at the very least may have memories of her to share.

Beatrice looked at the map of Poland on the office wall and saw that Elk was in the lake district, close to where she had been on holiday that Summer. The Embassy staff were due to go there again the next year, and Beatrice determined to make this her mission: to find Greta Blum.

CHAPTER 42

Bath, 1966

Rosamund's beloved son had returned from a long tour of Australasia which, judging by his letters, he had loved, even telling her about the Polynesian girls he had met – sometimes she felt he gave his mother more information than she really needed to know. At one point she worried that he was going to turn into Gaugin and stay there, so was relieved when his ship returned to Portsmouth and he came home at last. Rosamund and Eileen greeted him, overjoyed to see the tall, handsome, Lieutenant Cedric Mason, Royal Navy. He brought all manner of unusual gifts for them, causing great merriment, and entertaining them with his stories. When they settled down Rosamund asked, 'what are you going to do next?'

'I've been appointed to Greenwich for a year to attend the Staff Course, so I'll be closer to home.'

'Good, I remember your father doing the same.'

She looked fondly up at Mortimer's portrait, proud that his son was following in his footsteps, a naval officer, born to the sea.

After completing the first term at Greenwich, Cedric returned home with an announcement.

'I have some news. I'm engaged to be married!'

Rosamund was taken aback.

'What – who…?'

'It's Wendy – Wendy Fowler. You remember, Mummy, I brought her here to meet you, although you didn't get off on the right foot. We've been writing for years, and we've been seeing each other since I started at Greenwich. She lives in Oxford – she's an archaeologist.'

Rosamund bristled.

'Yes, I do remember her… a rather common girl, in a short dress. Are you quite sure about this, Cedric? I always thought you'd meet a nice, well-bred young lady - an Admiral's daughter, perhaps…'

'Like *you*?!'

He laughed and took his mother's hand.

'I've made up my mind. Wendy and I love each other, we're going to get married, and next weekend I'm bringing her here to see you.'

Rosamund was uncertain about meeting Wendy again but when the day came she made an effort to be civil, for her son's sake. She asked Wendy about her career and listened as she spoke animatedly about her passion for archaeology and the time she had spent in Malta, excavating Roman ruins. The young couple clearly adored each other and Rosamund had to admit that Wendy was very attractive, with vivid green eyes and red hair cascading around her shoulders.

The visit concluded and Rosamund stood with Eileen, watching the pair walk down the driveway together, hand in hand. At the end they both turned and waved. Rosamund sighed.

'What do you make of it all, Eileen?'

'Well, Mrs Mason, if she makes him happy that's all that matters, isn't it.'

'Yes, dear – I suppose you're right.'

France, 1966

In September, Philippe received a telegram:

YOU ARE TO REPORT TO THE BRITISH EMBASSY IN PARIS SOONEST FOR A SPECIAL MISSION. SULIS.

The message could only have come from Beatrice; it must be important, and urgent.

'Clare,' he said, 'I'm sorry but I've got to go.'

Leaving behind his bewildered wife, Philippe caught the train to Paris with a mix of curiosity and excitement. He went straight to the Embassy where he was referred to the Polish section and given a letter.

Dear Philippe,

Apologies for the cloak-and-dagger approach but security is vital.

I have traced your mother. She is living in Elk, in Poland, with a friend she made at Auschwitz. I have met them both. Amélie is frail but well and is desperate to see you again.

Travel behind the Iron Curtain is not permitted for the general public but we will put you back on the Foreign Office books so you can visit her under diplomatic protection. You will

travel by train to Warsaw where I will meet you, then I will take
you to her home. Do not tell anyone, it could put your mother
and her friend in danger. Take care, Sulis.

B.'

Philippe was overwhelmed.

His mother was alive, and living in Poland! He had a thousand questions to ask, but they would have to wait. Beatrice, what a wonderful woman you are.

Poland, 1966

After a seemingly endless rail journey across Europe, Philippe crossed the border into Poland and arrived in Warsaw. A car took him to the British Embassy where he was warmly greeted by a smiling Beatrice.

'Philippe! I'm so pleased you've arrived safely!'

'Yes – and I can't wait to see my mother. How can I ever thank you?'

'I'm delighted to help. Now, it's all fixed. You can stay with me tonight and tomorrow we'll catch the train to Elk. I've told Amélie to expect you.'

Beatrice smuggled Philippe into her apartment through the back entrance, avoiding the prying eyes of the secret police. Over several cognacs she told him everything she had found out about Amélie and Greta, Philippe listening intently and asking many questions to which Beatrice had only some of the answers. Towards bedtime she said, 'I don't have a spare room I'm afraid, but will you be all right on the sofa?'

'Of course.'

The next day they travelled away from the city towards the north-east. Rather like Beatrice, Philippe was impressed by the unexpected beauty of the Polish countryside, steaming through lush, green hills and valleys, across bridges, looking out at farmers working in the fields, harvesting their crops as they had for generations. After a four-hour journey they arrived in Elk and took the bus to Greta's address, a modest house in a quiet street. Beatrice stood back while Philippe knocked on the door and Greta answered.

'My name is Philippe Swann. I believe my mother lives here.'

'Come in! Come in!' then she called, 'Amélie – he's here!'

Greta welcomed Beatrice and showed Philippe into the lounge, then she and Beatrice withdrew to give mother and son some privacy. For a moment the two stood and looked at each other, then they embraced and the tears came. He held her tightly, aware of her frail body, while she wept with relief to see with her own eyes that her son, the artist, was safe and well. They sat down, noticing the changes in their faces, reflecting the lives they had lived, the things they had endured since they had last seen each other at the Gare du Nord, twenty-six years ago.

'I thought you were dead,' they said, and smiled at each other. She touched his face, more mature and rugged, but still her handsome son. He touched her face and her hair, and kissed her again.

'I lost my hair, then it grew back white.'

'It doesn't matter. I like you new style! Tell, me what happened to my grandfather?'

Amélie shook her head. 'He died at Drancy. It was a terrible time and he was so weak. But at least he was spared Auschwitz.'

Greta and Beatrice returned with tea and they spent the next hours talking and talking, Philippe and Amélie sitting next to each other, turning to look at one another, not letting each other go.

Later, Amélie said to Philippe and Beatrice, 'tell me again, how you two know each other.'

'We worked together during the war,' said Philippe.

'We were in the Resistance,' said Beatrice.

Philippe looked at her, surprised to hear her speak the words so openly, but in present company there was nothing to fear.

'So was I!' said Amélie, 'I used to run messages for Dr Fournier... Jean-Pierre...'

She stifled a sob.

'We were lovers, but the Nazis found out and it led to the network being broken up. Jean-Pierre and five others were shot. I learnt about it from a nurse I met at Drancy.'

Philippe held her hand tightly, then Amélie asked, 'Philippe, were you known as Pascal Lejeune?'

'Yes! How did you know?'

'I tried to find you in Paris. People told me someone by that name was looking for me, but I was sure it must be you. Then I heard you were dead. I had nothing left to live for. I nearly ended it all, but a kind man rescued me and eventually I found my way to my dearest friend, Greta.'

'And it's thanks to *my* dearest friend that we can be together now,' said Philippe, reaching over to take Beatrice's hand in his, and she returned his look of affection with a smile that lit up her face.

Amélie said, 'Beatrice, you are an angel.'

Greta gave Beatrice the spare room and Philippe passed another night on a sofa. The next day Amélie said, 'we want to take you somewhere special.'

The four of them caught a bus to a town called Orzysz and Amélie led them to the gate of a large, detached house.

'When your grandfather died at Drancy I found a photograph in his wallet of my mother standing outside a house when she was a little girl. This is the house, Philippe – this is where your grandmother was born. They were driven out by the Russians in the 1880s because they were Jewish, and fled to Paris. The same happened to Greta's family.'

'How tragic,' said Beatrice, then she added, 'perhaps the two families knew each other…'

'Yes! That's what we wondered!' said Greta.

Philippe stood, staring at the house.

'So this is why you suffered so much, Maman, because your mother – that little girl in the photograph – happened to be Jewish.'

'Yes - all the Jews who lived here were killed by the Nazis or taken to the camps.'

'Who lives in the house now?'

'A government official from Warsaw. He only comes here in the Summer. We haven't made ourselves known – we don't want to cause any trouble.'

The following day, Philippe and Beatrice had to leave. The four of them embraced, the air heavy with emotion, hoping to see each other again but knowing it may not be possible.

'We can write to each other, Maman, Beatrice will arrange it.'

'Yes,' said Beatrice. 'I'm due to stay at the Embassy for another year and I can pass letters through the diplomatic channels. And if I get the chance I'll come and visit you both next Summer.'

'That would be wonderful!' said Amélie and Greta, together.

Amélie kissed her son one last time and said, 'I love you.'

'I love you too, Maman.'

Philippe and Beatrice caught the train back to Warsaw, both overwhelmed by what they had learned about Amélie and Greta's lives and family history. Back at Beatrice's apartment after the journey of a lifetime they relaxed with a bottle of cognac and sat together, going over again what they had found, talking about the past, and about Poland. The two had grown close over the course of their trip, enjoying each other's company, and were sorry their adventure was coming to its end. Around midnight Beatrice said, 'we'd better go to bed – I've got to get you to the station in the morning.'

'I'll stay here, then,' said Philippe, stretching out on the sofa.

'Well…you don't have to…'

She turned to him and kissed him, and in the emotion of the moment he put his arms around her and returned her kiss. They looked at each other, remembering the night they had spent together before he had left for France to join the Resistance, and she smiled at him.

'Come on, *Sulis*,' she said, leading him to her bedroom.

CHAPTER 43

France, 1966

Philippe returned to La Rochelle, longing to tell Clare about his trip to Poland but knowing it must stay a secret – rather like the last night he had spent with Beatrice. Back home he simply told his wife, 'I have seen my mother, and she safe is well. I'm sorry, *chérie*, that's all I can tell you.'

Clare had always felt distanced from that part of his life, in the same way as she would never know what he had done in those years after the Bath Blitz. She struggled to understand the need for secrecy, but accepted it, along with the occasional faraway look in his eyes. She wondered if that odd woman Beatrice had something to do with it – she seemed to have some sort of hold over him.

She knew he wouldn't answer her questions so didn't ask, but gave him a hug and said, 'that's wonderful, darling! All these years you've been desperate to know what happened to her. Thank goodness she's alive. I'm so pleased for you.'

Poland, 1967

As Beatrice's appointment to Poland neared its end she made one last trip to see Amélie and Greta. They welcomed her warmly and Beatrice gave Amélie a clutch of letters from Philippe, safer to be delivered by hand.

'I'm only sorry I haven't been able to bring Philippe in person, the authorities warned that it was just too dangerous.'

Beatrice told the women all she knew about Philippe's latest art exhibitions and his family life, and listened in turn to Amélie and Greta's news. They discussed the political situation and the ever-changing boundaries of Eastern Europe, Beatrice feeling an empathy with the Polish people who had suffered for generations from invasions by Germans, Prussians and Russians, but for all of it had survived, their spirit undimmed, knowing that one day they would reclaim their country. Greta talked about her own family, whom, like Amélie's, had fled from East Prussia, as it was then known.

'But my parents always insisted they were Polish,' said Greta. 'As my mother used to say, "if a cat has kittens in a china cabinet, you don't call them teacups."'

When it came for Beatrice to leave she said, 'I'm due to return to London, but I may come back to Poland in the future – the Foreign Office has invested in my language training and won't want to waste it! I hope to see you both again.'

'You'll always be welcome here, Beatrice,' said Amélie.

The women hugged and said goodbye. As they watched her go Greta said, 'do you think Philippe realises how much she loves him?'

Amélie smiled. 'Probably not – but I'm sure he will, one day.'

Beatrice spent the rest of her holiday walking alone in the hills, thinking about Amélie and Greta, two courageous women who had survived the horrors of war and imprisonment, and found consolation with each other through the power of friendship. Reflecting on her own life, rooted in secrecy, intelligence and deception, she felt humbled by their humanity. What had begun as a mission to help the man she loved had become a deeply emotional experience that she would treasure for the rest of her life.

Strolling in the fresh, cleansing air, drinking in the beautiful scenery, Beatrice knew she had fallen under the spell of the Mazury lakes. The area was remote, timeless, offering as close to freedom as it was possible to get in Soviet-controlled Poland. She walked alongside a lake, observing a stork as it circled, its long gangly legs stretched out behind as it glided over the water. The bird suddenly dived downwards in its search for a fish, frog or rodent, then rose into the sky, holding its prey firmly in its long, orange beak. Watching the stork as it flew away Beatrice noticed in the distance a little cottage, by the lake. It drew her like a magnet. As she grew closer she could see it was derelict, but so promising, in a perfect setting.

A man was working in a field nearby and she asked, 'who owns this cottage?'

'My father. He doesn't use it now - we live in a new house, up there.'

He gestured to a hilltop where a few modern houses stood.

'Would he be interested in selling it?'

The man shrugged. 'Maybe. Come with me and you can ask him.'

She followed him up the hill and he introduced her to his father. They quickly agreed a price for the cottage which Beatrice considered a bargain; the owner thought this English woman was mad. They shook hands and Beatrice said, 'I promise I will return soon with the money.' The man didn't believe her, but it made no difference to him.

France, 1967

In September, Philippe received an invitation from the Embassy in Paris to mark the arrival of the new Ambassador.

'It looks awfully grand!' said Clare. 'I'd better wear a hat!'

The event took place in the Embassy gardens with many local dignitaries as well as politicians and officials from the UK and other European countries. The Ambassador and his wife greeted their guests.

'How lovely to meet you both,' said the Ambassador, shaking their hands enthusiastically, 'you're the artist who painted the portraits of my predecessor and his wife that hang in the library - very impressive. I hope you will do us the same honour!'

'Of course, it would be a pleasure!'

'My secretary will be in touch. Now, please, have a look round the garden and enjoy the buffet.'

'That's good, Philippe, another commission!' whispered Clare, elegant in a pale pink bouclé suit and matching pill box hat. As the couple mingled, Beatrice came to greet them, looking smart in a tailored navy blue dress, although her flat lace-ups rather spoilt the image. Philippe was pleased, but surprised, to see her.

'Beatrice! I thought you were back in London!'

'I am, but I came over especially for today. In fact there's some people here I'd like you to meet…'

She led them to the rose garden where a tall, fair-haired RAF officer was speaking to some other guests.

'This is Air Commodore Henry Roberts, the Air Attaché,' Beatrice said, as they shook hands, 'and this is his wife, Tilly.'

Philippe and Tilly smiled discreetly, unable to acknowledge that they knew each other from their SOE days.

'Philippe is an artist based in La Rochelle,' said Beatrice, and Henry picked up the conversation, saying, 'ah, the famous portrait painter!', while Tilly spoke to Clare. After commenting on the lovely Autumn weather they talked about their families.

'Our daughter Harriet is seventeen and our son Freddie is twelve,' said Tilly. 'They're at the International School and they love it. I always think children settle into new situations more quickly than their parents.'

'I agree. My son Alfred was five when we came to France and now he's like a native, thanks to Philippe – he adopted him, after my first husband died. The two of them get on so well together, they're as thick as thieves! Alfred graduated from the Sorbonne and now he's working as a geologist in Provence.'

'Lucky man – all that sunshine! And where did you live before coming to France, Clare?'

'In Bath.'

'Oh, that's where Henry grew up!'

'Really?'

'Yes, his father was a doctor, he retired some years ago. He lives in a place called Lower Weston. Henry's mother was killed in the Bath Blitz, it was terribly sad – I never had the chance to meet her.'

Clare felt her stomach lurch as she realised who Henry was.

'So you used to live in Bath?' asked Henry, turning to Clare and casting his eye over the attractive, fair-haired woman in her mid-forties.

Clare was careful to give nothing away.

'Yes – I lived in Larkhall. Can't say I miss it, though – I prefer the weather in France!' She smiled charmingly then said, 'if you'll excuse us…Philippe, I'm quite hungry – shall we try the buffet?'

Clare took Philippe's arm and as they walked towards the long tables laden with food Clare whispered, 'you know who he is, don't you – his father's Dr Roberts who lives opposite my old flat - he treated me in hospital. You don't think he'll make a connection, do you?'

'I doubt it – there's no reason to. And Henry probably hasn't lived in Bath for years. Don't let it worry you, Clare. Now, let's have something to eat – it looks delicious…'

But, with thoughts of her past life with Reg echoing in her mind, Clare had lost her appetite.

After Philippe had eaten his fill, a member of staff approached him and led him away, leaving Clare with one of the secretaries who could talk for Britain. Philippe was shown into the library where Beatrice was waiting with Tilly and the three were able to greet each other openly.

'It's good to see you again, Philippe!' exclaimed Tilly, 'we haven't met since VE Day!'

There was so much to catch up on. Tilly said, 'when I married Henry I never expected to be living in Paris! It makes a pleasant change from all those dreary RAF camps in England. We met after the war – Henry's a friend of my brother, they served in the same squadron and were POWs together. And you found your way to France with your lovely wife! I suppose you met when you went back to Bath?'

'Yes, that's right. After a couple of years I decided to move to France, and Clare and Alfred joined me. We're very happy in La Rochelle, and I've got plenty to do – I come to Paris regularly to see the owner of the gallery who shows my work. And I painted these…' he said, gesturing to the portraits on the wall.

'Philippe's had several successful exhibitions,' said Beatrice, proudly, 'he's made quite a name for himself in Paris.'

'Clare was telling me about your stepson, Alfred, the geologist.'

'Yes, he's passionate about his work. We're very close.'

'That's what Clare said! And I hear you've seen your mother, in Poland.'

'Thanks to Beatrice...'

Philippe looked at Beatrice, deep with gratitude, and she returned his gaze with a smile of acknowledgement and affection. Tilly noticed, aware of the special warmth and understanding they shared.

The three of them reminisced, remembering friends and colleagues who had died in the war, and talked about the current political situation.

'Will we ever learn?' asked Tilly, 'so much destruction. And now we have the Cold War to contend with.'

'We must protect our freedom at all costs,' said Philippe.

Beatrice said, 'there will always be some megalomaniac who wants power, to invade other countries and take their land, to right what they see as historic wrongs. All we can do is be prepared, keep our armed forces going, and put our faith in God and diplomacy...'

She poured them each a cognac and raising their glasses the three made a toast.

'The SOE.'

CHAPTER 44

Bath, 1971

Green Park station had been closed to passengers since 1966, the last goods train had run and now it was a scene of dereliction and creeping decay. Many proposals were put forward for the old station's future – offices, a hotel, a concert hall – but no investment was forthcoming. The Council decided to turn it into a car park and demolition work began, knocking down the old industrial buildings, ploughing through the old Fish House and other relics of the past. The workers cleared tons of concrete and debris, and as they delved deeper they crashed into the vaults at the far end of the platform, one of the old coal bunkers from years ago.

Bert Hogg was driving his bulldozer one foggy October morning, knocking down a wall, when he spotted something odd and stopped the engine. He climbed down from his cab to inspect the wreckage, noticing something strange amongst a pile of rubble and coal, and took a closer look. There was no mistaking: he could see bones, and what looked like the top of a skull. Bert shouted out to his foreman who ran over to see what was the matter.

'My God! It's a skeleton! We'd better stop work and call the police!'

The police arrived with a pathologist and cordoned off the area.

'Your first thoughts?' asked Detective Inspector Doyle.

'I'll be able to tell you more when I get it back to the lab, but I'd say, probably human, been here anything from upwards of twenty years.'

'Thanks…that should narrow it down a bit…'

The pathologist took photographs of the scene then carefully removed the remains and had them transported back to her laboratory. After a forensic examination she declared the skeleton to be that of a male, aged between twenty and sixty, the cause of death most likely to be from a broken neck. She had found no means of identification on the remains or in the immediate area where they were found.

'Can you say how long he's been there?' asked Doyle.

'More than twenty years, but probably less than a hundred, from his condition.'

'Any suggestion of foul play?'

'Hard to tell – the broken neck could be due to a fall. You'll need to contact the coroner. I'll try and trace his dental records to see if we can find out who he is, but it will take a while.'

The police issued a statement:

The remains of an adult male have been found on the site of the old Green Park railway station in Bath. The discovery is being treated as 'unexplained' and the incident has been referred to the coroner. Our priority is to identify the deceased. This could be a lengthy process and we will update the public in due course. The area has been sealed off to allow officers to carry out further searches. Members of the public with any information about this grim find are invited to come forward.'

The Press leapt on the story.

GRUESOME REMAINS FOUND BY WORKER IN GREEN PARK STATION

...ran the front page headline in the *Bath & Wilts Chronicle*, complete with an interview with Bert Hogg, the driver of the bulldozer, giving him his brief moment of fame. Speculation was rife:

'Probably a tramp who was drunk and fell.'

'The remains were skeletal – could have been there for centuries!'

'He might have been murdered and dumped there!'

David Roberts watched the reports on the local TV news with his son Henry and daughter-in-law Tilly who were down from Berkshire for the weekend. Filling his pipe and lighting it, his mind going back thirty years, he said, 'of course the whole area was bombed during the Bath Blitz. I wouldn't be surprised if he was a victim, lain hidden all these years.'

Rosamund had the same thought, remembering with horror the scene that had met her in Green Park that dreadful day, when she had gone there to find that Michael had been killed.

At their home in Corsham, Daniel said to Emma, 'I thought it felt ghostly when we went to fetch the canvases from the vaults. I can't believe that poor man was lying just a few yards away. We must pray for his soul.'

In Larkhall, Mary read the macabre story, thinking of the times she had walked past the station not knowing that a dead body was lying there... the thought made her shiver. She wished Derek was with her to discuss the news – she missed him so much. Following a few short years of happy retirement he had sadly succumbed to emphysema, leaving her bereft. Although he had been ten years her senior she hadn't anticipated widowhood quite so soon, and was finding it difficult to adjust to living alone, with just her new pet canary for company.

Mary read the article again. It was creepy, but exciting too, and in her next letter to Philippe she enclosed the press cutting.

France, 1971

'Oh my God!' exclaimed Philippe, reading Mary's letter. 'Clare - look - they've found him!'

Clare caught her breath. 'But how…?'

'They're demolishing the railway station and found the skeleton amongst the rubble.'

Philippe cussed to himself. He hadn't anticipated the station being torn down, exposing their long-buried secret.

'What if they find out who he is?' asked Clare, panicking, 'we'll be finished! What are we going to do?'

'Nothing. They'll never be able to identify him, and there's nothing to implicate us. It will blow over, you'll see.'

He took her in his arms, trying to reassure her.

'Don't worry, *chérie*, everything will be all right.'

But as she lay awake in bed, Clare's old fears returned. She recalled every detail of the events of that night, her shock at the ease with which Philippe had murdered Reg and her guilt at her part in it, but also the overwhelming relief that Reg would no longer harm her or Alfred. When she finally got to sleep it was only to be re-awakened a few hours later by her old nightmare, and once again she saw Reg's dead body lying in the hallway, his bloodshot eyes bulging from their sockets.

Bath, 1971

Detective Inspector Stanley Doyle, early fifties, balding and with an expanding waistline due to too many liquid lunches, was reviewing the responses to the Green Park inquiry with his Detective Sergeant, Alan Turner.

'We've had a few people come forward with suggestions as to the identity of the remains, but nothing definite that we can prove,' said Turner.

'Dental records?'

'Still searching.'

Doyle nodded - this was going to be a long job. His team were working through their list of missing persons, but with the victim being found at a railway station the scope was vast – he could have come from anywhere. They fed the Press the line that the remains were most likely those of a vagrant, and low-priority. The Coroner put the case on hold until the new year and the matter faded from public view, but behind the scenes Doyle was exploring other possibilities. He interviewed staff who had worked at the station over the years and established that, before the bulldozer had done its work, the area where the remains were found had been a sealed vault, accessed by a shute from the street. A drunk may have managed to climb in and fall to his death, but Doyle wasn't convinced.

'Keep searching the record of missing persons,' Doyle told his Detective Sergeant. 'I reckon our man's in there somewhere.'

Like a dog with a bone, once Stanley Doyle began an investigation he wouldn't let it go until he had achieved a satisfactory result, and as far as he was concerned his work had only just begun.

CHAPTER 45

Bath, 1972

At the start of the year Daniel suggested to Richard that they hold an exhibition in April to mark the thirtieth anniversary of the Bath Blitz.

'You remember our *'Bath At War'* exhibition that we held in '41? I thought we could show some of the old canvases we brought back from storage at Green Park.'

'What an excellent idea!'

'And it would be a good way to mark your retirement, to thank you and Ann for everything you have done all these years.'

Richard and Ann were reluctant to relinquish the jobs they loved, but the odd bout of ill-health had finally persuaded them it was time to hand over the running of the School to the next generation – and who better to take it on than Daniel and Emma. The couple and their four children had established themselves in Corsham and were well-respected in the local community. Daniel was forever grateful for the patience and understanding with which Richard had helped him emerge from his dark days after the Bath Blitz, and his teaching career had flourished under his guidance.

'Right!' said Richard, 'I'll organise the venue and you choose the paintings!'

Over the next weeks Daniel, aided by Lizzie James, his star pupil, unpacked the canvases and examined them, carrying out restoration and cleaning where needed. They selected fifty of the best, representing a range of work produced by the students from that era, several of whom had perished in the raids. As they recorded the details in a catalogue Daniel remembered his old friends and Lizzie listened avidly as he told her about the fun they'd had as students. Daniel found it helpful to have a younger person working with him, offering a new perspective on the depictions of Bath at that time in its history.

'I love these of the old railway station,' she said, 'aren't they spooky! Especially when you think about what they found there last year…'

Daniel had a disturbing thought and hesitated for a moment. 'Perhaps we shouldn't include them…'

'No, I think they should stay. Let the paintings speak for themselves!'

On the opening day of the exhibition Richard made a short speech in memory of those who had lost their lives in the Bath Blitz. He then announced his and Ann's retirement, adding, 'I am pleased to tell you that the new Head of the School will be Daniel Johns, supported by his wife Emma. With this dedicated and talented couple at the helm we can be sure that the future of the School is in good hands.'

Everyone clapped and congratulated Daniel and Emma, honoured to take on their new role.

Mary went along to the exhibition, recalling when she and Derek had come to the original show. She came across Philippe's depiction of the vaults at Green Park and shuddered. It always did give me the creeps, that one, she thought, particularly now, with that skeleton they'd found... Then, she saw Philippe's portrait of Clare at work on the station platform, sensing the rapport between artist and subject, and fell into thinking about the couple. She was sure they were in love, and could never understand why Philippe had given up on her so easily after Reg disappeared. She had often wondered what happened to Clare and Alfred after they moved to London. Philippe had returned to France, but Clare, the woman he loved, wasn't with him.

A shiver ran up her spine.

Or was she?

David Roberts was also at the exhibition. He enjoyed art, and the scenes of wartime Bath brought back memories of his dear wife, lost in the Blitz. He was looking at paintings of life at Green Park station when someone appeared beside him.

'Rosamund! What a pleasant surprise.'

Since retiring, David had more time for socialising and occasionally met up with Rosamund. Now in their seventies, they had grown closer since David had attended Cedric's wedding four years ago.

Rosamund's first impression of her future daughter-in-law had not been favourable, but when she learned that Wendy was an old family friend of David's she had gone up in her estimation. Rosamund was now proud to tell people that Wendy had gained her Doctorate in Archaeology and was conducting important research at the Roman Baths.

'David! How nice to see you. Are you enjoying the exhibition?'

She liked being with David. There was a lingering smell of pipe tobacco about him which reminded her of her late husband, Mortimer.

'I certainly am - the artists portrayed that wartime period so well. I love this one of the railway station, it captures all the hustle and bustle of the day. And I recognise the woman, here – '

He pointed to a figure sweeping the platform.

'It's Clare Watkins - she was a neighbour of mine, and a patient. A sad case, actually - her husband Reg was a violent man and quite frankly I was pleased when he left her.' He remembered the look on Reg's face after Clare had lost her baby, and shivered. 'I heard later that Clare and her son had moved to London.'

'She's a pretty thing,' said Rosamund, who had a vague feeling that she'd seen the young woman before. 'Who's the artist?'

David consulted the catalogue.

'A Philippe Swann. It says here that he returned to his native France after the war and is making quite a name for himself in Paris.'

'Really?'

The name rang a bell with Rosamund and she remembered that terrible morning after the raid when she had gone in search of Michael. Philippe was the kind Frenchman, Michael's friend, who had told her he was dead and held her in his arms as she sobbed.

They wandered along to the next display which included a painting of the large air raid shelter outside the Scala cinema in Oldfield Park.

'This is the shelter that was destroyed in the second raid - so tragic. More than twenty people lost their lives there,' said David.

'Yes, I remember.'

David looked at the catalogue. 'It says the artist, Michael White, was killed at Green Park in the third raid.'

'I know,' said Rosamund, haltingly. 'So sad…'

France, 1972

Mary wrote to Philippe, telling him about the exhibition and how much she enjoyed seeing his work again. Then she added something which he found rather odd:

'…I love your paintings of Clare working at the railway station, so natural - you two always got on so well. To be honest, Philippe, I wish you had stayed with her and Alfred after Reg had gone - you would have made a lovely family together. By the way, I read in the paper a while ago that the police suspect the body found at Green Park was most likely a vagrant and they're downgrading their inquiry, so there is no more need to worry.'

He read the letter to Clare.

'What does she mean, *'no more need to worry'*? Good God, Philippe, do you think she knows?'

He sat, stroking his beard as he did when he was thinking. 'I think it's her way of telling us that she suspects we're living together, and approves, but whether she's worked out what happened to Reg, I don't know...'

'Perhaps we're reading too much into it.'

'Yes... and as long as she keeps her thoughts to herself it doesn't matter, does it?'

But that night Clare awoke, suddenly, her heart thumping, and sat bolt upright in bed. She took some deep breaths and a drink of water to calm herself. It was her old nightmare, but this time, as she stared at Reg's body he turned his head towards her, bared his teeth and laughed.

*

A few weeks later Philippe received another envelope from England, this time from the Foreign Office enclosing a letter from Beatrice who was coming to the end of her second tour to Poland. Unfortunately, it was bad news.

'...I'm sorry to tell you that your mother has died. She had a fall at home last month and broke her hip, then whilst in hospital she contracted pneumonia and didn't recover. Greta was with her and saw to the funeral arrangements. You will be pleased to know that Amélie was buried in the Catholic tradition. I was hoping to visit her again, but it was while making the arrangements that Greta told me the sad news. My condolences, Philippe. Your mother was a brave and inspirational woman.'

Philippe showed Clare the letter – there was no need to hide anything now and he told her how Beatrice had arranged for him to see Amélie in Poland. Clare hugged him, saying, 'I'm so sorry, darling, I know you loved your mother very much. Thank goodness you saw her before it was too late – and I understand now why you couldn't say anything, it might have put her in danger. Although you could have trusted me to keep quiet...'

'Of course - but I was sworn to secrecy.'

'You were lucky that Beatrice managed to get you out there – she's been so helpful to you.'

'Yes, she has – she's a good friend.'

Even as Clare held him in her arms, Philippe looked beyond her, remembering the trip to Poland. He felt a sudden yearning to see Beatrice, aware of a fondness and the strong bond between them, to seek comfort in her company and wise counsel. He wrote a long, affectionate letter to her, thanking her for her efforts in reuniting him and his mother and telling her how fortunate he was to have such a special friend. Without her he would never have seen his mother again.

The next Sunday, Philippe went to Mass and lit a candle in memory of Amélie Swann who was born in Paris, married an Englishman, survived Auschwitz and died in Poland with a Jewess by her side, but proclaimed to the end that she was proud to be French, and Catholic.

CHAPTER 46

Bath, 1972

Dr Alfred Swann's career was thriving. When he was approached by a professor from Aix University about a special assignment he accepted without hesitation: it fell exactly within his area of expertise, gained in the hills around Aix, and for once, speaking English would be an advantage. He was to be seconded to Bath University for two years to conduct geochemical studies into the carboniferous limestone which dominated the Mendip Hills, the origin of the springs which fed the Roman Baths. He was disappointed in his parents' reaction - normally so supportive and enthusiastic about his career, for some reason they had reservations about him returning to the city of his birth. But, approaching thirty, a free agent, and having separated from his long-time girlfriend Bernadette, this career opportunity was too good to miss.

Alfred looked out the window as his train approached Bath, the green hills and yellow-grey terraces re-awakening memories, some of which he preferred to leave dormant. He had been allocated accommodation at Bath University on Claverton

Down, so made his way there and reported to the Geology Department. Once settled, he was free to explore. It was mid-Summer and Bath was full of tourists from all over the world, Alfred feeling like one of them, his home city had changed so much since he'd left. Although many of the old landmarks were familiar he felt like a newcomer among the high-rise blocks of flats and offices, vast housing estates and the new shopping centre in Southgate.

Alfred divided his time between field trips to the Mendips, taking rock samples and analysing them at the university laboratory, and the Roman Baths where he was part of a small international team excavating newly-exposed parts of the Baths and Pump Room. He was working alongside Dr Wendy Mason, an expert in the archaeology of the Roman period, who shared his enthusiasm for the ancient world, albeit her interests were measured in thousands, rather than millions, of years. She was also an attractive redhead around his own age.

One evening Wendy invited the team to her house in Lower Weston for supper. On his way Alfred passed the flat where he used to live and it made him shudder, reminding him of his father's bouts of anger, how he used to lash out at him and his mother for no reason. Perhaps that was why Philippe had warned him against coming back.

Wendy welcomed her visitors, wanting to make them feel at home. She told them about her family.

'I was born in Bath, in the middle of the Blitz! My father was lost at sea in the war, then my mother and aunt moved to Bristol where I grew up. I met

Cedric, my husband – he's an officer in the Royal Navy and we've been married for four years. He's based in Portsmouth, in command of a minehunter, doing trials in the English Channel. Can't say I envy him that, although he has been to some fascinating places.'

Alfred, who had retained his accent, couldn't deny he was a Bathonian and told his colleagues he had been born in Larkhall, the place of his fondest memories, not mentioning the flat in Lower Weston.

'Then my father died and I moved to France with my mother, and she remarried.'

'Do you think of yourself as more French than English?' asked Gina, a stunning, dark-eyed beauty from Rimini in northern Italy who was also a geologist. This team had more than its fair share of interesting women, Alfred thought.

'Yes, I do,' he replied, 'I was only five when I left England so all my growing up was in France, and I'm very close to my stepfather.'

'I can understand that. My father was an English soldier who met my mother during the war, but he was killed in action. I am Italian – although sometimes, I think my English side comes out…'

Gina smiled at him and Alfred was smitten.

A young student who was working with them asked Alfred, 'were you in Paris in '68?'

'No, I was in Aix - but there was the same unrest everywhere in France, riots in the streets, and students occupied the University. It was a strange time.'

In May of that year, students in Paris had rebelled against the establishment, barricading the streets, and trades unions called a general strike. The government feared a revolution. The whole of France came to a standstill until demands were met, a general election held and the violence evaporated as quickly as it had begun.

'You French are always protesting about something!' said the student.

Alfred shrugged. 'It is normal. I remember going on my first demonstration when I was eighteen, my first year at the Sorbonne. We marched along the left bank, chanting slogans and had a fight with the police! Happy days…' he sighed, nostalgically.

After their meal they smoked cigarettes and drank whisky, chatting about their careers and sharing their stories. Wendy talked about her experiences in Malta and Gozo, excavating a Roman villa and other ancient sites.

'It was fascinating - it's amazing what surprises you find when you start digging up the past…'

*

Away from the public gaze, Detective Inspector Doyle's investigation was progressing apace. When the name Reginald Watkins came to the top of the list of missing persons, Doyle felt it was worth pursuing. Mr Watkins, from Bath, had been reported missing by his wife, described in the notes as 'distraught', and it was concluded he had left her for another woman. He had never been seen again. The report stated that he had served as a Corporal in the Royal Engineers during the war, so when civilian dental records drew a blank Doyle had an idea.

'Get on to the Army records office, will you?'
he told Detective Sergeant Turner. 'See if they have any
information about Corporal Watkins and the state of
his teeth…'

Doyle's team looked into Mrs Watkins'
background and found that during the war she had
been employed at Green Park station.

'Interesting coincidence, these remains turning
up where she used to work!' Turner commented.

Detective Constable Jennie Jones investigated
Mrs Watkins' medical records which showed that in
September 1946 she had been taken to hospital with a
miscarriage. According to the doctor's notes, bruising
was found on her body, possibly due to domestic
violence.

'She reported her husband missing in the
November,' said Jones. 'A year later she applied for a
passport, left Bath and there's no further trace of her,
or her son, Alfred.'

'Really?' said Doyle, stretching back in his chair
and clasping his hands behind his head. 'You, know,
I've got a feeling in my gut about this one…'

France, 1972

October came, and with it the great migration
of greylag geese from their Summer home in
Scandinavia to the warmer climes of Spain. They flew
over the coast of Western France, directly above their
house, Clare reckoned, and she loved watching the
scores and scores of geese as they massed together,
high in the sky, circling and honking, before flying

south in their distinctive 'V' formation. When one group had flown another would take its place, then another, endless threads of grey stretching into the distance. Sometimes hunters would shoot the geese, looking for any that flew too low or swept down to feed on the saltings next to the sea. One morning on her way to the *boulangerie* Clare was distressed to find a dead goose lying by the side of the road, its neck twisted and feathers bloodied from a bullet wound. She looked away, fastening her coat as a chill wind suddenly blew in from the sea, making her shiver and filling her with a sense of foreboding.

Back home, Clare answered a knock at the door to find the postman with a registered letter. She signed for it and examined the envelope which was addressed to Monsieur P. Swann and postmarked from Bath, stamped with the name of a solicitors' office in Queen Square. Intrigued, she took it straight to Philippe who was at work in his studio.

'Look, it's from Bath! I wonder what it is?'

'Let's see,' he said, picking up a rag and carefully wiping paint off his hands. He opened the envelope and read:

'Dear Monsieur Swann,

I regret to inform you that our client, Mrs Mary Joan Stevens, of Larkhall, Bath, has passed away following a short illness. As the sole beneficiary of her estate, your presence is requested at the above address in order to sign the necessary documents and to settle Mrs Stevens' affairs which include the sale of her house and possessions.

Yours sincerely etc…'

Philippe sat down, in shock. Coming so soon after the news of his mother's death this was a double blow, although Mary's passing was more problematic.

'Does that mean you've got to go to Bath?' asked Clare, also shocked and saddened by the news.

'I don't see as I have much option!'

'We always said we'd never go back, it would be too dangerous…'

Philippe stroked his greying beard, considering the situation, then said, 'look, the only person we thought might suspect something was Mary, and now she's gone, sadly, and the police have put the case on hold. I could go to Bath, deal with the legal business and be back within the week – that should be safe enough. And I could see Alfred!'

Clare missed her son and longed to see him. She couldn't pass up this opportunity.

'I can't let you go on your own – let me come with you! I'd love to see Alfred, too. I could help sort out the house and Mary's things – I had to do the same for my own mother, remember.'

'All right, we'll go together. You can travel with me on my French passport.'

They decided they should go as soon as possible, and Philippe made the travel arrangements. By the following week everything was in place and Clare wrote to Alfred with details of when to expect them.

Philippe wrote to Beatrice, telling her about his Aunt's death and his forthcoming trip to Bath. She read his letter with interest, and some concern. It was never a good idea to return to the scene of the crime…

CHAPTER 47

Bath, 1972

It was a lengthy journey by rail and ferry, but finally Philippe and Clare arrived in Bath, feeling like strangers after twenty-five years away. Their concerns about the past dissipated as they took in the changes around them - the world had moved on and it was unlikely they would meet anyone who remembered this couple in their fifties or had any interest in events that had happened just after the war. Many people didn't even know that Bath had been blitzed.

Philippe and Clare checked into a hotel in the city centre then met Alfred who was renting a room above a shop nearby, having grown tired of student accommodation. The three were excited to see each other again, finding it hard to believe that they were together, in Bath. Philippe told him more about the reason for their visit.

'Aunt Mary was good to me when I came here during the war. I was sorry to learn that she'd died, and as her heir I'm responsible for sorting out her estate.'

'We used to go to her house sometimes, on Saturdays – do you remember?' said Clare.

'Yes, vaguely...' said Alfred. 'That's when we used to see Philippe - Papa.'

Recalling the happy times only served to remind Alfred of the misery of living with his violent father, so to change the subject he said, 'I'd like to take you both out to dinner tonight, my treat - there's a new Italian restaurant which is very good. The food in England is much better now, Papa!'

'Only because it's foreign!'

Alfred laughed, then added, 'the other thing is, I'm pleased you're here because next week there's going to be an awards ceremony at the Pump Room. It's all to do with our work at the Roman Baths and I'm in the running for a prize. I'd love you to come, and there's someone special I'd like you to meet...'

The following day Philippe went to the solicitor's office to conduct the legal proceedings and collect the key to Mary's house. He and Clare went there together, unsure what they might find, but everything inside was in good order. A neighbour knocked on the door and Philippe introduced himself.

'So you're her nephew, the artist! She used to talk about you, out in France – she was proud of you. I used to keep an eye out for Mrs Stevens, it was so sad when she passed away. I took the canary, I hope that was all right.'

'Of course! Thank you for everything you have done.'

Not wanting to get further involved, Philippe politely closed the door so he and Clare could get on with their task of sorting out Mary's possessions and getting the house ready to put on the market. A few days should do it, then they could attend Alfred's bash at the Pump Room and get home to France.

Alone in Mary's house while Philippe was dealing with the estate agents, Clare busied herself cleaning, putting clothes into bags for the charity shop and collecting up items Philippe may want to keep, including some framed photographs of his father and his family. She took Philippe's painting of Pulteney bridge down from the wall, remembering standing next to him, looking at that same view an age ago.

Clare popped down to the new local shop to buy a few groceries and was suddenly aware of how lovely it was to be back among her own people, hearing and speaking her own language. Even in the dreary November weather it felt good to be home.

Returning to Mary's she thought of when she had first met Philippe in Mary and Derek's old house, the one that was destroyed in the Blitz. She'd found him attractive, but she was married, so what could she do? It was only when Reg's violent outbursts became intolerable that she'd finally let herself be seduced by Philippe, although she'd never dreamt that it would lead to murder…

Clare needed a break and went for a walk around Larkhall, remembering the places she and Reg had frequented when they were courting, before he'd joined the Army. They had been so young, so happy, and she blamed his experiences in the war for turning him from a normal lad into a vicious bully. She thought back to the last months of their marriage, reminding herself of Reg's cruelty, the loss of her baby and how much she had hated and feared him.

Philippe had put an end to that and they had lived lovingly together ever since, with a quality of life in France they could never have experienced in England. And yet… she couldn't help thinking, did Reg really deserve to die such a violent death? And would she ever stop feeling guilty about her part in it?

*

The Army came up trumps: dental records showed that the charting of Corporal Watkins' teeth and fillings aligned with the remains which had been recovered at Green Park station, and a positive identification was confirmed. Doyle breathed a sigh of satisfaction and called his team together.

'We've got him! So, the question is, did he break his neck in a fall? Or did someone do it for him?'

'The wife had a motive, if he was violent to her. All this business about her being distraught could have been play-acting,' said Turner.

'Indeed! Now, if it was murder, and we still can't be sure, Mrs Watkins couldn't have done it on her own – there must be an accomplice, a boyfriend perhaps? We need to find Mrs Watkins and speak to her, and her son, Alfred. He was aged four when his father went missing so he must be – what – thirty, by now.'

Turner added, 'after the war Watkins went to work for a company in Bristol, dealing in Army surplus. I've checked it out – the Managing Director is a Roy Baker. He's still in business.'

'My old stamping ground!' said Doyle, who hailed from Bristol and worked there when he was in uniform. 'I'll go and pay him a visit. Anything else?'

Detective Constable Jennie Jones spoke up.

'Just a small thing, sir – I don't know whether it's relevant. I was going back through the interviews with staff at Green Park station and one of them mentioned that an artist was working there for a few months at the same time as Mrs Watkins was employed there. Name of Philippe Swann – a Frenchman. They were quite friendly, apparently.'

'A Frenchman? Now, that's interesting…'

Doyle hadn't been over to Bristol for a while and was pleased to be back on his old patch. During the war he had served in the Royal Navy, in the Malta convoys, and he recalled his horror at coming home to find huge swathes of his city razed to the ground by Nazi bombs. Since then the place had been re-built, and it was in a brand-new tower block that he found the plush offices of Baker and Sons Ltd. He took the lift to the Managing Director's office.

Doyle had established that Roy Baker was in his mid-fifties, the same vintage as himself. A sergeant in the Royal Engineers, he had started trading after the war and was now head of his own private limited company. Baker, a short man wearing a three-piece pinstripe suit with wide lapels and a kipper tie, stood up to greet Doyle and smiled, revealing his gold fillings. Doyle instinctively disliked him; there was something oily about him, untrustworthy – an old-fashioned spiv.

For his part, Roy Baker did not like dealing with the police. His business interests were – well, wide-ranging – and there were certain parts of his portfolio in which he would not wish them to be involved. He needed to be very careful.

'I understand you used to employ a Reginald Watkins.'

Baker breathed a little more easily. This, he could handle.

'Yes – we served together in Italy – he was one of my Corporals - then I took him on after the war. Good bloke, till he did a runner.'

Doyle raised his eyebrows.

'He deserted his wife – she rang me in a real panic. Word was he took up with another woman and I never saw him again. Why are you asking?'

'A general inquiry, sir. What can you tell me about Mrs Watkins?'

Baker thought back. He remembered her slapping his face at the dinner dance in Bristol. 'I'd say she was good-looking but stuck-up – got a bit above herself in my view. She changed her tune when Reg left, though. Came over all tearful.'

'Really?'

Baker laughed, coarsely.

'Women, eh?'

Doyle smiled complicitly, and said, 'thank you, Mr Baker, you've been very helpful.'

They shook hands and Doyle returned to the station, satisfied that Baker had told him all he knew about Reg and Clare Watkins, but there was something else on his mind. He made a call to an old friend in the Fraud department.

'I've got no evidence, but there's a nasty smell at the offices of Baker and Sons Ltd. in Bristol. Might be worth your chaps taking a look…'

Jennie Jones was driving up to Corsham Court when she slammed on the brakes as a peacock appeared from nowhere and strutted across the road right in front of her, his iridescent tail feathers trailing behind him. Recovering her breath, Jennie put the car in gear then parked by the main entrance where Daniel Johns, the head of the School of Art, came out to meet her. He was feeling uneasy about her visit but tried not to show it, and took her to his office.

'Do you know someone called Philippe Swann?' she asked.

'Yes - we were students together, during the war.'

Daniel the Quaker was as honest as the day is long, but a warning bell rang inside his head. His instinct was to protect his old friend and his answers became circumspect.

'What's this about?'

'A general inquiry, sir. Do you know whether Mr Swann had any connection to a Mr Reginald and Mrs Clare Watkins?'

Daniel thought carefully. 'He knew Clare – she featured in some of his paintings – but I don't think he knew her husband.'

'Would that have been when Mrs Watkins was working at Green Park station?'

'Yes, that's right.'

'Do you know Mr Swann's whereabouts?'

'No - after the war Philippe returned to France and we lost touch.'

The detective probed a little further but Daniel had nothing to add, so she said, 'very well, Mr Johns. If you do remember anything, please let me know – this is my phone number.' She smiled and gave him her card.

Jennie Jones drove away, sure that Daniel was holding something back. She would do some digging herself and return when she had more to go on.

Emma, curious, came into the office.

'What did she want?'

'She was asking whether I was in touch with Philippe Swann!'

'Really? I hope he's not in any trouble...'

Back at the station, Doyle reviewed the latest findings.

'I'm convinced Mrs Watkins holds the key to this. We need help to find her. It's time to go public!'

CHAPTER 48

Bath, 1972

The Pump Room was as grand as ever, arranged for the occasion with cabaret-style tables for the guests and a stage where the prizes, sponsored by Bath University, were to be presented. Clare had put away her gloomy thoughts and cheered herself up, buying a new dress for the unexpected event. She was glad to be at Philippe's side, the two of them remembering when he'd taken her there for tea, and in her eyes he was just as handsome, his greying hair and beard lending him a distinguished look. Alfred showed them to their table where he presented Gina, his Italian beauty.

'We've been going out together for a while...'

Gina smiled and gazed at Alfred adoringly.

'Lovely to meet you,' said Clare, pleased to see her son so happy, and Philippe said, 'ah, the someone special!', impressed by the stunning young woman. Next, Alfred introduced them to his colleague Dr Wendy Mason, saying, 'Wendy's made me very welcome here, and she's so knowledgeable about the Roman Baths and their history.'

'It's good to meet you both, Alfred's told me all about you. You're over from France?'

'Yes! We're here on business, so Alfred asked us to come tonight,' said Philippe, admiring the smart redhead with her pre-Raphaelite looks. He was suddenly struck by the thought that she was just the type Michael would have gone for, then, there he was, right in front of him - Michael. Or Michael's ghost.

'This is my husband, Cedric,' said Wendy, unaware of the turmoil unleashed in Philippe's head at the sight of the tall, slim, fair-haired young man with piercing blue eyes. He was Michael's double.

'Cedric's come up from Portsmouth especially for the prize giving.'

'I wouldn't have missed it for the world!' he said, putting his arm around his lovely wife. Wendy introduced Cedric to Alfred and as they chatted the three were amused to find that they had been born within a few months and a few miles of each other, but had taken very different paths to reach where they were tonight.

While Philippe tried not to stare at him, Cedric said, 'my mother should be here somewhere…'

Rosamund appeared and Wendy said to her, 'Alfred Swann works with me at the Roman Baths. This is Clare, his mother, and his stepfather, Philippe – he's a famous artist from France!'

Rosamund and Philippe looked at each other in recognition, memories stirring and minds whirring. She took a breath and, giving Philippe a pointed look, said, 'how nice to meet you. I'm pleased Cedric was able to get leave from his ship to come here tonight -

he's in the Royal Navy, like his father, my late husband the Captain.'

Philippe smiled at her, understanding perfectly.

The party took their seats, applauding as nominees were read out and awards presented, Wendy winning a prize for her work on identification and dating of Roman artefacts, and Alfred recognised for setting up a programme of hydrogeological studies. Clare dabbed a tear from her eye, so proud of Alfred's achievements here in Bath. She couldn't help but wonder what Reg would have made of it, although she kept her thoughts to herself.

After the ceremony Rosamund approached Philippe, saying, 'may I have a word?'

He excused himself, leaving Clare chatting to Alfred and Gina, and followed her outside to the lobby where they could speak in private.

'I've seen how you keep looking at Cedric,' Rosamund said, leaning towards him confidentially. 'I know who you are. You were Michael's friend and you comforted me after he was killed in the raid.'

'Yes…I remember you, Mrs Mason.'

'You are the only person who knows…'

'…that Michael is Cedric's father.'

Rosamund's heart raced at hearing the truth.

'I have brought him up, on my own, all these years, in the knowledge that his father is my late husband, Captain Mortimer Mason.'

'And you have done a marvellous job, he is a credit to you.'

'Thank you.'

'Michael was a good friend to me. Such a waste, so talented – I was devastated when he was killed.'

'So was I.'

'Cedric is the image of him.'

'I know.' Rosamund touched Philippe's arm and said, softly, 'I'm sure I can trust you to keep this information to yourself?'

'Yes, of course. I have nothing to gain by revealing it, and you have a lot to lose.'

Rosamund was visibly relieved. 'I'm pleased we understand each other.'

Then she added, 'I saw your paintings at the exhibition earlier this year – they really are very good. The young woman in them – is that your wife?'

'Yes.'

'And Alfred…?'

'Clare's son, by her previous marriage. Her husband died.'

Cedric suddenly appeared beside them.

'Sorry to interrupt! I wondered where you'd gone, Mummy. Can I get you some drinks?'

'Please, dear. I was just telling Philippe what a marvellous man your father was…'

Later, at home, Rosamund remembered that she had seen Clare before, at the memorial service in the Abbey. She had broken down in tears, and Clare was the kind woman who had comforted her.

*

The day after the prize giving, Alfred and Wendy were back at work at the Roman Baths. At lunchtime, Wendy went out to buy herself a sandwich and picked up a copy of the *Bath & Wilts Chronicle*. Reading the headlines as she ate, she exclaimed, 'Oh! The police have identified the remains at Green Park station!'

Alfred looked up, unaware of the story.

'They were found last year and it's taken this long to find out who he is. There's even a picture of him, the poor man – he's called Reginald Watkins.'

Alfred started at the name.

'May I see?'

Wendy passed him the newspaper and Alfred was confronted by a young Reg in his Army uniform, staring back at him.

Daddy.

Alfred was a child again.

Feeling nauseous, he read:

HUMAN REMAINS FOUND AT GREEN PARK IDENTIFIED

The remains found at Green Park station in October 1971 have been identified as Mr Reginald Watkins from Bath who went missing in November 1946. Mr Watkins, a Corporal in the Royal Engineers, was a hero of Dunkirk and the Italian campaign during the Second World War. The police are keen to contact his widow, Clare Watkins, and his son, Alfred, who was four years old at the time of his father's disappearance, to help with their inquiries. Any member of the public with any information relating to the case is requested to come forward and speak to the police.

Under his breath, Alfred uttered, '*merde!*' He threw the newspaper down and said, 'I'm sorry, Wendy, but I have to go. I'm not feeling well…'

His mind a whirl of anger and disbelief, Alfred went straight to the hotel to confront his parents and demand that they tell him the truth.

Clare had gone out for one last look at the local shops before returning to France. When she saw the headline in the newspaper she felt the blood drain from her face. Shaking with nerves, she bought a copy and hurried back to show Philippe.

'Look! It's all here - Reg's name, and even a photograph! The police want me and Alfred to help with their inquiries. What are we going to do?'

He snatched the newspaper from her and read the article.

'We'll leave, tomorrow, as planned. We're travelling under the name Swann and there's no reason for anyone to be suspicious as long as we stay calm.'

Clare, panic rising, said, 'but I don't think I can ignore it, now it's out there!'

'Now, come on, Clare! The police can't prove anything.'

'But it's *my* name that's in the paper! Someone's going to remember me, or Alfred, and say something…'

'Not necessarily – it's a long time ago.'

There was a knock on their door and Clare froze.

'Oh God, is that the police? Have they found out I'm here?'

'Don't be ridiculous! It's probably the maid, come to tidy the room.'

Philippe answered the door to find Alfred who burst in, saying, 'I've seen the newspaper - what's all this about, Mum? Did you know Reg had been left for dead? Did you and Papa kill him?'

Clare started to cry. There was no point in denying it. 'It was Philippe's idea! Reg was violent, we had to do something!'

Philippe said, 'now, quieten down, both of you. Yes, Alfred, I murdered Reg and hid his body. We had no choice, that man was a monster!'

'I know he was! And I'm pleased he's dead. But I wish you'd told me. You lied to me, both of you!'

Clare was in tears and said to her son, 'I'm sorry, but you were too young to understand…'

'But how can you have pretended all this time, as if it never happened?'

She shook her head in distress. 'The years went by, and there seemed no point in saying anything…'

'Until now!'

'Don't tell me you wish you'd stayed in England with him!' exclaimed Philippe.

'Of course not! I love you, Papa. It's just come as a shock…'

'I knew it would catch up with us one day!' cried Clare, 'no wonder I keep having nightmares!'

Philippe gave her his handkerchief, saying, 'wipe your eyes, *chérie*, we've nothing to fear. The police have no evidence – there's nothing to tie the events of that night to us. We'll return to France and we'll be safe.'

Alfred said, 'but I'm not going back – I have my job here – and Gina!'

'And there's no reason for you to go. You are Alfred Swann, not Alfred Watkins. As long as we keep quiet, nobody need ever know.'

Between sobs Clare said, 'but those people we met last night – they might put two and two together. And that woman, Rosamund Mason – I recognised her. I met her in Bath, briefly, years ago, and I think she remembered me…'

'You knew Rosamund?'

Philippe turned to her in surprise, then said, 'well you needn't worry about her. She won't say anything…'

Clare looked at him, trying to read his expression, feeling her stomach churn.

'Oh no, Philippe, not more secrets, surely? What else have you been hiding from me? I can't bear it!'

In despair she threw herself onto the bed, weeping, refusing to be comforted.

*

Eileen came back to The Oaks with the newspaper and excitedly showed Rosamund the report. A shiver ran through her as she realised the people the police were looking for were those she'd met the previous night at the Pump Room. Should she tell the police? She was wondering what to do when the doorbell rang. Eileen went to answer and Rosamund heard her say, 'hello Dr Roberts, yes, Mrs Mason's in the drawing room', and in he came.

David saw her with the newspaper and sat down next to her.

'You've seen it too…'

'Yes…Reginald Watkins…'

'I had to come, Rosamund – there's something on my mind and I need to talk to someone. Reading this has brought it all back to me. You see, one night around the time Reg disappeared I heard a car pull up outside, then it left and returned a little later. I looked out the window and saw Clare Watkins and a man - not her husband - go into her flat, opposite my house. Then he drove away. It was late, gone midnight. What do you think it means? I wonder whether I should tell the police?'

Rosamund's head was spinning. Was the man David had seen Philippe Swann? Had he and Clare conspired to kill Reg and hide his body, freeing themselves to make a new life in France? From what David had told her Reg was the most horrible man and if murder could ever be justified, this was it. She struggled to imagine Philippe, the artist, committing a violent act, nor could she see the kind and gentle Clare helping him, but love did strange things to people, as she well knew…

Philippe had promised to keep silent about Cedric, and she owed him for that. The least she could do was protect him from coming under suspicion. And as for David's concern, who was she to insist that other people come forward with the truth, when she had built Cedric's life on a lie?

Rosamund had rarely seen David so uncertain and wanted to reassure him, so after some consideration she said, 'it's all circumstantial though, isn't it, David - I mean, you don't know who the man was, and you can't be sure of what night it happened. There might be any manner of reason for a man calling on the woman late at night…it might not do her reputation any good, either…'

'That's a fair point - I hadn't thought of it like that. Thank you, Rosamund. I'll sleep on it…'

*

In Corsham, Daniel and Emma looked at the newspaper and each other in astonishment.

'Is that why the detective was asking questions? Do you think Philippe had anything to do with this?'

Daniel had a feeling of dread. Surely his friend wouldn't have done something as terrible as this: to kill a man and take his wife?

'It was probably a horrible accident. Let's say a prayer, Emma, for the soul of Reginald Watkins.'

And, in the event that Reg had been murdered, Daniel privately added a prayer for the soul of the man who killed him.

CHAPTER 49

Bath, 1972

Alfred went back to his room to try and come to terms with everything he had learned, and Philippe took a walk to clear his mind. His feet led him to Green Park, where all these events had begun, and towards the River Avon, passing through a run-down area where a group of vagrants were sitting on a bench drinking the local favourite - cider and methylated spirits. They shouted incoherently at him and he walked on, avoiding discarded needles, broken bottles and other detritus from life on the street.

Being November it soon grew dark and cold, and he returned to the hotel to an hysterical Clare.

'It's been on the local TV – there was an interview with a detective. They kept repeating my name and Alfred's! Someone's bound to recognise us…'

'But you're Clare Swann, now, not Watkins. People won't remember.'

Trembling, she said, 'I've decided – I'm going to the police, *tonight*. I'm going to hand myself in.'

'You're not serious! They don't have a shred of evidence against us. We'll soon be safely back in France and no one will find us there.'

'I don't think so – the police aren't stupid. They'll make the connection between us, sooner or later, and track us down. I can't go on living, waiting for that knock on the door. I don't think we'll ever be safe, even in France.'

'But they can't prove anything!'

'That's not the point! I can't stand it any longer - the lies, the deception - I've had enough! I've got to own up.'

'But you can't, *chérie*! Not after all we've been through. I did it for you and Alfred. Remember how cruel Reg was, how violent…you lost your baby…'

'I know, but it was wrong, to kill him in cold blood. I can still see his eyes… I should never have let you talk me into it - I should have found another way out. It's my fault. You might be used to murder, with whatever you got up to in the war - but I'm not. I'm sorry, I just can't go on!'

She broke down, sobbing. Philippe took her by the shoulders and tried to shake some sense into her.

'You mustn't do this! We've had a happy life together, haven't we?'

'Of course we have – it's been wonderful.'

'I love you!'

'I love you too! But I'm sorry, this is something I have to do.'

Philippe was exasperated. He paced the room, clenching his fists in frustration, swearing to himself in French, his native instinct taking over.

'We'll lose everything, Clare – everything! If you confess they'll take me too. You'll get away with a short sentence as an accessory, but it was I who killed him. They can't hang me, but they'll put me in prison for the rest of my life!'

'I know, but I have no choice - I can't live with myself!'

Philippe tried to regain his self-control, taking deep breaths to calm himself and the two sat on the edge of the bed, Clare wiping the tears from her face. Then he said, quietly, 'all right - if this is what you want, fine, but it will be final. We won't be able to see each other again. There's no going back.'

Clare swallowed and put her head in her hands. At last she said, 'I know, and I hate that it's the end for us. But I can't go on like this, it's driving me insane!'

'And I'll go insane if they put me in prison for something I don't regret.'

Philippe lit a cigarette to calm his nerves, inhaling deeply, then said, 'very well. You must do what your conscience is telling you. But my conscience is clear. Reg was a monster who deserved to die. If you want to give yourself up, that's for you to decide. But I ask one thing of you: for the sake of all we have ever meant to each other, don't go to the police tonight. Wait until the morning.'

She hesitated.

'Clare, for all our years together, our love for each other - please!'

She took a deep breath.

'Very well, I'll wait until the morning.'

'Thank you.'

He walked around the room once more and finished his cigarette in silence. She stood up and they held one another for the last time, struggling to believe this was the end, then released their embrace and looked at each other.

'Goodbye, *chérie.*'

'Goodbye, my love.'

Philippe put on his coat and left the hotel room without looking back. He walked through the city centre, his emotions in turmoil, but from within the desperate maelstrom of his mind he formed a plan. It was towards eleven o'clock and people were leaving the pubs and rolling home. He took an empty bottle out of a litter bin and staggered along, pretending to swig from it, and as he passed a drunken group of lads he deliberately pushed into one of the men who turned on him.

'I'm sorry!' said Philippe, holding up his hands. 'I stumbled, sorry my friend.'

The man ignored him and the group went on their way.

Retracing his steps from earlier that evening he went to Green Park where he met another boozy party and repeated his performance, shoving one of them off the pavement then apologising profusely. The man turned and threatened to punch him but his friend said, 'leave it, he's drunk!'

He returned to the place where alcoholics and the homeless gathered, then sat down at a distance in the shelter of some bushes, wrapping his coat around him against the cold night. There was a full moon – a bombers' moon – and he had a clear view of the drinkers as they came and went. In the early hours Philippe spotted who he was looking for – a vagrant about the same age and build as himself who came to relieve himself in the bushes. Philippe stood up and spoke to him in a drunken drawl.

'Want some cider, mate?'

The vagrant saw the bottle Philippe was holding in his hand and walked towards him. He didn't stand a chance: Philippe smashed the bottle over the man's head, knocking him unconscious, and he fell to the ground. Philippe swiftly removed his own wristwatch and fastened it onto the man's wrist, checked his victim's pockets for any sign of identification and found none. He took off his coat and, with difficulty, dressed the vagrant in it, then dragged him to the edge of the riverbank. Just as his eyes opened and he started to protest, Philippe pushed him into the Avon, prodding him with a stick to move him along with the current.

Next, Philippe made his way through the empty streets to Alfred's room and hammered on the door. A bemused Alfred, awoken from his sleep shouted, 'who is it?', opening the door to see his stepfather, bedraggled and cold.

'Papa! What are you doing here? It's four o'clock in the morning!'

Philippe entered and said, 'Alfred - I need your help. Please, listen - for the sake of all the years we have spent together, and for the love we have for each other – there is something I need you to do for me…'

Later, as they said goodbye, Alfred asked, 'but where will you go, Papa?'

'To London. I'll catch the first train. I have a friend there, she will help me.'

They embraced, in tears, knowing they would never see each other again.

'I love you, Alfred.'

'I love you, Papa. *Adieu.*'

*

Clare barely slept that night, but during the brief time she drifted off she dreamt about the young Reg, the fun, sandy-haired lad she'd fallen in love with. He took her hand, smiled at her and said,

'Go and tell them, babe.'

She awoke with Reg's voice ringing in her ears and her conscience clear. As dawn broke she got up to make some tea, then prepared for the day ahead. She hadn't changed her mind. She'd given Philippe the time he'd asked for. Now she was going through with it.

With a serenity that came with a decision made, Clare checked out of the hotel, walked to the police station and calmly said to the desk sergeant, 'I'm the person you're looking for. My name is Clare Swann, but I used to be Clare Watkins. I know who killed my husband Reg, and I was an accessory to the crime. I want to give myself up.'

The astounded policeman recognised the name and called for Detective Inspector Doyle. In the interview room Doyle asked her to repeat her claim. He had heard too many false confessions in his time and wanted to make sure she was the genuine article.

'The body that was found in Green Park station last year - he was my husband, Reg Watkins. He was murdered by Philippe Swann in my flat and I helped him take the body to the railway station and put it down the shute. Philippe took Reg's clothes and destroyed them, then I told the police that Reg had left me.'

Doyle said nothing, just looked at her and waited for more.

'Philippe and I didn't see each other for a while, then he went to France and my son Alfred and I joined him later. We lived as husband and wife and Philippe adopted Alfred. He loves him like his own.'

He stared at her and she got angry.

'I'm not making it up! I swear I'm telling you the truth!'

Doyle took a deep breath.

'I believe you.'

The police took Clare into custody and issued a warrant for the arrest of Philippe Swann. Clare provided a photo of him which was published in the newspaper and on TV and the police notified the ports, assuming the fugitive would head for France.

Clare made a call to Alfred who arrived at the police station, devastated that his mother had given herself up and betrayed Philippe. He said nothing about the visit he had paid him in the early hours of that morning. The police interviewed Alfred about Reg's murder, but he protested that he was only a child when it happened and had known nothing about it until the last couple of days. He did, however, testify to Reg's violence and his relief when he'd disappeared.

Clare spent the next nights in a cell at the police station, and in spite of the uncomfortable bed slept soundly for the first time in years, with no nightmares to disturb her peace of mind.

Having seen the reports in the press, some young men came forward to say they had seen a man resembling Philippe Swann walking drunkenly along the road near Green Park and heading towards the river. Doyle questioned Clare as to Philippe's state of mind when she had last seen him and she said, 'he was in a terrible state, very upset. He maintained that he was right to kill Reg and couldn't face the rest of his life in prison.'

Doyle accepted what she said and developed a theory. He would wait a week or so and see what popped up.

*

Ten days later a woman was walking her dog alongside the riverbank in Saltford, a few miles west of Bath. She noticed something strange caught in the grating by the weir – a bundle of clothes - and as she grew closer she caught her breath. It was a body.

*

The Bath police were sadly familiar with young men falling into the Avon and drowning after going out on the town and having too much to drink. This particular case was different in that the man was in his fifties, but his fate had been the same. The pathologist examined the bloated, deformed body and declared drowning as the cause of death, although the man had suffered severe cuts, bruises and a head injury during his turbulent passage down the river. She retrieved his coat which was torn and battered, but which had been of good quality and of French manufacture, according to the just-legible label. Most importantly she recovered the man's wristwatch, engraved on the back with the initials 'P.S.' and a date.

Doyle showed the watch to Clare.

'It's Philippe's!' she said. 'I gave it to him for his fortieth birthday. Where did you find it?'

He told her as kindly as he could.

Clare began to sob, because for all of it she still loved Philippe and couldn't believe he was dead.

'We think he was drunk and stumbled into the river,' said Doyle. 'I'm so sorry.'

'Or he may have done it on purpose...' she cried, knowing he would rather drown himself than end his days locked in a cell. Now she had *his* death on her conscience. Would she never be able to find peace?

Doyle left Clare with her thoughts, but he was satisfied. He had his man.

The body had to be formally identified and with Clare in detention, Alfred, distraught to learn of Philippe's death, came forward. He went to the morgue and stood as the pathologist drew back the sheet covering the corpse.

'Yes,' said Alfred, sorrowfully, 'yes, that is my stepfather, Philippe Swann.'

Nobody noticed that a vagrant was missing.

CHAPTER 50

Bath, 1972

Philippe was laid to rest at Perrymead, Bath's Catholic cemetery, in the presence of those who had known and loved him. Clare was allowed to attend the service, handcuffed to a WPC, with a sombre Alfred by her side. Daniel came with Emma to pay respects to his old friend, knowing he was safely in the arms of the Lord, and Richard and Ann mourned the sad loss of a talented artist.

Afterwards the devastated Clare was taken back to her police cell. Alfred said goodbye to her then returned to his room, reflecting on the events of the last weeks. His mother had made her choice by giving herself up and betraying Philippe in the process; Alfred had made his choice by covering for him and was pleased he had done so. No matter what his mother felt, Alfred would always see Reg as the enemy and Philippe as his saviour. He lit a cigarette, poured himself a large cognac and made a silent toast to his beloved Papa, wherever he may be.

An inquest was held into the death of Reginald Watkins, and based on Clare's confession, the coroner returned a verdict of unlawful killing. A separate inquest determined that Swann's death was accidental. The case against Clare for her part in Reg's murder was heard quickly by the court. In view of the time that had elapsed since the offence and given the mitigating circumstances - that Reg had been violent to her, that she had confessed to being an accessory, and that it was Philippe who had planned and executed the act - she was given a suspended sentence.

After the trial Alfred asked, 'what are you going to do now, Mum?'

'I don't want to go back to France, I'll stay in Bath. I'm going to live in Mary's house – it's mine now, with Philippe gone…'

Her eyes filled with tears and Alfred put his arm around her.

'And I'd like to stay close to you…' she said, then smiling at him, added, 'and Gina...'

*

The press covered the controversial case in lurid detail, some journalists questioning the validity of Clare's confession, saying it was easy to put the blame for Watkins' death on Swann who wasn't there to defend himself. Others conjectured that Swann had committed suicide because he was guilty of murder and could not face justice.

At The Oaks, Rosamund and Eileen devoured the reports. Rosamund was shocked that the loving family she'd met at the Pump Room only a few short weeks ago had torn themselves apart. Clare must have had Reg's murder on her conscience all these years, and when it came to it her need to confess, to expose the truth, had outweighed her love for Philippe.

'I think Clare was better off with her first husband dead,' said Eileen. 'What do you think, Mrs Mason?'

'It's difficult – I mean, murder is wrong, but in the circumstances, with Reg being so horrid, I can understand how it came to that. They might have got away with it if they'd gone back to France, but there we are – Clare chose to confess, and now Philippe is dead.'

Rosamund didn't say that her sadness at Philippe's death was moderated by relief, for with him gone, her own secret was safe.

David Roberts' instinct told him that Reg Watkins had been a monster who deserved everything he'd got. At the same time, he knew that Philippe had been wrong to take the law into his own hands and had sympathy with Clare's position. It was sad, though, for an artist of Philippe's standing to end his life drowned in a river.

When David's son Henry and his wife Tilly came down to Eagle House for the weekend he told them about the case. Lighting his pipe, he said, 'you might remember me mentioning it when the remains were discovered, last year. I knew Clare and Reg Watkins – they lived in one of the flats opposite - but I never met Philippe Swann.'

Tilly was listening keenly and said to her husband, 'Henry, we met Philippe at a garden party at the Embassy in Paris. It would be - what - five years ago. Do you remember?'

'Now you say it, I do - Philippe and his wife Clare, an attractive woman. He was a well-known artist in Paris - he painted the ambassador's portrait.'

Tilly thought back to the garden party, the last time she, Philippe and Beatrice had been together, old friends and comrades from the SOE. She had always liked Philippe, a charming man and a brave Resistance fighter, not one to give up easily. She knew he and Beatrice were close and wondered what she would make of his death. A tingle ran up the back of her neck.

'I hadn't realised you'd met them!' said David. 'It's a small world...'

Henry read the report in the newspaper.

'They reckon the police had Philippe on their radar and it was only a matter of time until he was caught. It says he may have drowned himself on purpose, not wanting to face prison – but there we are, whether it was a deliberate act or an accident, Philippe Swann is dead.'

'Out of interest, who identified his body?' asked Tilly.

Henry looked at the report.

'His stepson, Alfred Swann.'

'Really...?'

Tilly raised her eyebrows, remembering something Clare had said.

'What?' asked Henry.

'Oh, nothing... it's just that, sometimes, people get another chance at life...'

CHAPTER 51

Poland, 1972

The man came to the cottage by the lake at the start of the long Polish Winter. In the same way as a new hen is introduced to a coop at night, by the time Spring arrived he was accepted as if he had always been there. He busied himself, re-building and repairing the cottage and cultivating the land around it. For a few years the woman spent her Summers with him, then she stayed for good.

The couple kept themselves to themselves. Nobody from the nearby village knew who they were; they thought the woman was English and the man probably French, but people showed little interest beyond that. The woman had bought the cottage in the '60s as a holiday home and seemed happy in her own company, but when the man came to live with her she was positively delighted. It was clear to see that they held a deep regard and love for one another.

Occasionally the pair would venture out to the local market but otherwise they were self-sufficient, getting by on what they grew on their land, fish from the lake and their chickens. While she looked after the vegetable plot he would paint, and very well – he was an accomplished artist. One woman said the man was the spitting image of her Uncle Freidrich Kosinski from Orzysz but that was clearly ridiculous.

The couple lived contentedly, growing old together, finding joy among the beautiful lakes and green landscape of the Mazury region of north-east Poland. During the Summer they would spend their time walking in the hills, gathering wild mushrooms in the forests and sailing their boat on the lake. During the long, dark Winters they would sit indoors by the fire, reading, talking and listening to music, enjoying one another's companionship. He never tired of painting her portrait, trying to capture her strong character, her enigmatic quality, the inner beauty which belied her plain looks.

At the end of each day he would pour two glasses of cognac from their stash in the cellar and they would smile at each other, remembering past times and enjoying the present, then they would make a toast, clinking glasses and saying just one word: '*Sulis*'.

In April 2022 events were held to commemorate the eightieth anniversary of the Bath Blitz. Bathonians came together to remember the 417 people who were killed and the hundreds who were injured.

Professor Alfred Swann, still sprightly in his eightieth year, and his lovely wife, Gina, were standing at the memorial at the entrance to Victoria Park with their daughter, Francesca, their son Giorgio, and their families. Giorgio was pushing his grandmother, Clare, in a wheelchair. At the grand age of a hundred and one she felt honoured to be able to attend the ceremony, to remember that period of her life and those she had lost during the raids. She counted her blessings, so lucky to have a loving son, grandchildren and great-grandchildren.

She had spent the latter part of her life in Bath and loved her city. Giorgio would take her out occasionally to see the sights and the latest generation of shopping centres in Southgate. The only places she had no desire to visit were the supermarket, cafés and market stalls which occupy the site of the old railway station at Green Park.

About the Author

Originally from Kent, Maggie moved to Bath at the age of eleven and lived and worked in the city for many years.

She is now retired and lives in Wiltshire.

'After the Bath Blitz'

The third part of the 'Bath At War' trilogy.

Original artwork by Maggie Rayner

Copyright © 2022

Also available from Amazon:

'When Bombs Fell On Bath'

The first part of the 'Bath At War' trilogy.

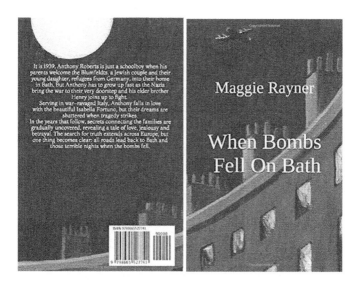

Also available from Amazon:

'Bath Ablaze'

The second part of the 'Bath At War' trilogy.

Original artwork by Maggie Rayner

Also available from Amazon:

'Moonflight and Other Tales from Wiltshire and the West'

Original artwork by Maggie Rayner

Copyright © 2020